Interior Format by The Killion Group, Inc.
www.thekilliongroupinc.com

A Road Back to Grace

BOOK 2, THE KEEPER SERIES

ROBIN P. NOLET

For Mom

"

Like prayer—you go to it in sorrow more than joy,
for help, a road back to 'grace'."
~Anne Morrow Lindbergh

One

IF SHE CLOSED HER EYES, just let go, and didn't over-think it, Claire could almost imagine she was lying beside a tropical waterfall, its warm waters splashing nearby. In the distance unknown birds called from the tops of what she imagined were palm trees swaying in the gentle trade winds. She could even smell the hyacinth. Yes, if she closed her eyes, she could almost imagine...

"Breathe deep, ladies," a woman's voice whispered, "feel prana flow through you, cleansing tension and bringing clarity. In...out...in...out..."

Clarity? Jesus, she could use clarity. In fact, wasn't that why the hell she was here? Hadn't she been working on deep-sixing the tension and finding friggin' clarity since she arrived five months ago?

"Breathe out negative chi. Release all cares, all thoughts," the woman continued, in a calm, soothing voice.

Maybe I'll get an iced chai tea after class. Geez! I'm not supposed to be thinking but here I am thinking about not thinking. "Shut-Up," she said to herself.

"Claire?" the woman's voice asked.

"Sorry, talking to myself."

"Good to know," she said softly. "Well, ladies, I think we've come to the end of today's class."

The tropical forest and all its delights suddenly ended. Gone was the waterfall, the birds, the breeze in the palms. Claire opened her eyes and saw Calysta, her yoga teacher, tucking her iPod into a backpack and blowing out the candles; so long, hyacinths.

After a few minutes of stretches to get the circulation back into her now uncrossed legs, Claire rolled up her lime green yoga matt, tucked it into a brightly colored paisley tote and pulled a lightweight saffron-shaded Patagonia sweat top over her head. She flipped free her ponytail, pushing back an errant strand of hair from her face, and stood, looking at herself in the wall mirror. Was that a gray hair?

Not long ago her thick, black hair would have hung in an easy, professionally styled wave that grazed the shoulders of a neatly tailored, black DKNY suit. Her fair complexion and dark eyes would have been expertly enhanced with the aide of 40-something-friendly Bobbi Brown. An Hermes scarf would have draped elegantly at her neck, a black leather briefcase holding her laptop in one hand, a Coach handbag over her shoulder. She would have been 40 and fabulous!

"Who the hell *are* you?" she asked her reflection.

"What, Claire?" asked another woman, packing up beside her.

"Nothing, sorry, talking to myself again." *Since when do I talk to myself?*

She walked out the front door of the yoga studio and stood in the early August heat, looking up at the mesa facade of the Book Cliffs. They towered over the picturesque town of Grande River, named for the tributary that flowed through the valley that was the bustling heart of Colorado's wine industry.

"Since you moved here," she whispered.

"I'VE GLUED AND SCREWED THE rickety out of this thing," Andy said, carrying a small cafe table from the bakery's back room.

A patch of sawdust clung to his close-cropped wiry blonde hair and Gwen noticed a spot of something— glue?—on the pocket of his blue, buttoned-down shirt. Her husband's new work day wardrobe leaned toward khakis and a nice shirt, but he left the collar open and rolled up the sleeves; dressy enough to meet with customers but dressed down enough to pitch in wherever he was needed.

It was a nice change from his previous profession as a long-haul trucker. Now, his near endless summer days were spent managing the vineyards, giving his complexion a burnished glow. She wondered, not for the first time, why it was some men grew more attractive in middle age rather than less.

"Thank you, honey," Gwen called from behind the register where she was steaming coffee for a customer's latte. "You're a life saver. I owe you!"

"Promises, promises!" he said with a smile. "I'll put it back on the front patio, but next year I think we should spring for some new tables and chairs out there. These garage sale specials are only gonna last so long."

"Next year maybe we can afford it."

The sale of her old bakery the previous January in the mountain town of Blue River had brought in a little nest egg for this new endeavor. And since they were only renting their current space, they had saved a great deal of up-front cash, but the hard times they'd gone through the previous year made her gun-shy of any unnecessary expenses.

She no longer worried about trucking strikes or icy stretches of mountain roads that might send her husband's rig careening out of control and land him in the hospital again...or worse; that reality was in the past. Their friend, Bob, had offered to make Andy the new site manager at his winery, Columbine Vineyards. Andy accepted and Gwen had closed the book on her Blue River Bakery. Together, they'd started a new chapter in Grande River.

It didn't hurt that Bob had also lured Gwen's friend, Claire, to town. Claire was recovering after a vicious assault last winter and Bob offered Grande River as the perfect place for some R&R. Clearly, Bob was hoping it would bring him and Claire closer together but Gwen still wasn't sure the staunchly independent Claire was ready to deepen their relationship.

Gwen had expanded from her previous bakery concept, adding in the coffee house theme, and acquiring a large Gaggia espresso machine. In the two months since their June grand-opening Gwen had worked to gain a sense of competency as a true barista.

The latte served, Gwen stood a moment, surveying the current state of affairs. Some days she felt like she was bubbling with emotions inside, so much had been accomplished and so much was left to be done. Sure, she was anxious, she thought, who wouldn't be?

But she was excited too, excited about all the possibilities their future held in this new town and all the possibilities her new business held. It was satisfying to survey her domain, she thought, and she smiled as she did.

Out front, customers walked through the gate of a low, split rail fence onto a patio where cafe tables and chairs were nestled within the edges of a wild mountain garden. Up a few steps and past a porch swing they entered the front room, where, on the right side, her bakery cases, register and Gaggia served all comers.

This first room had a small potbelly stove against the far wall, and an array of overstuffed chairs circled a five-foot round, mahogany coffee table. At the back, a wide flight of three steps took customers into a larger room, with tables and chairs of varying sizes upfront and an oversized sofa at the back, facing a floor-to-ceiling stone fireplace. It was summer now, so only candles glowed within, but Gwen anticipated the blazing fires that chilly winter afternoons would bring.

To the left of the stairs a swinging door took employees into the long, side kitchen—the heart of Gwen's new business home—its work tables occupied by baked goods in various stages of creation, its ovens warm from their daily tasks. Aging oak floors creaked throughout the building.

Large windows along the outside walls revealed views of the cliffs above town, and the river across the street.

She'd closed her old bakery and moved a hundred miles west, from the ski town of Blue River, to where the Rocky Mountains opened up to mesas and the vistas switched from mountain-rimmed to big sky.

In celebration of a new life and big changes, Gwen had cut her hair short, discovering a suggestion of natural curl and accepting the few gray hairs that now nibbled at the temples of her brown locks. By August the summer's sun had given a glow to her cheeks and brought out a few freckles that hinted at her Irish heritage. The move and all the extra efforts that a new business required also meant she'd lost enough pounds to now consider herself trim, even in her tightest jeans.

Andy worked in the fresh air under nature's elements while Gwen labored before flour dusted counters and ovens that only cooled at night. She still fretted over too many things, big and small, and she'd noticed that the *worry-wrinkles* between her brows seemed more pronounced. *Had Andy noticed them too?*

Settling into her new business plan was more difficult than she'd expected. The expansion from her original bakery format to include the coffee shop had seemed like a small addition at first. But Gwen discovered that it took a great deal more effort and pulled in more customers than she'd anticipated.

Not that that was a bad thing. But it did take her away from her kitchen and, for better or worse, she really enjoyed the interaction with customers that the new format allowed. Unfortunately, she found herself interacting more than she should. That meant working extra hours catching up in the kitchen.

She'd hired two employees to help out front. Carolyn came in the mornings. She was Claire's age, with the slight plump of middle age and softly curling short brown hair that framed a freckled and cheerful face. She was a popular local watercolor artist, but said she needed to get out of her studio once in a while and visit the real world. Becca, a student at the local high school, filled in afternoons and weekends.

When things slowed, Gwen retreated to the kitchen, baking up treats to fill the case out front. More and more she found herself sorry to leave the front room. Like a child being sent away from the party.

They'd bought an old, three-story Victorian home that the previous owner had brought up to code and upgraded with a kitchen that felt like something out of an IKEA catalog. Gwen would have said she was a traditional sort, so even she was surprised how much she loved that new kitchen.

Her new nest was still as empty as her old one. Jeff, her only child, had helped with the move, then flown off to spend the bulk of his summer on a church mission trip in Haiti. A quick trip home last summer was barely long enough for Gwen to do his laundry before he returned to his sophomore year at Colorado State University in Fort Collins, four hours east of home.

Gwen thought she was handling this new phase of life pretty well. Still, though it was logically impossible, it felt to her that Jeff left home more often than he returned!

Their new home was midway between the bakery and Andy's new job at their friend's winery, Columbine Estates. In an odd twist of fate, that friend, Bob, was also the love interest of Gwen's good friend, Claire.

It's crazy that Claire has any love interest at all.

Not too long ago she'd been a committed relationship-phobe, every waking moment dedicated to her real estate business. That had changed the day a client attacked her, leaving her body and spirit weakened. Bob invited her to spend some time with him in

Grande Valley. No, coerced was more like it.

She had to admit that though they'd left their mutual friend, Del, back in Blue River, the move was easier with Claire's sharp wit and sharper tongue nearby.
Watching Claire decompress had been an amazing,
sometimes painful, but still entertaining sight. She
hoped her formerly driven friend survived all the relaxation the summer had provided.

G WEN GLANCED AT THE TIME, then toward the
sidewalk out front. Like clockwork, Claire emerged
from the yoga studio across the street and headed toward
the bakery. She smiled as she watched her type-A friend,
though dressed down for her workout, still striding with
purpose, as if on her way to negotiate a million dollar
offer with a tough competitor.

Gwen knew Claire was struggling with her doctor's
orders to find a less stressful routine. For someone who
fed on the pressures of her job, achieving a laid-back
lifestyle was its own form of stress.

"Good morning...almost." Claire dumped her bag
on the coffee table and collapsed into one of the arm
chairs.

"It's nine o'clock, I think that counts as morning."
Gwen sat across from her on the coffee table. "Since
when are you not a morning person?"

"Since I didn't fall asleep until almost 2 am."

"How come?"

"I don't know. It's not like I have anything to worry
about. Jesus, it's not like I have anything—period. I
spend my days doing yoga, reading books, hiking in

the mesas and visiting with you—not that you aren't delightful company, kiddo."

"Why thank you, I can almost take that as a compliment." They shared a rueful smile. "What about Bob? Aren't you two...?"

"Bob's great, but he's got his own life. And it's a busy time, gearing up for harvest."

"Tell me about it. I'm lucky to get a few minutes of Andy's time for my honey-do list, let alone any up-close-and-personal time. He's just beat at night. I managed to snag him for a little while this morning, but he'll be heading out soon. You didn't see him coming in?"

"Nope. He's not on the patio."

Gwen looked out the windows behind the counter and saw her husband trimming bushes at the side of the building. He looked up, winked at her, and returned to his task. "Looks like he's working his way down the list. I shouldn't complain, but even when we are together, we're both either too busy or too exhausted."

"Bob's on overdrive, too. He gets off late. We don't always see each other."

Gwen knew Bob wanted Claire to move in with him, but that was a little more reality than Claire could handle, so she was renting a small—very small—house that sat at the intersection of two peach orchards, on a ridge overlooking the valley. The view was breath-taking, but Gwen wondered if the isolation was both a blessing and a curse for Claire.

"How's your garden?" This was a question Gwen never thought she'd be asking of Claire, but Claire had planted her garden almost immediately upon arrival, saying she needed a reason to get up every day and a damned garden seems like as good a friggin' excuse to get my ass out of bed every morning as anything else.

"Weedy and needy. I'm thinking of opening up a garden shop by that name, it seems to be the theme for gardens. But it is productive." Claire reached into her bag and pulled out a zucchini that was nearly a foot long. "Here. It's a zucchini. I've got a bunch of them but you can only eat so much of this stuff, you know?"

"Thanks…although I think you're supposed to pick them when they're smaller."

"Oh? Well, I've got lots of those too, I'll bring you some. I thought they were kind of seedy, compared to the stuff I've had in restaurants."

"These big ones are good for zucchini bread."

"Bread? Out of zucchini? Who knew."

Gwen smiled. "I'll make you some. Or you could take cooking lessons…that might give you something to do."

"Cooking? Not much of a kitchen in the hut I live in. The Unabomber probably had a bigger kitchen."

"You can always use the kitchen here," Gwen said. She was willing to offer any help for her friend, though she didn't really think Claire was likely to embrace a culinary adventure. "That is, if you want to learn to cook…more."

Claire laughed. "It's okay, you can ask it. You're wondering if I really am a complete incompetent in the kitchen, aren't you?"

"Well…."

"I'm not. Not completely, at least. I've just gotten in the habit of eating out or taking out or at the most, reheating. I'm a veritable genius with a microwave. But I could cook a meal in a pinch…just haven't wanted to for a long time."

"And do you want to now?"

"Not particularly," Claire confessed. "It's only that I want to do something! I'm used to being busy, you know?"

Gwen nodded sympathy and patted Claire's knee comfortingly.

"You're a good friend, Gwen. I know you mean well, but Jesus, I have to find something to do with myself or I'm gonna go nuts!"

"Are you thinking of going back to Blue River?" Gwen asked the question that had been worrying at the back of her thoughts for some time now.

"Oh, I don't know. Maybe. If I go back I can pick up my business there, but I'm not sure that's what I want to do anymore."

"Are you...afraid?" Gwen wondered if the memory of the attack had frightened Claire out of real estate.

"Afraid? No. I don't think so. Besides, once I got my hands on my Tazer I did a job on that guy—probably fried any chance he ever had of having kids," she said, a trace of a smile crossing her face as she remembered...then it was gone. "He just beat me up pretty damn good beforehand," she added softly. Then, louder, "What doesn't kill you makes you stronger, isn't that the saying?"

"Sure," Gwen said, still concerned.

Claire leaned back in the chair and pulled a throw pillow into her arms, hugging it protectively against her chest. "Anyway, when I was in the hospital—and since then—I've had plenty of time to think. These last few years I was going and going and I couldn't help wondering just where it had gotten me. Sure, my checking account was happy, but was I? Looking back, I feel like I made my clients' dreams come true…but did I make *my* dreams come true?"

"Well, you did help Sally and Jordan, and that was a dream of yours, right?" Gwen knew Claire had helped to support her younger sister and her son, who had a learning disability. She'd dedicated herself to making their lives better, but Sally had taken over that responsibility, found a good job, a good school for Jordan and met a wonderful new husband. Sally didn't need Claire's help anymore.

Claire stared out the window at the garden, watching a hummingbird hover and dash between lavender petunia blossoms. "Yeah, it was…."

"So." Gwen stood, arms on her hips, staring down at her friend.

"So." Claire stared up at her. "Can I have an iced chai?"

"You've had some version of herbal teas every day for weeks now and I know you hate it."

"Doctor's orders were no coffee."

"No, doctor's orders were not to live on it. I think you're ready for a nice iced coffee. With a little cream. It's kind of what you had before, but it's different. And Dr. Gwen prescribes something different!"

Claire stared up at her friend for a few seconds. "Huh. You might be right."

IF THERE WAS ONE THING the valley was known for, besides wine, it was second chances. So many of the vineyards were started and staffed by people who had switched their lives in midstream, taken a leap of faith or retired to a new and more fulfilling way of life. Bob fit the profile.

He was tall, his dark hair worn short but always ready for a trim. Even features and brown eyes gave him a friendly but steady look like a good-natured German Shepard. He was trim and tan and moved with a comfortable easiness acquired only recently.

Tireless years in the demanding world of finance left him a wealthy man but in the end had cost him his marriage along with his personal illusion of success. In the months after his divorce he'd cleansed himself of all vestiges of his former career and home. He'd gone on a modern-day walk-about and ended up at the vineyard home of a friend in Napa Valley. With little purpose beyond the moment, he worked in the fields and the winery, learning the craft and the art of the vintner.

What began as a way to get from one day to the next turned into a passion that eventually brought him to Grande Valley, heart of Colorado's growing wine industry. He bought an aging winery and dedicated himself to building the renamed venture, Columbine Estates, into its current status as the producer and purveyor of award winning wines.

Life was good for Bob, and it got even better when a visit to his off season home in Blue River led to Claire. She was a friend of friends, and the moment he met her he saw beyond the walls she'd worked so hard to erect around her life and heart. Bob recognized the symptoms; they had once been his own.

But he'd learned patience in the vineyard, cultivating vines that rewarded tender care under hot summer suns and through freezing spring nights. He'd learned that time spent nurturing something of value brought rewards well worth the effort. Bob knew instinctually that Claire was like those vines; sinewy and tough at the core, but able to bear a luscious fruit if she could break free of her self-imposed winter.

He also knew that she'd been struggling with her temporary visit to the valley. Bob had hoped that the time spent in its laid-back atmosphere, recovering physically and emotionally from an assault that had occurred while she was holding an open house the previous winter, would transform her outlook on life, as his time in the vineyards of Napa had. Some days, he thought, it was working its magic. Though she'd refused to move in with him, they'd been together often.

On clear, dark nights when the full starlit skies burned down upon them and everything seemed possible, he felt certain the woman he held in his arms would never leave. But just as fully as he felt that moment in his heart, there were other moments; hot afternoons watching Claire dig at her garden, clearly tearing away at more than the visible weeds; late afternoons as she sat in his winery's tasting room watching others so preoccupied with their purpose-her own lack of purpose painfully clear on her face; early mornings when he woke to find her standing at the window, watching the sunrise with unexplainable tears welling in her eyes.

Even Claire couldn't express the multitude of conflicting feelings she struggled with daily. He'd suggested a psychologist, but she'd tossed off the idea, intent that she could solve her own problems; Type A all the way. Bob knew he couldn't find the answers for her, but dammit, if he could do anything to help her find her way, he would.

August was a time of anticipation in the vineyards. Veraison, when the grapes switched their efforts from growth to ripening, was beginning. Walking through the vineyard, the clusters of berries were mottled green to purple to an almost deep burgundy for some. The Merlot grapes were past half turned, but the Cabernet were only getting started. Soon they'd be draping nets to keep the birds from eating the sugary fruit and the air would take on a sweeter scent as well.

Bob spent early mornings visiting fields to gauge the progress and calculate the timetable to harvest. Now, back at the winery, he assisted in setting up glasses and bottles for the tourists who would soon descend for the daily rounds of tastings, one winery at a time. Claire had slipped in earlier and was seated at a small table, concentrating intently on the Kindle in her hands, seemingly oblivious to their activity at the bar.

"Hey, Boss," called Terra, Columbine Estates' manager of sales and customer outreach, "when you're done there, can you take a look at the plans for next month's wine tasting dinner?"

Terra was young, only a couple years out of college where she'd majored in marketing. But she loved the earth, having grown up on a farm in the Midwest. A visit during summer break led to her new life in Colorado, and Bob appreciated the enthusiasm and New Age ideas this tech-savvy marketer brought to his company. Her small but athletic frame, topped with a frizzy mane of red hair nearly always tamed into long braids, sporting a bandana, along with shorts, tank-top and hiking boots gave the impression of someone at ease in a workroom, vineyard or orchestrating a tasting event. She was in her element.

"The dinner for the festival?" Bob asked referring to the valley's annual Wine Festival to be held in mid-September.

"Yep, we've gotten a lot more bookings than planned. I'm not sure how we're going to squeeze everyone into the space."

"Can we hold it outside?"

"Possibly. But I think we'd need some good tents, you never know."

"That's the truth." September days could be anything from summer heat to winter chill and possibly even snow. Fall was an unpredictable season in the mountains and mesas of Colorado. "Look into it. I'm willing to consider it as long as we don't leave ourselves unprepared."

"Will do," she said, heading off as if on a mission,

clipboard in hand.

Bob chose three wines for the day's tastings; a rosé, a merlot and a cabernet franc reserve, chilling the rosé, but opening the others to breathe a bit. Then he pulled a can of peach flavored tea from the fridge, filled two glasses with ice and sat beside Claire at her table.

"How was yoga this morning?"

"Stretchy," she said, not looking up from her Kindle.

Bob poured their teas, took a sip and sat back, watching her read, a crease of concentration above her nose, a slight frown at the corners of her lips. "Whacha readin'?"

She heaved a sigh, looked up from under downcast eyes and handed him the Kindle. He read the book title across the top of the screen: Creating Inner Peace: the beginner's guide to a quiet mind and active meditation.

"You're kidding?" he asked.

"You said I should see a shrink. This is pretty much the same thing."

"I did not say you should see a shrink. I said you might benefit from talking to someone."

"Again, same thing."

"Claire." He set the reader on the table and reached to take her hands in his, feeling her hesitate, then relent. "Baby, I know you're not happy and I don't know what to do about it."

"No one asked you to do anything, Bob. It's not your responsibility to figure me out, it's mine."

"But I want to help; I just don't know what to do. I only thought…maybe you should talk to someone who knows the answer. Or at least knows how to help you find it."

"This book is stupid." She pulled her hands from his and crammed the reader into her yoga bag. "It's all about lighting my inner flame to illuminate my life's journey. Is that bullshit or what?"

She looked at him so earnestly for a moment he wondered if she actually wanted an answer to her question. Then he struggled not to laugh at what he assumed was her usual less than politically correct take on the issue. "Well, Ace, then I'd say you should find someone who talks your language, not the Dalai Lama's. There's gotta be someone, have you looked?"

"Well, I did hear one of the gals in my yoga class talking about someone her husband saw. He got laid off and needed job counseling, but it sounded like more than that."

"That's great—I mean for you. Can you get a name? Give him-or her a call?"

"I suppose….shit."

"What?"

"Jesus, Bob. Who am I? I never needed anyone else to tell me what to do? I was always in charge. Where did that woman go?" Tears welled up in her eyes and she wanted to reach out and feel Bob's arms around her, comforting her, but the knowledge that she craved that comfort only made her more frustrated. "Dammit, this sucks."

Bob wrapped an arm around her, pushing a stray strand of hair from her eyes and wiping a tear's trail from her cheek. "That woman's still here, Ace. But I think you're on your own version of a walk-about now. Just like when I went to Napa. It doesn't so much change you as it transforms you. Claire. That's who you're looking for, and you'll find her. You know I'll help anyway I can, right?"

"I know," Claire whispered, allowing herself a few deep breaths into the warm comfort of his shoulder before pulling herself together. "I gotta go." She stood, hauling her bag over her shoulder.

"Where you off to?"

"My damn garden needs watering."

THE NEXT MORNING DEL SIPPED her tea and, scanning the local paper for news of last night's festivities, found an article half-way down the second page.

ST. FRANCIS HOSPITAL PLANS CONSTRUCTION OF CHILDREN'S WING

She'd invited the reporter to join her and thirty of the hospital's largest donors for a cocktail party at her home the night before. Del had been working long hours over the last few months leading up to last night. She'd pulled together a plan to raise several million dollars for construction of the first child-centered facility in the Colorado mountain, mini-metropolis of Blue River and last night had been the official kick-off.

Del smiled as she read the many positive comments her guests had shared with the reporter. Clearly everyone was on board with her first fundraising event, scheduled for the holiday season. It would be a Gala style Christmas ball incorporating both silent and live auctions.

Several of those in attendance the night before had

pledged a variety of auction items: a week at a water-front condo on Maui, a ski vacation in Steamboat, a catered dinner for twelve. One donor even pledged a Bichon puppy from her pet's future litter. All these goodies were donated to the cause, and would not only bring the hospital needed funds for construction, but provide their givers with convenient tax deductions next April. It was a win-win for all, and a very successful evening for the new head of fundraising for St. Francis Hospital in Blue River.

A year ago Del had been one big mess, but she'd literally crashed into the lives of Gwen and Claire after losing control of her car and plowing into a large planter in front of Gwen's bakery while Claire was inside getting a coffee. She knew now what a blessing in disguise that had been.

With the encouragement of her new friends she'd survived a divorce, found her footing as a single mom to her two kids, started out in the job world and the dating world as well.

She'd gone from disheveled mess to stylish social-ite. Her shoulder length blonde bob complimented a heart-shaped face with hazel eyes and full, naturally peach-shaded lips. Freckles hinted at her maiden name, Donahue, but despite the divorce, she'd kept Micky's last name, Rufino, so she'd match her son and daughter's.

Then one day she'd been miraculously handed her dream job with St. Francis. After years of managing fundraisers for PTO's and the local Women's League, Del was just the person to tackle fundraising for the new children's wing. Her heart and her detail-oriented head were most definitely in the perfect place for the challenge. It was the other challenges she'd lately faced that were throwing her this morning.

Del reached across the table and touched the petals of a bouquet of lavender roses that had arrived only an hour earlier, then picked up the card and read it again.

Lovely flowers for the lovely hostess! Carl

Del glanced at the clock; almost nine-thirty. She thought Gwen would be past the early morning rush at her coffee shop and might be able to spare time for a short chat. Since both Gwen and Claire had moved to Grande Valley Del sometimes struggled with an empty feeling that ached in her chest.

She knew she was doing well with all the changes of the last year, but her friends had become her support system. Del was happy for them, for the good changes the move brought them both, but their absence left her with that ache that overwhelmed her at the most surprising moments. Like this morning.

THE PHONE RANG SEVERAL TIMES before Gwen finally answered.

"Good Morning, Gwen's Bakery, how can I help you?"

"Hi, Gwen!"

"Hey Del, how are you, sweetie? How'd the party go?" Gwen asked. She held the phone between her shoulder and chin while she sprinkled cinnamon on top of a toffee latte and handed it to her customer.

"It was a big hit. Everybody was really excited about

the plan. And we've already received several commitments for the auction."

"That's great," Gwen said, waiting as her customer swiped a debit card and finished the transaction. "Thanks so much, have a great day," she said, half-covering the mouth piece.

"Oh, I'm so sorry," Del said, "I thought you'd be kinda on a break by now. I can call back."

"No, no, that was my last customer."

"Where's Carolyn?" Del knew Gwen had hired at least two part-timers to help during the busier hours of her day.

"Pink eye."

"Oh, Gwen! That can be very contagious!"

"Not Carolyn, her daughter. She had to take her to the doctor so I'm flying solo this morning."

"I wish I were close by. You know I'd come help," Del said earnestly.

"I know. But when you're new to town you have to be resilient."

"What about Claire? Could she help?"

"I don't think so. Claire's kinda…not Claire these days."

"What do you mean?"

"Well, she's doing yoga, gardening and talking about taking classes in wine making and I think she said something the other day about learning to brew beer."

"Beer?! Claire doesn't drink beer, she's a wine lover, through and through. Are you sure? That does not sound like Claire."

"I know, but craft breweries are big these days so she was just toying with the idea. I think. Honestly,

Del, I think she's having sort of an identity crisis."

"Poor Claire," Del said.

"Oh, sorry!" Gwen said, "here you go."

"What? What are you sorry for?" Del asked, clearly confused by the turn in the conversation.

"No, not you sweetie. It was a customer-needed a coffee cup sleeve. Guess the cup was too hot."

"Maybe I should call back another time, when you're—"

"No, really, I think we've hit a lull now anyway. Everyone is either out the door or sitting and sipping. Tell me more about your evening." Gwen knew Del was lonesome for her friends. She'd felt badly when she and Andy had decided to move and then, for better or worse, Claire had come for the summer and left Del, she sometimes thought, adrift in Blue River.

"It was so good, Gwen. Everything went well and the reporter even wrote a great story for today's paper; lots of wonderful, positive things. I think it will really help get more people interested in being involved. I want everyone, no matter how much, or how little they can give, to be a part of the project. I mean, don't we all have kids, or know kids or—"

"Hey, I'm sold! I don't know what I can do, but you let me know, okay?"

"Thank you, Gwen. I appreciate it, you know. You—and Claire— have been so supportive. Poor Claire," Del said again. "I really wish I were there to help you both."

"I'll be fine," Gwen assured her, though inside she still felt unsettled about her own dissatisfaction with her new business plan, but she didn't want Del to worry about that, not that she could have really put it into words. Or wanted to.

"You are always such a rock, Gwen, but I worry about you all the same. And Claire, too."

"Oh, you know her. At first I thought taking it easy for a while would be good for her. I'm sure the time with Bob was good, too. But now she's healed, physically at least, and Bob's occupied with the harvest coming up-Andy too. It's a busy time of the year. I can tell she's feeling restless, starting to need something to do."

"She's always been a busy kind of person, don't you think? Maybe she doesn't feel like herself if she's not working on a project. How's her garden?"

"Funny you should mention that," Gwen said, suddenly remembering the zucchini cakes that were baking in the kitchen. "The garden is having a bumper crop. Claire might actually have a green thumb. Only problem is she doesn't know what to do with the results. But I'm not so sure going back to real estate is what she wants to do, either. Honestly, I don't think she knows what she wants, and that's starting to drive her crazy, I can tell."

"Oh, poor Claire," Del said yet again. "I should call her. I haven't stayed in touch like I wanted to be."

"Dell, you've been busy enough for all of us with this project for the hospital. I'm sure she doesn't resent not hearing from you as often as she used to."

Gwen smiled to herself, she knew Claire often thought of Del as a little bird that fell from its nest. Claire's tough exterior certainly cracked when it came to looking after Del. Still, she knew Claire's private nature and Del's outgoing one sometimes had left Claire exasperated. Del tended to share her every thought.

Not so, Claire. Gwen had seen Claire cringe on more than one occasion when her phone rang and Del's name was on the screen. She loved Del, but in moderation, which seemed to be how Claire loved in general.

"I'm sure she understands. We're both just happy there are so many reasons for you to smile these days."

"Oh, there are," Del said, "In fact, you should see the beautiful flowers I got this morning!"

"Flowers? From Jimmy? That's thoughtful. Was he at the fundraiser, too?" Gwen knew Del had seen a lot of Jimmy since she'd met the owner of the Dockside Restaurant on one of their girls' nights out the previous fall. She'd thought it was getting pretty serious by the time she and Andy had moved.

"Um, well, no. Actually, they are from Carl. Carl Henderson. He's a member of the board, for St. Francis. "

"I see," Gwen said, not quite sure she actually did. "So, this is someone you're working with on the fundraiser?"

"Yes, he is but—"

Del was cut short by a sudden blaring noise on Gwen's end of the conversation.

"Oh my God! I have to go, Del! The smoke alarm in the kitchen it going off-oh geez, I totally forgot about the cakes. Sorry-bye!"

"I'll call later to see if you're okay!" Del shouted into her phone, but the line was already dead.

"**O**THER THAN SOME MINOR SMOKE damage, I think you're fine, ma'am. You are fine, aren't you, ma'am?" The firefighter stooped beside the chair Gwen clung to, seated in the coffee shop's front garden. She'd retreated there as soon as the fire truck arrived and sat, gripping the chairs wrought iron back as she watched their comings and goings.

That's where Claire found her when she heard the fire truck's sirens and leapt from her yoga matt in the studio across the street, sprinting over, barefooted, to comfort and support her friend.

"Hey, kiddo, you in there?" Claire asked, touching her friend's knee lightly.

Gwen felt numb. "I almost burned the place down…" she whispered.

"Well, I don't think I'd go that far," the fireman said. "Frankly, if it hadn't been for the automatic alarm your security system sounds at the fire station, you might not have even felt the need to call us, once you'd gotten the cakes out of the oven. Not that I'd have recommended that; smoke was pretty dense in there by the time we went in. It's always better to let the professionals handle anything fire or smoke related. But really, just smoke damage, I'd say, aside from some pretty burned cakes–and the pans. I think the pans are a total loss, but a little soap and water and the place will be fine. Really." He looked over at Claire, eyebrows raised, and shrugged his shoulders.

"That's right, see? There's some cleaning to do, and some pans are toast–literally–but that's all."

"Exactly," the fireman added, standing up. "Your friend is right, ma'am." He glanced inside. "Just gonna clean up the mess we made and we'll be out of your hair in no time. You feel free to call if you have any questions."

He met Claire's eyes, she nodded, and he left.

"So, here's what I'm gonna do," Claire held Gwen's hand as she spoke. "I'm gonna run back to the studio, get changed and then I'll be back to help. We'll get this place scrubbed up and ready in time for the lunch crowd."

Gwen looked down at her, a scowl on her face and wrinkles on her un-botoxed brow.

"Okay, maybe in time for tomorrow's lunch crowd, how's that for realistic?"

"Better." Gwen sighed and leaned back, closing her eyes for a moment.

"Did you call Andy?"

"Yep." Gwen rubbed the back of her neck and rested her head against her palm. "He didn't answer, probably didn't hear his cell-he puts it on silent in meetings and then he forgets to change it back. He's busy. I left a message." She swept both hands up across her face and ran her fingers through her short hair, dusting off a stray bit of ash into her hand. "Great," she said, looking at the ash in her palm, "more gray."

"That gray washes right out, sweetie. And I'm sure Andy will be here soon." Claire said, making a mental note to call Bob as soon as she left and tell him to find out where the hell Andy was.

"Yeah. Well…" Gwen stood. "I better go thank the firemen before they start worrying that I'm comatose or something." Another sigh.

"Hey."

"Hmm?" Gwen looked distractedly toward her.

"It's just smoke," Claire said, "and a few pans. That's

all."

"I know. But Claire, it could have been worse."

"But it wasn't."

"No thanks to me."

"Gwen, nobody is perfect. You were busy, it happens. We'll figure out a better system, one that keeps you more in touch with the back of the house when you're up in the front, sound good?"

"Maybe, but I've got to be realistic about what I can and can't do," she said, suddenly stern. "I have to face facts!"

"What do you mean? Don't you think you're being a little hard on yourself, kiddo? Accidents happen."

Something clanged loudly in the kitchen, drawing Gwen's attention. "I know but…oh, sorry, I'd better get in there." She turned and walked quickly back into the shop and away from Claire.

"I'll be back soon!" Claire called after her, but she was through the swinging door and gone into her kitchen.

Four

THE OLD FOREMAN'S HOUSE HAD been empty over a year when Claire moved in. Bob's winery leased it by default, having leased the land it stood on. Claire wound her car along an easement that allowed for the long drive through peach orchards, still tended by the owner. Beyond them were acres of vineyards, their grapes growing heavy as harvest neared. She'd come to love the late evenings when the sun set and the cooler air seemed to push the sweet perfume of all the ripening fruit across her doorstep. Breathing was a lush pleasure.

It was late by the time she finally returned home from helping with the clean-up at the bakery. Gwen had been unusually quiet throughout, despite Claire's efforts to ferret out her thoughts. Her friend was accustomed to long hours, just as she had been...before. But Claire was worried that Gwen's long hours were taking the joy out her business. Still, Gwen was the type to ask for help if she needed it, wasn't she?

Bob had found Andy walking through vineyards up on the mesa side of the river and driven him into town himself, staying long enough to survey the damage and leaving Claire with a promise to stop by her place later.

But it was already late and still no Bob. Claire thought that was just as well. She'd planned a bath along with a large glass of something red and then off to bed after the long day. The funny thing was, she wasn't as tired as she thought she would be. In fact, she felt energized, a feeling that hadn't been a part of her mental lexicon for some time.

Claire chose a Columbine Estates reserve cabernet, one of Bob's favorites, and decanted it into the narrow neck of a wide, flat crystal bottle that Bob had given her as a gift upon her arrival in the valley. She laid out her yoga matt and decided to do some stretches to wind down the kinks of the day while the wine breathed.

There was just enough room to stretch without hitting furniture once she'd spread the sage green matt onto the floor of the large main room of her little, farm-house-in-the-vineyards. Not that there was a lot of it to hit.

Bob's staff had cleaned out the house ahead of time and found a few basics, including an antique, metal infirmary-style bed. The bed was a twin size, something Bob apologized for from the start, but Claire suspected he'd planned it that way to encourage her frequent stays at his home. It worked often enough, but she found herself wanting her own space and really, though small, it was a comfortable bed.

Claire had brought some things from home: a dark chocolate, cashmere throw, a few watercolor prints, two crystal candle holders and some pottery bowls and vases. Lately she'd found comfort in the more rustic and organic items she owned, opting to leave much of her modern decor at her home in Blue River, nearly everything in fact, except a contemporary chair and ottoman made of wood and pale yellow, buttery soft leather chair.

Over the years she'd spent many hours in that chair with her laptop, working late into the night. Now she climbed into it to read, to rest, to listen to her iPod and try to figure out what the rest of her life should be about.

These things made the rooms feel more like her home, though often as not, it still felt as though she was, not so much away from home, as in search of it.

The large room she now addressed with a sun salutation opened on one end to a small porch, complete with swing, and ended with a fireplace hearth surrounded by rocks hewn from the mesas the home sat upon. Large windows looking out onto peach orchards. A short hall led to her small bedroom and a modest bathroom with only a clawfoot tub. Claire wondered if Bob had also hoped she'd be lured by the promise of a shower at his house but again he'd failed. For the first time in years she found she enjoyed the slow, soothing pace of a bath.

Off the small kitchen was side door to a carport where she'd parked her high-end, sleek black Euro-SUV. To Claire it looked as out of place in its new surroundings as she often felt.

She was winding down from her yoga routine and thinking of finally pouring a glass of wine when the sound of tires on gravel alerted her to the approach of a car. Claire stood, stretching as she walked, and opened the door, expecting Bob's Silverado pick-up in her drive.

Instead, she saw the old, green pick-up she knew belonged to her neighbors, two elderly sisters who lived alone in the large, once elegant Victorian home whose peaks she could see over the tops of the orchards to the west.

Claire had met them briefly a few times, with just the pleasantries neighbors exchanged in passing. She knew little about them, aside from a natural good-naturedness.

"Hello, dear!" came a voice from the pick-up, and she heard the squeak of the door as it opened. Claire recognized Cora Larson, the more out-going of the Larson sisters. Claire had always imagined Cora as the 'life of the party' in their youth, while her sister, Evie, likely baked the cakes, greeted the guests and tended to everyone's comfort. They both seemed comfortable within their own skins, or at least the years had made them so.

Cora wore a light blue barn coat over beige khakis and serviceable shoes. She had a bright fuchsia, silk scarf wrapped around her white hair and tied under her chin, giving Claire the impression of an elderly Grace Kelly, just come from mucking out the stalls.

"Cora, what are you doing out at this hour? Is everything alright?"

"Don't worry, dear. Evie and I are fine. It's just a small problem, and I was wondering if I could use your phone. You do have one, don't you?" she asked, approaching the door. "I know Walt, who lived here before, never had lines put in, but I figured you kids now-a-days all have cell phones. Thought you'd likely be able to help us out."

"Sure," Claire said, opening her door to let her

neighbor in. "Let me get it. Is there a problem?"

"Just a little one. Our phone line went out during that last storm and we kept thinking about getting it fixed but, well, it was so nice without it ringing that we never got around to it."

"Huh." Claire said, retrieving her phone from the kitchen counter. It had never occurred to her-ever-that the lack of a phone could be so pleasing. "I think it might be a little late to call for phone service, don't you?" she asked, handing her the phone.

"Oh my, yes. I think I'll have to see to that tomorrow. I only need to call the doctor."

"The doctor? What the—what's wrong, is it Evie?" Claire barely knew the women but suddenly she felt a protective impulse rush through her.

"I'm sure she'll be fine. She took a little tumble when the lights went out—"

"She fell? What—what about your lights?"

"Well, that generator is getting old."

"Don't you have, you know, utilities? Don't you use the power company?" Claire was having a hard time imagining their large home being completely off the grid.

"Of course, dear. It's only that we mislaid the bill...a few months ago and then a couple days ago the power was turned off."

"What? Did you call them?" Claire's concerns were growing with every word. Should these sweet little old ladies be living on their own?

"Well, we meant to, but then there's the phone service going out. But we have Mother's gas lamps— and candles of course. It's really quite charming. I had planned to stop by the electric company next time I got into town for groceries, but the garden has been so abundant this year. Isn't your garden doing extremely well, also?"

"God is it ever—"

"Now Claire, you shouldn't invoke the Lord for a thing as simple as you garden." Cora's voice took on an admonishing tone, but she smiled in a way that softened the effect.

"Um, sorry..." Claire smiled, recalling the elderly clients she'd worked with in the past, remembering what seemed like a time far away from this night.

"Abundant?" Cora asked.

"Pardon?"

"Your garden?"

"Yes, yes. Insanely abundant, I even—" Claire's thoughts suddenly returned to where this encounter had started. "Wait! Evie fell? Is she okay? Can I help?"

"Why yes, dear. You can let me use your phone to call the doctor. He might want to send an ambulance. You know how fussy they get when you break something."

"What?" Claire stood with her mouth open for a second processing the train of the conversation and then, once it all kicked in, she picked up her cell and punched in 911. "Here!" She handed Cora her phone. "When they answer tell them your address. I'll get my coat and you come with me, we'll be at your house long before the ambulance."

Claire hustled Cora, despite protests, into her SUV and in minutes they were on the dirt drive leading to the Larson's home. An expansive covered porch, with double columns at each turn surrounded most of the first floor of the large white home. The third story was topped with multiple peaks and gables and generous gingerbread trim in what Claire recalled was a faded burgundy and green. A wide stair led to the front door with its large, beveled glass oval.

In the moonlight Claire could see that it had been a proud house once, but time and neglect had had its way with the exterior. She wondered what she'd find inside.

Cora climbed the steps and opened the door, calling out, "Evie! I've brought help, and more's on the way. Where are you?"

"On the couch where you left me, Cora," said a small voice from a room off the front hall.

"So you are," Cora said, gently stooping beside her. "I've brought Claire back with me—or actually, she brought me!"

"Why thank you, Claire," Evie said, taking Claire's hand in her own, giving it a small squeeze. "I do hope I'm not inconveniencing anyone."

"I'm sure you're not," Claire assured her.

Claire felt the thin bones beneath the slight grasp and hesitated to squeeze back too firmly. Evie was a slighter version of her sister. Claire wondered who was older, or if they might be twins. Each had glorious white hair. Cora's was tied up on her head, but Evie's fell about her shoulders. While Claire could imagine Cora had once owned—and managed—the largest spread of fruit orchards in the Grand Valley, Evie seemed delicate in comparison, and her complexion a paler version of her sister's fuller, ruddier looks.

"How's it feel?" Cora asked, looking down at Evie's leg, stretched out on the ottoman before her.

"Remember the time Daddy's hand, Kade, was

bucked by the sorrel—broke his shinbone clean through?"

Cora nodded, a frown on her face for the first time.

"I have new sympathy for him tonight, God rest his soul."

The two sat quiet for a moment and Claire wondered if they might actually be praying for the guy with the broken leg. In the distance she could hear sirens.

"Ladies," she said, breaking their silence, "I think the cavalry's coming."

"What?" they both said in unison. Then realizing what she meant, Cora said, "Very good, Claire! Yes." she patted Evie's hand. "Claire has organized your rescue, darling. She's a woman of purpose after my own heart, I must say."

"Oh?" Evie looked up at Claire. "Thank you so much for helping Cora. I was very worried about her."

"No problem," Claire said, somewhat amazed and almost tempted to laugh when she realized that they were each equally concerned for the other. "So, Evie," she said, "is there anything you want to take with you to the hospital? The ambulance is almost here."

"Excellent idea, Claire," Cora said, and turning to her sister, "Would you like your housecoat? Perhaps some personal items? Do you think I can ride with her in the ambulance?" she asked Claire.

"Well…probably."

"Oh, dear!" said Cora suddenly.

"What?" Claire asked.

"I can't leave, there are so many lamps lit, and I need to lock up and—"

"I'll do it, don't worry. I'll take care of it," Claire

said, surrendering to the fact that there was no bath or glass of wine in her future tonight.

I T WAS VERY LATE BY the time Claire finally locked up the Larson sisters' home. Once the ambulance had driven away it occurred to her that she might as well call the power company's emergency line to alert them to the troubles. The sisters were well known in the valley and Claire's assurances that that bill would soon be brought up to date invoked great sympathy that Claire found surprisingly touching, though she'd needed to give them her own account information, should it not. Business was business, apparently, no matter how small the town. It turned out there was an emergency crew nearby, wrapping up a call and they could be there within an hour; could she wait? She could.

Claire sat at the bottom of the staircase, watching through the glass of the front door for the lights of the repair truck. She could have waited in the living room, curled up on the couch, but she knew if she did that her exhaustion would catch up with her and sleep would be too tempting.

Perched on the steps, she surveyed the house. It was everything an elegant old home should be, from its graceful sweeping staircase with turned and curved walnut rails and balusters, to the large crystal chandelier that hung over the entry hall to the spacious old parlor, with its oak floors warmed by oriental rugs and a large stone hearth.

She wondered if the rest of the home was equally inviting and, feeling the curiosity that her years of selling homes had instilled in her, she made a quick sweep of the rooms, on the pretext of turning out the lights. She found two more oil lamps and also found the rest of the home up to her expectations. Her realtor's mind tagged it as gracious but in need of some TLC.

The bones of the house were clearly spacious and good, though time and aging décor had left it with a feeling of melancholy, as if the ghosts of the departed lingered with both love and lethargy.

She wondered if there were family nearby to help and made a mental note to ask if the opportunity arose. The arrival of Grand Valley Power put an end to her inspection, though she was only beginning to wonder about the practicality that such a large home played in the future of two elderly spinsters.

"SORRY FOR THE DELAY, DEL. Let's do the Dockside—12:30. I'm heading into another meeting, but I'm greatly anticipating our luncheon date."

"Oh." Del listened to Carl's voicemail with growing anxiety. She pushed the button on her cell for reply but found herself immediately deposited in Carl's voicemail. "Oh no," she said, wishing she'd carried her cell phone with her. Instead, she'd left it on her desk while visiting the ladies room down the hall from her office at St. Francis Hospital.

Del waited a few minutes and tried again, but still no luck. Carl must have silenced his phone while in the meeting. This was not good. Of all the places he could have chosen, what were the odds it would be the restaurant owned by Jimmy, her...what, she wondered, her former boyfriend, her former lover? She was still confused about what they had been to each other, though the ache in her heart told her it had mattered.

She had thought herself such a professional, agreeing to Carl's request for a lunch meeting, despite her instincts that Carl was hungry for more than lunch and a part in her latest fundraiser.

There were the flowers he'd sent yesterday morning after the event he'd attended at her home. And the many kind words of support and agreement during frequent meetings with the hospital board, of which Carl was a member. And of course there was his very generous donation to her fundraising cause; that was hard to ignore.

So when Carl had called asking if they could meet for lunch, Del had done her best to push what she considered immature and unprofessional concerns to the back of her mind. It was not a date, she reminded herself, it was business.

Still, she'd been caught off guard and, when Carl asked where she'd like to eat Del was unsure whether the restaurants she normally chose for luncheon with her friends would be appropriate. She'd told him to pick and she'd meet him there. He'd been in a rush and promised to call later with a spot. She'd agreed.

Now what? It was almost noon, and the Dockside was only a short drive from the hospital. She could leave him a message, but what if he didn't check it in time? And what if he did? How would she explain why she couldn't meet him there for lunch-but could meet him elsewhere?

Was the food bad? No, everyone in town loved the place. Was the staff rude? No, they'd won the 'best service' award five years running in the local paper. Really, there was no reasonable, adult way to explain that she couldn't meet him there for lunch because the owner, Jimmy, was—what? What exactly was Jimmy to Del these days?

A month ago they'd been close; extremely close.

"Oh shoot," Del said, slumping back into the sage and pink striped armchair that filled one corner of her office. She pulled a floral chintz pillow from beneath her and hugged it to her chest. A small mewing sound involuntarily escaped, followed by a sigh.

A month ago Del had been in love; happier than she'd been in years. Then suddenly she'd felt the whole relationship was moving too fast. Several years had passed since Jimmy's wife died and now, with Del, he apparently felt like he was ready to settle down again.

Del, however, was finally feeling comfortable with her new found freedom after the divorce. She'd adjusted to being a single parent when Cara and Nate were home, and she loved her incredible new job. Heck, she loved where she was in her life, she'd thought, and Jimmy just made it all the sweeter. That was until he'd started talking seriously about merging their lives.

More and more Del noticed conversations modified by monogamous statements like in our home or when we go on vacation. At first it was fun. Like playing house. But then she realized Jimmy wanted to play house for real-and soon. But did she?

One thing led to another and little disagreements started popping up over the smallest things, like what movie to watch on a Friday night or even, one evening, which vegetable they'd have with dinner!

"What the hell are we talking about here?" Jimmy finally blurted out over the broccoli.

"Jimmy, I-I like asparagus!" Even Del knew that answer was lame.

"Babe," he'd said, standing in the middle of his kitchen, his eyes speaking what they both knew.

But still she avoided the topic. "Broccoli is fine," she

said at last, turning her back on him.

"Del, this isn't about broccoli or asparagus, and you know it." He tried to wrap his arms around her but she broke away.

"No, Jimmy," she said, frightened by the direction the conversation was going. She felt like she'd been caught in some trap, smothered under Jimmy's attention and care. "It is," she said, "it's about having…my own asparagus in my own home—by myself!"

She'd said it finally, instantly sorry she had. When she turned to look at him and saw her own confusion reflected in his expression, suddenly Del felt the pounding of her heart and the need to be away from this moment, this place and this man. She'd grabbed her purse, made some quick excuse and fled.

Since then they'd had a couple conversations, the gist of which were that maybe they both needed a little space for a while. Maybe they should take some time to be alone and figure out just what it was they wanted.

Del wasn't sure that was exactly what she wanted. She missed Jimmy, but she'd agreed.

THE DOCKSIDE RESTAURANT AND BAR overlooked Blue River reservoir and had been the site of many happy moments spent not only with Jimmy, but with Gwen and Claire, as well. In a way, it was where Del had truly 'come out' as a social single. When she walked through the door to meet Carl the establishment's woodsy, mountain/nautical décor wrapped her in nostalgia. It was warm and inviting—until she saw

Jimmy behind the bar.

He hadn't seen her yet, so she asked the hostess to seat her at an out-of-the-way table, beside the windows and overlooking the docks with her back to the bar. Maybe she couldn't avoid Jimmy, but at least she could stay out of his direct line of sight.

She was just settling into her chair when she jumped at the sound of Carl's voice.

"Hello lovely lady!" he said in a loud voice as he approached their table.

Del smiled and cringed, glancing toward the bar in hopes that Jimmy hadn't noticed. He hadn't. She was safe…for now.

"Carl," she said, lifting her hand to shake his. He took her hand in both of his and gave it a squeeze that Del felt was just a little too intimate for a business meeting.

Carl had a dapper successful corporate executive appearance. His impeccably tailored, beige suit had a pale, cream pinstripe running through it. Its coloring, along with his sun-burnished, fair features and close cropped cornsilk-colored hair would have made him fade into the woodwork, but he'd chosen a lavender shirt and topped it with deeper lavender tie. There was even a matching pocket square.

What's wrong if man took time to put himself together in the morning, Del thought, she did the same, after all. There wasn't anything wrong with wanting to look nice. It was a tasteful combination that made him look like the well moneyed, successful man he was. And really, Del, reflected, nothing in Carl's personality would ever make him a wall flower. Quite the contrary.

"What a delightful break in my day, Adele. Your

smiling face makes up for all the bull hockey I've been putting up with all morning."

"Oh?" Del instantly imagined what Claire would say about Carl's choice of terms. That is, if she ever told Claire about this lunch. Well, she thought, why shouldn't she? It's just business, and certainly Claire would understand that.

"Pardon my French," Carl added, laughing at his own joke, "but I've spent the morning with a roomful of timid investors. Let me tell you, if there's one thing I learned at Wharton it was to strike while the iron is hot! These jokers are letting this deal cool until it's frigid."

"Are these investors for the hospital?" Del asked, hopefully.

"No dice. This is another board I'm on. But I'm working on funding for your project, lovely Adele," he said, reaching across the table to take her hand.

Del froze, a smile on her face, took a breath and gave his hand what she hoped would look like a firm, business-like squeeze before deliberately extracting it to reach for the menu. Though she had no way of knowing, she felt certain Jimmy's eyes were boring into her back.

She managed to steer the conversation down more professional paths as their lunch progressed, but Carl had what Del found a slightly disturbing manner of reaching to touch her hand, or pausing to compliment her at every opportunity. It was unnerving, considering the circumstances, but really, she thought to herself, she and Jimmy were taking a break, weren't they? And if she'd met Carl for lunch anywhere else, would the same behavior really bother her? He was, after all, being very complimentary and attentive.

In fact, Del realized, she was enjoying her lunch with Carl very much. Their shared interest in the hospital gave them plenty to talk about and the time passed quickly. Of course, there were several pauses while Carl checked his emails and texts. Apparently the meeting he'd left to join her for lunch had reconvened without him and his expression grew darker with each buzz of his phone.

Finally, after some firm tapping on his cell he said, "Adele, I'm really sorry about this, but I'm going to have to cut our lunch date short."

"Something serious?" she asked, glancing from his face to his phone.

"Unfortunately, without me there to steer things in the right direction, I'm afraid the board is about to make a very serious mistake. I need to get over there."

He placed his napkin on the table and stood. Del had thought he meant to wrap their lunch up and leave, but apparently he was going straight for the exit.

"Oh, well, certainly, if you must." She reached for her purse and glanced for their waitress in order to get the bill.

"No, no. You stay and finish your lunch," Carl said. "And enjoy the view—it's great, isn't it? And it's on me. I'm the one who insisted you join me and now, I'm leaving early."

"No, Carl, really. I'm finished," she said, looking down at her half-finished lunch. She'd ordered the honeyed-pecan crusted, salmon salad, her favorite item on the menu. She usually finished it all. "I'll get a doggie bag," she added and started to rise, but Carl was already crossing to the bar and, much to Del's horror, heading straight for Jimmy.

"Hey, Jimmy,"he said,"can you have your girl put our lunch on my tab? I have to leave early but I'd like my companion to be able to finish without me." He pointed across the room and directly at Del.

Jimmy's dark eyes followed and, apparently seeing Del for the first time since she'd arrived, he looked from her to Carl and back again. The surprised expression on his face quickly turned to something harder, making Del's heart race. She felt her face flush like a sixteen-year-olds' and quickly turned her back to them both.

"You bet," was all Jimmy said.

"Isn't she something?" Carl added.

Del glanced back, shocked Carl would say something like that about her. As if he had the right to consider her anything, let alone something!

Jimmy stared back at her and said, "Yeah, she's something all right."

At that Del turned away again, but this time she wasn't shocked, she was mad. She could only think of the many tender things Jimmy had said to her when they were together. She'd never heard him use that tone of voice with regard to her. If his intention was to hurt her, he had, she thought. But two could play that game. And so she turned again to wave at the departing Carl. "Good luck with your meeting!" she called after him. He managed a quick wave and was gone, leaving Del to deliberately settle back into her chair with every intention of enjoying all of her lunch.

And she almost did, until Jimmy suddenly arrived.

"Adele," he said, sitting across from her, his hands clasped on the table before him.

"Hi, Jimmy." She noticed his lean frame seemed slighter and wondered if he had been ill. His luscious black hair that she'd so enjoyed running her fingers through when they were making love looked like it was overdue for a cut. He'd always had some gray at his temples…was there more? She longed to reach out and touch a curl that fell loose above his eyes, but resisted, forcing her gaze back to her salad.

"Enjoying your lunch?" he asked, coolly.

"Yes. I love the salmon salad. Um, you know I do."

"I was referring to your company," he said, looking off toward the door Carl had exited through. "I see him in here a lot. He's pretty popular…with the ladies."

His lips were pursed tightly and Del had the feeling strong emotions ran right below the surface, but she felt a growing resentment toward the implication of his words.

"Carl is a member of the hospital board, and we were having a business lunch," she said primly, making every effort to seem nonchalant about the whole matter, even taking a bite of salad, hoping her chewing didn't look as uncomfortable as the rest of her felt. Jimmy never used to make her feel uncomfortable, she thought.

"It didn't look like business from my angle."

He nodded his head toward the bar and she realized he'd been well aware of her presence during the entire lunch.

"Looked like he was having a hard time keeping his hands off you, Adele."

"Well you're just—just wrong, that's all. Carl's just like that," she said, inwardly astounded at herself for defending Carl's touchy behavior that only a short while ago had made her uncomfortable. "Some people are," she waved a hand in the air, looking for the right words, "the 'touchy-feely' type," and knew instantly she'd chosen her words poorly.

"Really."

He tilted his head and raised his brows in a way she knew well. He'd tease her with the same expression whenever he felt she was being naïve. In the past, there had always been a smile, too. Now the smile was gone.

"Really. And really, Jimmy, what's it matter if it was more. You know, we're not seeing each other anymore. That was your decision." Del regretted those words also, knowing it had been both of their decisions. How had she managed to turn what they'd both considered an amicable temporary pause in their relationship into what now felt like a permanent break?

She took a sip of iced tea to ease the growing knot in her stomach.

"If that's how you truly feel, Adele, then I can't argue with you there." Jimmy stood. "Just be careful, babe. It might be business, like you said. Just be careful you don't get played."

He left before she could say anymore and, in truth, she didn't want to say more. She grabbed her purse and left as quickly as possible, not looking back to see if Jimmy watched her exit. Not wanting him to see the tears that almost overflowed. She wanted to leave, to go home, to crawl into her bed and hide from the reality of how terrible this conversation made her feel. To sooth the ache inside where she'd once felt only loved.

Six

VISITORS WHO UNFORTUNATELY FOUND THEMSELVES at Grand Valley General couldn't help but to feel that the name was a bit of a misnomer. They expected a city-sized hospital but what they found was more a clinic on steroids. Still, it served the valley's needs. Several doctors covered the various specialties. What wasn't available could be choppered in on short notice from St. Francis Hospital in Blue River.

Claire had managed a couple hours sleep before rising early. A long hot shower had cleared some cobwebs along with a heavy dose of black coffee afterward. She found the Larson sisters in one of these rooms, Evie resting comfortably, her broken leg set in what looked more like a splint than a cast. Cora sat in a chair beside her sleeping sister, fully focused on a passage in a Gideon bible that Claire assumed she'd found in the room.

"Oh! Claire, dear, what a delightful surprise!" Cora said, setting the bible aside and patting the seat of the chair beside her. The early morning sun was pushing through the slats of the the room's blinds.

"I brought Evie some flowers." Claire set the vase of pink roses she'd purchased in the facilities gift shop on a counter within sight of the bed.

"What a lovely thought. I'm sure they will brighten up Evie's spirits."

"The nurse said the operation went well, that the break wasn't too bad?" Claire glanced at Evie, resting so peacefully, then back to Cora as she sat beside her.

"Dr. Burquist said she was a real trooper. He expects she'll be hopping around good as new in a few months."

"Months?"

"Yes, taking into consideration the healing time, then some additional therapy after this splint, or whatever it is, is removed." Cora cast a concerned look toward her sister's leg.

"I've seen those before," Claire said. "They're supposed to allow some movement, I think."

"Yes, the doctor says she'll have to work with a therapist daily, but they want her to walk on it as it heals. Can you imagine?" Cora paused, shaking her head. "Certainly not what Doc Wulf would have done, but I know he chose Dr. Burquist to replace him in his practice, so I feel we must put our trust in his judgment."

"I'm sure it must have the best end result, if that's what he's recommending," Claire said, placing her hand lightly over Cora's deeply veined, slender hands.

Cora seemed so vulnerable, concern for her sister written across her face despite her efforts to sound upbeat. Claire felt she was peeking through a window to the real woman behind the no-nonsense façade and felt almost ashamed, as if she were invading her privacy. Cora sighed deeply and then, in a second, the façade returned and she took Claire's hand in hers, turning the reassurance back on its giver.

"Not to worry, all will be fine, I'm certain of that. Evie may appear frail, but she has steel in her bones—broken or not."

Cora held Claire's hand so tightly Claire was amazed at the strength and warmth of the grip.

"We two have weathered many challenges since our dear father passed all those years ago. Much hard work…and heartache as well." Cora glanced at Evie, then down to the floor, as if remembering a loss. Then picking her spirits back up she patted Claire's hand once more before releasing it. "We could not have run the largest orchards in the valley for all those years without the tenacity to survive and thrive." She sat back in her seat and ran one hand softly across the cover of the bible. "And faith, faith has been our guide."

Claire noticed the weary look in Cora's eyes and asked if she'd slept at all since she'd arrived last night.

"Cat naps, there's been quite a great deal of activity, what with nurses and the doctor coming and going."

"Do you want me to fix up the bed?" Claire asked, nodding toward the cushioned couch built into the wall. Claire recognized it from her stay in another hospital earlier in the year, remembering how her sister, Sally, had slept there many nights watching over her.

"Bed?" Cora looked at her with confusion.

"The couch makes into a bed—you could sleep too, and be right here for Evie when she wakes up."

"Quite!" Cora said with some amazement.

"I'm surprised the nurses didn't tell you," Claire said, rearranging the cushions and digging out sheets, pillows and blankets from a drawer beneath the bench.

"It does seem familiar. They may have said something about a bed but I confess I shooed them away. I didn't want them to disturb Evie. And I spent many a night in the chair at father's bedside during his illness. It never occurred to me..." Her words trailed off as she watched Claire transform the couch into a bed.

Claire eased an exhausted Cora into the makeshift bed, with promises to return in a little while to take her home so Cora could pick up a few items before returning to her sister's side.

On her way out of the hospital she stopped at the nurses' desk to inform them that they'd have both sisters for the time being and would they please add meals for Cora to the plan.

The head nurse pointed out that meals for family members were a private expense, not covered by their insurance, and Cora would have to pay separately for those. Instead, Claire gave her her own credit card information and instructed the nurses to put anything Cora needed on her account-and that they should not tell her that Claire was paying for the extra expense.

"Just keep them both comfortable," Claire instructed before finally returning home. The bubble bath she'd planned the night before was long forgotten as was her early morning yoga class. The only item on her day's agenda was an overdue date with her bed.

GWEN HUNG UP THE PHONE and sat, wondering if she was doing the right thing. It seemed like the best course of action and Gwen had always believed in taking action swiftly when a problem presented itself.

Yesterday's fire had certainly been a problem and,

after a long discussion with Andy about her options, she tossed and turned most of the night until she'd finally given in at last to what she knew she must do.

First, however, she'd arrived before daylight to post a sign on the front door of the coffee shop advising her patrons that the shop would unfortunately be closed for a couple of days for repairs, but assuring them it would reopen. There was no reason to explain what had happened. Grand Valley was a small town and bad news traveled fast enough to spare her the uncomfortable necessity of an explanation. Hopefully the news, as it spread, didn't say that she'd been so distracted by her multiple responsibilities that she'd totally space out the zucchini cakes burning in her oven!

After putting up the notice Gwen called the local paper and placed a want ad for a baker. All that tossing and turning had finally convinced her that if she continued to try to do everything at her new shop she'd sacrifice doing it well. It was time to give in and get help.

Of course, turning over the baking to someone else was a hard step to take. Gwen's baking skills had brought her this far. They'd made it possible to open her own shop and find independence and a good life for herself and her son, Jeff, after her first marriage fell apart. They'd also been the heart of a new life with Andy, since their first home together in Blue River was right behind her bakery and their daily lives revolved around the bakery's schedule.

With a new baker in the kitchen Gwen could take on more of a supervisor's role, dipping into and out of baking duties as she wished and as her scheduled allowed. It would also free her up to work the front coffee counter and mingle more with her customers, something she'd been surprised to find she actually enjoyed!

But the bottom line meant the bakery needed to be a success now, more than ever, since she'd have the added expense of another salary. It was a challenge, but one that a sleepless night had convinced her she was up for.

Once the ad was set she returned to the task at hand: scouring every last sign and scent of smoke damage out of Gwen's Coffee Shop and Bakery. She'd set herself the target goal of two days before she reopened and Gwen always met her goals.

Around mid-morning she heard tapping on the front window and, when it didn't stop, decided there must be someone out there who couldn't read her sign. She climbed down from the ladder she'd used to reach a top shelf in her storage closet and headed for the door.

"Coming!" Gwen yelled, the tapping turning into heavier knocking as she pushed through the kitchen door. "Did you see the sign?" she yelled and then stopped, looking through the front window where Del stood, looking back.

Gwen unlocked the door and the two friends fell into each other's arms, laughter and tears joining into a chorus of surprise.

"What on earth are you doing here?" Gwen asked when she finally pulled back with a sigh to gaze into her friend's face. She thought Del's eyes looked red and her face tired.

"I tried to call you but you didn't pick up!"

"Oh shoot! I left my cell under the front counter.

In my purse! And I had music playing in the kitchen. I never heard it. I'm sorry, but what are you doing here?"

"Remember, you were on the phone with me yesterday when the fire started—"

"Oh Del! I'm so sorry, it never occurred to me to call you. Wait, how did you know there was a fire? I don't think I—"

"You didn't. I tried you last night but—"

"I turned my phone off…"

"I figured. So I called Claire this morning. She must have really tied one on last night-I think she was still in bed—and hung-over! She sure sounded beat, but she told me what happened and I, well, it was just a good time for me to get out of town and I thought why not come help you? I could use a day or two of scrubbing and cleaning to clear my cobwebs. That is… if you need the help."

"I'd love the help! But are you alright taking off from work? And what about the kids?"

"No one will miss me at work for a couple of days, and I answer my phone when it rings," she said, with a teasing tone that made Gwen smile. "The kids are on vacation with Micky and the latest squeeze. Oh, does that sound bitchy of me?"

"I think you're due a bitch or two, considering all he did to you!"

"I know, but I'm trying to be a better person," Del said with an honest earnestness that made Gwen smile. "Besides, when the you-know-what hits the fan, friends need friends. So I'm here!"

At that Gwen teared up and almost lost it altogether. She hadn't realized how on the edge her feelings were about the whole mess. It only took Del's thoughtfulness to release the anxiety and fears she'd struggled with daily and, for a moment, she accepted another hug from Del, before pulling away and back into control.

"Okay, boss, put me to work!" she said at last.

"You asked for it!" Gwen laughed.

"Oh, and I hope you can put me up too, because I didn't budget for a hotel room."

"There is no way I would let you stay in a hotel, even if you weren't coming to help. And you know that."

"I know. Thanks." Del walked past her into the kitchen.

Gwen locked the front door and followed her friend, remembering the red eyes she'd noticed at first and wondering if, perhaps, Del needed a friend as much as Gwen did.

Seven

"HEY BABE, I'VE BEEN CALLING you all day. Where've you been? Call me…I'm starting to worry. May have to send out the troops to find you if I don't hear back soon."

Claire listened to Bob's voicemail, realizing she really needed to call him back. She couldn't figure out why she hadn't just answered her phone when he'd called, rather than letting it go to voicemail. He'd called several times and already left two messages.

Bob had been so busy lately with the harvest and plans for the festival. Claire understood about being busy. It had been her wheelhouse for years before the attack sent her to the western slope in search of… what?

Claire wasn't sure what exactly she'd lost, which of course made it all the harder to find. And Bob wanted so badly for her to find it. She could feel it when she was with him. Clearly he'd expected more of a breakthrough by now. Instead, she continued to drift between yoga and gardening and even a quick—and wisely aborted— try at sculpting.

She knew Bob loved her; he'd said as much. And

he waited for her to say it in return. She felt it, she knew she did. But saying it was another thing; a very solid, traditional, vulnerable thing. Claire wondered how long she could go on in this limbo of personal transformation and if Bob would still be there when she came out the other side. If that day ever came, what would their relationship look like? That was the question she knew Bob needed answered and that was why she'd found herself avoiding him more and more. She didn't have the answer yet. And she wasn't sure she ever would.

Still, for now, Claire couldn't let Bob go on worrying. She ran a few errands and then took Cora for a short trip home to pick up some things. Cora had insisted on making Claire a cup of tea before returning to Evie's side. Claire accepted. Really, she thought, what else was there that she needed to be doing?

Once the tea cups were rinsed and set to dry on the sideboard, Claire carried Cora's bag to the car. She made a quick trip in to be certain they'd turned off all the lights and discovered, to her surprise, a candle burning in one of the upstairs bedrooms. She snuffed it out and finished locking up, then joined Cora for the drive into town.

"Cora," Claire began as they pulled away from the house, "did you light a candle upstairs while you were packing?"

"Yes, dear. It was so stuffy up there and Evie loves the scent. It's honeysuckle, you know. When Evie returns home it will smell delightful and lift her spirits."

"Ah, yes, but you left it burning."

"Oh, I…I thought I'd…you put it out?"

Claire looked at her and nodded.

"Well then, all's fine. No need to worry." She sat back in her seat, an easy smile on her face. The last of the orchards faded from view as they pulled onto the main road.

Claire looked at Cora and wondered if her cares were so few as they seemed. Cora was the rock of the two sisters. What would happen to the Larson sisters if the rock weakened?

SEVERAL CARS FILLED THE PARKING lot at Columbine vineyards. Claire wasn't used to hunting for a parking spot, even with the summer crowds. But as the harvest picked up and the festival neared, tourists had begun their annual migration in celebration of the vine and its fruit.

Claire found Bob in his office, sitting deep in conversation—almost head to head—with Terra, whose handed rested too comfortably on Bob's shoulder. Bob looked up distractedly when he heard the door open, but jumped up immediately when he saw her.

"Claire! At last!" He strode across the room and hugged her hard, then stepped back, looking her over. "You okay?"

"Well, of course, why wouldn't I be?"

"I've been calling and calling. I was worried."

"I'm sorry...I had my phone turned off," Claire lied. "I was at the hospital."

"What? Did you—are you—" Bob looked her over, clearly expecting some sign of injury or illness.

"No, I'm fine. Not me, the Larson sisters. Actually, Evie, she broke her leg and I drove them both to

Grand Valley late last night."

"You should have called me. I would have helped."

"I was fine. I'm a big girl." Claire could hear her walls going up but caught herself, realizing Terra followed their conversation with great interest. "Hi, Terra," she said, pointedly.

"Hey, Claire. Sorry to hear your friend hurt herself; really nice of you to pitch in and all." Terra was twirling the end of her braid, where strands of red hair freed themselves from the pink rubber band that bound them. As usual, she wore a form-fitting t-shirt that was just revealing enough without being objectionable.

Claire could see her slender legs, extending from very short cut-offs into mid-calf Ugg boots. She supposed the boots were Terra's nod to the colder temps along with the two noticeable protrusions at the tip of each breast. Claire couldn't help wondering what part of Bob's brain must shut down in Terra's presence despite a dress code he strictly enforced in the Tasting room. Sure, Terra was more often working in the vineyards than inside, but still…

"Thanks, Terra. Could I steal Bob away from you for a minute?" Claire glanced at Bob who seemed unaware that kicking Terra out of the office so they could be alone was really more his task than hers.

"Sure. I'll just wait here." Terra smiled brightly.

"Great." Bob wrapped an arm around Claire's waist and pulling her toward the door. "I'll be right back." He whisked Claire into the hall, pulled the door behind him and turned to give her a kiss, only to be met with a hard stare that dared him to try. "What?"

"You're kidding."

"About what?"

"Isn't that your office?"

"Yeah. Oh, well, we've got all the notes for the festival dinner laid out on the table and I'll be right back so I figured, well, you know…"

"I know what you figured. Kiss the little lady and send her on her way and out of your hair."

"Claire, honey, that's not fair, that's not true—I was worried about you. And you know how busy I've been."

"Oh, I definitely know that. Your extremely busy schedule is hard to miss!" Claire pushed away from him, feeling the steam blow into her attitude while simultaneously wondering what the hell she was doing.

"You know it's my busiest season. And we've got so many reservations for this dinner. We don't know how we're gonna fit everyone in."

"Can't you rent a hall or something?"

"Everything's booked, not that there's a whole lot to book in this town. I may have to gamble with our crazy fall weather and hold it outside. And that's a whole new set of problems if we do. You know if I had a choice I'd rather be with you than anything else, I wouldn't have any free time at all if it weren't for Terra, come on, Ace."

"Don't Ace me, and you looked pretty cozy in there with Terra if you ask me!"

"Terra's a kid!"

"You're telling me? She's a very well developed kid, in case you haven't noticed! She seemed very at home snuggling up over paperwork and schedules behind your desk."

Bob stood, mouth agape, trying to understand how the hell his worry and concern over her well-being had devolved into this conversation. He couldn't figure out how to un-do where it was heading and he was afraid that anything he said at this point would either come out wrong or be taken wrong so he took the most logical next step—for Bob.

He took her in his arms, kissed her—despite initial protests—then, held her at arms-length as he spoke. "I love you. There is nothing going on with Terra and I have to get back to work. I'll call you later. There's something I need to explain about—"

Bob's office door flew open and Terra stood there, holding his cell phone in one hand. "Sorry boss," she whispered, moving the cell behind her back, "I tried to put them off but they have to talk to you—pronto!"

Bob cast an apologetic look at Claire, then leaned in to kiss the tip of her nose but she leaned back and glared, speechless at last.

"I'll call you later," he said again, then returned to his office, shutting the door and leaving Claire alone in the hallway, struggling to understand if she was mad at Bob, at Terra, or at herself, or if she really was mad at all. Once again she was in a place she didn't recognize and, being a creature of habit, she bolted.

"I CAN'T BELIEVE IT'S ALL THE way in here!" Del yelled from inside the cabinet beneath Gwen's cash register.

"It's everywhere." Gwen climbed down from the ladder she'd been atop, wiping down the brass light fixtures near the fireplace. "The fireman told me to expect to be wiping black residue from the fire's smoke out of corners and cabinets for months. If the air got in there so did the smoke."

"Well, there was plenty of air in here." Del pulled herself out, tossing her sponge into a nearby bucket of water and sitting back against the wall. "But I think I got it all."

"It's almost one—you hungry?" Gwen asked.

"I'm starving. And my back is starting to kill me. I could use a change of position. I think I've crawled in and around all your cabinets out here."

"And I am so grateful, Del. I hugely appreciate it. Between Claire's help last night and yours today, I think I'll actually be able to re-open in another day, as promised."

"Speaking of Claire, I'm kinda surprised she didn't

drop by. It's not like she's swamped with work these days, is it?"

"Come to think of it, I'm surprised too. Other than her morning yoga class and weeding her garden she really doesn't have any commitments. She usually stops by after her morning class."

"Maybe she got tied up with Bob."

"Ha! You mean she wishes she had Bob tied up!"

"Gwen, don't go there. I'll never be able to look at the two of them together again without blushing!"

"Sorry. Besides, I doubt Bob was her distraction. He's just as busy as Andy is these days. We are both wine widows! If I didn't have this place to keep me busy I'd go nuts."

Del stretched her arms over her head, bending side-to-side. As stiff as she was, the hard work felt good. And it felt more than good to be spending time with Gwen. She'd missed her, and Claire, but being with her made her realize just how much. "Don't worry, we'll finish it tomorrow and it'll be sparkling clean to open up the next day! And I'll be the first one in line for a latte when you do."

"That latte will be on the house."

"That's a deal."

Tapping on the glass of the bakery's front window caught their attention and Gwen glanced up.

"Well, speak of the devil, it's our long lost yogini!" She pulled open the front door just as Del popped up from behind the counter.

"Claire!" Del called.

"Sweetie! What the hell are you doing here?" Claire swept past Gwen to embrace Del in a long hug.

"Gwen needed help so I came."

Claire eased back and eyed Del's soot smudged face with joy. "Of course you did. I should have expected it." She turned to Gwen. "I'm sorry I haven't been here all day. I meant to come, but it's been one crazy day—since last night!"

"Last night?" Gwen asked. "This sounds like a long story."

"Indeed." Claire sighed.

"Well, Del and I were just saying we need a break—and food. How about we three have lunch out? The bakery can treat us."

"Sounds great," Claire said, "but I'm doing the treating. I will feel much less guilty about not helping you Cinderellas." She reached out and rubbed at a smudge on Del's face. "Besides, it's cheaper than therapy."

"Lunch out with girlfriends *is* therapy, Claire." Del smiled sincerely. "We probably all need a little lunch therapy anyway."

"Oh?" Claire said, looking from Del to Gwen.

Gwen shrugged and shook her head, looking back at Del. "What's up?"

"Oh, no, I mean, well…"

Del brushed at her face, swiping at the soot, but Gwen thought there might have been a small tear at the edge of her eye.

Del looked down at her clothes, avoiding both of their eyes. "Oh, look how dirty I am! Why don't Gwen and I clean up fast and then we can go."

"Sounds like a plan," Claire said. "I'll go ahead and get us a table. How about Peaches?"

"Perfect," Gwen said, "we'll meet you there in half an hour-tops!"

THE PEACH CITY BISTRO FILLED a long narrow space in one of Grand Valley's oldest buildings fronting the main drag through town. Walls were exposed brick, and heavy sheets of white paper topped tables that sat on wood floors worn with the history of the place. What it lacked in space it made up for with good taste and fabulous food—including a dessert menu filled with nearly every peach concoction imaginable.

Claire ordered a bottle of Columbine Estates merlot. She smiled at the steep price the Bistro charged, even though the winery was just down the road, and her fridge up the hill had three bottles of the same vintage that Bob had personally delivered-gratis. Claire was a big advocate of the free market so if customers paid for it she thought the Bistro, and Bob, ought to reap whatever rewards they could. And these were top-dollar rewards.

"Are you sure?" Del glanced at the price in the wine list.

"Sweetie, how often do we three get to dine together; anymore at least?"

"Very true," Gwen winked at Del.

The waiter finally succeeded in getting their order on his third try. After the second try Gwen had firmly established a no talking rule until they had all chosen an entrée. She had always expressed special sympathy for the patience it sometimes took to get a group of friends to focus on their orders instead of each other.

Finally, they sat back to enjoy Claire's merlot and the company of friends.

"I've missed this," Claire said at last. "I know, I'm the last one to get weepy over crap like this but…there it is."

"Oh, Claire." Del gave her friend's hand a squeeze.

"I think we've all missed this," Gwen said. "I mean, Claire, you and I see each almost every day. And Del, we talk a couple times a week on the phone, but…"

"It's not the same." Claire breathed in the merlot's blackberry, plum and oak scents, then took a sip. "You know, I drink this at home a lot. And lately alone a lot, what with Bob's schedule, but it's not the same as drinking it with friends. What is it that makes a good wine great in the right company?"

"I know." Gwen swirled the glass, watching the fluid fingers fall back in clear red rivulets. "Andy says whiskey is a drink for lonely solitary nights, but wine is meant to be celebrated with friends."

"That's lovely, Gwen."

"Isn't it? Bob even said he's gonna put it in their brochure. My guy is pretty deep when you give him a chance. Of course, you have to catch him first to do that and that's not easy these days."

"Boy, this is so strange," Del said, almost to herself.

"What is kiddo?" Claire asked.

"Well, here I've been thinking how lucky you two were, having Andy and Bob, but it turns out you're just as lonely as I am."

"It's the season," Gwen started to say, "it won't always be like this—hey, what do you mean as lonely as you are? What happened to Jimmy?"

"Oh, Del." Claire put down her glass. "What's happened? I can't believe this. Jimmy always seemed like a great guy. What an idiot to let someone like you go. That asshole, I'm almost tempted to call him and—"

"No!" Del said so loudly the patrons at the nearest table stopped talking and looked over at her. "No," she said, again, almost whispering. "It's not Jimmy's fault. If it's anybody's fault it's mine."

"I find that hard to believe, kiddo," Claire said, emphatically.

"Tell us what happened, Del," Gwen said softly. She'd been aware all day that Del wasn't her normal perky self, and this new development would definitely explain it.

Del took a large gulp of her wine, sighed heavily and dove quickly and efficiently into the short and painful version of her separation from Jimmy. "I was so stupid."

"No, you weren't," Gwen said. "You were just scared, and I don't blame you. I mean, after all, you've had quite a year: a divorce, a new career, a new man in your life."

"That's a triple whammy." Claire smiled at Del. "You need to cut yourself some slack. You were like a deer in the headlights the day we met you, right Gwen?"

Claire looked to Gwen who nodded hesitantly. "You were definitely overwhelmed."

"You are the only person I ever knew who did relaxation therapy while driving a two ton minivan!" Claire said, recalling how Del had crashed into a giant flowerpot in front of Gwen's bakery in Blue River and, as a result, they had all met for the first time.

"You certainly did a job on that pot in the intersection. After you hit it the road crew was cleaning up potshards half a block away."

"Here's to shattered flower pots." Claire tipped her glass to theirs, the soft ting of crystal on crystal filling the air.

"You're probably right," Del said at last, "but I'm starting to think it was stupid of me. I'm starting to think breaking it off with Jimmy will go down as one of the dumbest choices I've made in the last year."

"Then you should talk to him," Gwen said earnestly, sharing a gentle and encouraging smile.

"I don't' know…it was so uncomfortable when he came over to the table after Carl left. I mean, if he wanted to get back together, wouldn't he have been kinder?"

"Del, sweetie," Claire said, "guys get hurt just like we do. You expect 'em to buck up and be gentlemen, but in my experience when a man is upset with a woman, rather than channeling his inner Dalai Lama he channels his inner asshole."

"That's pretty cynical, don't you think?" Gwen said.

"Doesn't make it any less true."

"Well…maybe you're right, but it was very uncomfortable all the same, and I saw the look on his face. I don't know where that conversation would start. And meanwhile, Carl has left me two messages asking me to dinner."

"Upping the ante." Claire smiled.

"You're going to have to make a decision and then have a conversation," Gwen said. "One way or another. And until you do, you won't know what's true and what's not. Just because you saw something doesn't mean it's what you think you saw. "

"Unless it does…" Claire said almost under her breath, reaching for the bottle.

"Huh?" Del looked over at her.

"What?" Gwen shifted her focus to Claire.

"I'm only saying that sometimes you see something and, well, you want to think it's not what you think it is but…experience tells you maybe it is."

"We're not talking about Del now, are we?" Gwen asked. "What happened?"

Claire shook her head and sipped her wine. "Nothing. Probably nothing."

"Claire, honey, are you okay?"

Now it was Del reaching out to comfort her, and Claire knew she shouldn't have said anything. "It's stupid, really. Not worth talking about."

"What?" Gwen and Del both said so quickly and firmly it almost made them laugh before they turned back to Claire, intent on the facts.

"I'm telling you it's nothing. It's just me reading into stuff, I'm sure Bob is not fooling around, I'm sure he's just busy."

"What on earth would make you think he's fooling around?" Gwen asked. "When would he have the time?"

"I know he's busy, it's only…he's seemed more distant lately. When I first came here he was always there. And if he couldn't be there, he was calling, texting, emailing. Always in touch, always concerned: Was I feeling okay? Was I happy today? Did I enjoy yoga? Stupid, I know…but always there. I think I might have complained a little that he was hovering."

"Well, there," Del said, "that's all it is. He got your message and backed off a little. He's giving you some space."

"I've got space all right. Now he forgets to call at night, or when he does, he's just checking in. That's what he says, 'hey Ace, just checking in'. We compare quick notes and he's off again. He has a late meeting, or he's so beat he's going straight to bed. And during the day, if I hear from him at all it's really just more of the same. We were practically inseparable when I first got here, now I'm lucky if I get a phone call. It's been almost a week since we actually sat down to dinner together and...well, even longer since we spent the night together."

"Claire, he's really busy," Gwen said, "I know that's all it is. I know he loves you."

"Yeah, well, that's the other thing. He does love me; he told me he loves me."

"That's wonderful!" Del said, practically bubbling over.

"No."

"Why?" Gwen asked.

"Because I friggin' couldn't say it back. Shit. I just couldn't say I love you. How stupid is that? Who wouldn't love a guy like him?"

"So....you don't love him?" Del asked.

"I don't know, yes, maybe. Oh Del, it's just not that simple. It's been a long time since I've felt comfortable enough to even consider feeling like that. Still, I was willing to, you know, consider the possibility that maybe I really did love Bob. That's why I went there today. I needed to talk to him, I needed to explain how my head works, ask him to be patient with me. I was practically ready to grovel. Then I saw him with her."

"Her?" Again Del and Gwen spoke in unison.

"You two really need to take your show on the road." Claire eased back into her chair.

"Sorry." Gwen looked at Del who clearly had been just about to say the same thing. "Okay, who are we talking about here?"

"Terra."

"Who's she?" Del asked.

"His sales manager," Gwen explained. "She's kind of a...granola version of a—"

"Bimbette." Claire said.

"Well, maybe not that bad. She seems intelligent and she's just a kid, really. How old can she be?"

"She's twenty-three," Claire said. "She joined the winery right out of college. I walked in on them this afternoon—very close, head to head, and Terra was more than cozy with her hand on his shoulder. It felt like they were almost cuddling for Christ's sake. I called him on it and he says oh, it's nothing, it's just work. Well, it didn't feel like work to me." Claire crossed her arms and set a grim look on her face for a few seconds before reaching for her wine glass and downing its contents in one gulp.

"Whoa." Gwen said. "Claire, watch it. Remember your health—and your ulcer. You're still in recovery. And I'm sure it's not what it seems, there's got to be a good explanation. Remember when we first met Del and she thought that police officer was her ex-husband's girlfriend? Remember," Gwen looked at Del, "you were wrong, she wasn't his girlfriend after all."

"That's true," Del said, "but I wasn't wrong about him fooling around. I knew something was up, I just had the wrong someone."

The friends sat silent, contemplating the possibilities.

"No. I don't buy it, Claire," Gwen said at last. "It's just not like Bob."

"I think I agree with Gwen, but then again, I never thought my ex would do what he did. Until I found out he did and suddenly I realized all the time it was so obvious to everyone but me. Oh, Claire, honey, I hope it's not true, and I think it's not true…"

"But." Claire sat back again in her chair, arms crossed tightly, her expression grim. "But you don't know. And neither do I. And worse yet, I hate that I don't just instinctively know. I mean, if I loved him and truly believed he loved me, why would I even entertain the idea? Why wouldn't I at least be clueless, like you were Del? I don't know if that's any better, but shouldn't a good, solid relationship be so true, so solid that it wouldn't even occur to you that he'd cheat? What's missing that I would think that?"

"I don't think something is missing in your relationship, Claire." Gwen slid her outreached hand across the table, like a lifeline to a sinking ship. "I think it's simply that you don't have a lot of practice being in a relationship like that. It takes time. I think you need to talk to Bob about this."

"Better to be sure than go around wondering," Del said. "This is something I am an expert on."

Claire sighed heavily, reaching over to take Gwen's hand. "I'll think about it."

The waiter arrived to deliver their meals and Gwen watched her friends, dealing with their worries, and decided, for now, that she wouldn't mention the ad she'd just placed or the new plans she was making.

"So, is this what kept you up all night?" Gwen asked.

"Oh, God, that's another thing—the Larson sisters." Claire proceeded to fill them in on the events of the night before. "They are two very sweet little old ladies. Very independent, but I think they ought to have someone around. Cora is very take charge, and Evie, who seems so delicate at first is probably made of sterner stuff than any of us. I know they ran the largest orchards in the region for decades. And they live in this big house all by themselves."

"I've seen it," Gwen interjected, "what an incredible old Victorian home."

"Shit, that house is almost like another sister. It's seen better days, but it's got pride. Still, it's a big house for those two to take care of."

"Do they have a handyman or gardener or anything like that?" Del dipped her fork into a large salad with grilled chicken, raspberries, and sugared almonds that was dressed with a tangy peach vinaigrette.

"Not sure." Claire tasted her dinner of grilled salmon with a sweet but pungent peach salsa. "Honestly, I really don't know anything about them. We nod and smile when we pass on the road, but until last night I'd never been in the house or had any sort of lengthy conversation with them."

"Do they have relatives nearby?" Gwen sliced off a bite of a tender elk steak with a side of acorn squash with caramelized peaches and red onion.

"No clue," Claire said, "but neither of them mentioned anyone they had to contact." Claire realized that for all the time she'd spent with the sisters in the last twenty-four hours, there was still a lot she didn't know. And much more she wanted to find out.

Nine

BY THE TIME CLAIRE FINISHED the long lunch with her friends the afternoon was growing late and she still wanted to visit Cora and Evie. She hoped she could learn a little more about their living arrangement so that she could stop her totally uncharacteristic concern for their well-being.

Late afternoon in the hospital was a quiet time. Lunch service had concluded and patients were either resting or greeting visitors. Claire pushed open the door to Evie's room, expecting to see them both sleeping, one in the bed and one in the chair. Instead, the room was empty, the bed made and all signs of the sisters gone.

At the nurse's desk Claire was told that Miss Larson had checked herself out.

"You've got to be friggin' kidding me. How on earth could she have been ready to go home?"

"Are you a relative?" the nurse asked, hesitantly. The portly woman wore her dark hair pulled back in a bun and was dressed in red scrubs with black polka dots. Claire thought she looked like a giant ladybug.

"No," Claire said, realizing the wall that must go up

according to the rules.

"I'm sorry. I really can't discuss the case with you. But you might stop by their home, if you're a friend, to see how they are."

"Oh?"

"Yes," the nurse hesitated and looked around before lowering her voice. "If I were a friend, I'd definitely stop in to be sure she's alright. Perhaps some professional in-home care would be worth looking into as well?"

Another nurse came around the corner and, though younger, it was clear she had some seniority because the ladybug straightened up and said more loudly. "But as I said, since you aren't a relative, I really can't give you any particulars."

"Thanks." Claire winked at the nurse before she turned and left. Clearly she was going to have to get the answers for herself.

"CLAIR." CORA SMILED WIDELY, OPENING the door wide to welcome Claire into their front foyer. "I'm so glad you stopped by. We felt terrible leaving the hospital without telling you, but we didn't know how to get in touch. Evie just wanted to come home. And the lights are on and the phone is working. You are such a dear!"

Cora quickly wrapped her arms around Claire's waist, tucking her head beneath Claire's chin, she squeezed so tightly that Claire almost dropped the bag she was carrying.

"Oh, well," Claire sputtered, "really, that's not necessary…" She was hardly accustomed to thank-you hugs from anyone, let alone little old ladies in need.

"Nonsense, we're ever so grateful for your consideration. Do come in and visit."

"Of course, but first I'd better unpack this." Claire held up the large grocery bag she was carrying. "Have you had dinner?"

"Well, there wasn't much, actually. Most of what we had spoiled when the electricity went out so…I did manage to find some nice greens in the garden for a salad, and there were beans, too. I planned to visit the grocers tomorrow."

"Then it's a good thing I stopped by Tonti's Deli on the way," Claire said. "I've gotten you some soup, a couple sandwiches and a few other things, just in case."

"So thoughtful!" Cora turned toward the front parlor. "Did you hear that Evie? Claire's brought us dinner!"

"So thoughtful!" came a faint voice from within, an echo of her sister's.

"I need to check on her…" Cora's voice trailed off, visibly torn between escorting Claire to the kitchen or returning to her sister.

"Go, go," Claire said, "I know my way. I'll join you in a second."

The kitchen lights were on, but there was still a candle burning, stuck onto a saucer in the middle of the kitchen table. Claire shook her head, wondering if perhaps the sisters actually preferred candlelight to electricity. She leaned closer and noticed it did have a nice scent, as Cora had mentioned, and supposed it was some comfort to Evie. Claire made a mental note to look for an air freshener with a similar smell, and then blew it out.

The kitchen itself was part modern convenience, part days-gone-by. Clearly it had started out in one era and came along over the years with additions here and there to accommodate progress.

The smooth white cupboard doors were clean but worn, decades of hands opening and closing them had left their mark. Likewise the gray and white flecked Formica countertop was nicked on the edges and, beside the sink, the pattern nearly erased from years of chopping vegetables and drying dishes. The floor had once been brilliant red linoleum, judging by the less faded corners, but now it was mostly a pale, pink version of its original self.

Claire pulled the latch on the door of the vintage white refrigerator. Inside it was scrubbed and clean, but nearly empty except for a small bowl of assorted lettuces and a paper towel on which a handful of green beans rested.

The lack of a microwave didn't surprise her, so she looked for a pot to reheat the soup in and found it in the drawer of a large Hoosier cabinet in the corner by the table.

"Wow," Claire said to herself, looking over the relic of kitchen convenience from another time. "Probably could sell that puppy for a nice price on eBay."

She put the soup on to heat and joined the sisters in the parlor.

"Claire, please sit beside me." Evie patted the unoccupied half of the small red velvet couch she sat on. Her leg was propped atop a red and gold, fringed pillow that had been placed on the mahogany coffee table in front of her. "I can't tell you how much we do appreciate all you've done for us. I hope we didn't worry you unduly when you found us gone."

"Well…" Claire eased herself down beside Evie, careful not to jostle her. "I was concerned. That's why I came right away."

"We really can't thank you enough for everything you've done!" Cora said.

"Our lights are on," Evie added.

"And the phone is once again working," Cora added. "In our time of need, you not only found us assistance, but came to our home's aide as well."

"What a good neighbor. What a good friend!" Evie smiled, summing up their joint thoughts.

"Really, I'm happy to help. But do you think it was really a good idea to leave the hospital?"

"I just…needed to come home…" Evie said in a soft voice, looking down at her hands, clasped tightly in her lap.

Claire looked at Cora, who shrugged and shook her head slightly, a worried look on her face. For the first time, Claire thought she saw some inkling of recognition that they acknowledged the realities of their situation.

"Don't you have to go for therapy every day, Evie?" Claire asked.

"Dr. Burquist said the therapist could stop by a few times a week," Cora explained.

"When I'm up to it, we can visit the therapist on the off days."

"I'm sure it will all work out just fine." Cora seemed to have regained some confidence in their decision. "Is the soup warming, dear?" Cora asked Claire.

"Oh, yes, I'll go check on it. I hope you like chicken and rice, it's all they had left."

"It will be perfect, I'm certain," Cora assured her. "Why don't I help you with the bowls."

Cora followed Claire into the kitchen and, no sooner had the door swung shut behind them than her voice regained its worried tone.

"I must explain, Claire. Evie is very…uncomfortable in hospitals." She opened a cabinet door and retrieved three white china bowls, their golden trim long faded and chips about their edges.

"I'm fine. I have dinner plans," Claire lied, pointing to the bowls. She was starting to worry that the sisters might not be able to afford enough food.

"Oh, well, if you're sure?" Claire nodded and Cora returned the third bowl to the shelf.

"Did Evie have a bad experience in a hospital?"

"Quite. We both did, in fact." She stood at the counter, watching Claire spoon out the soup, her arms crossed in front and wrapped about her waist. "Our dear father suffered terribly before his death. It was prolonged and required many hospital visits. In the end…he couldn't return home to pass. He was far too ill."

"I'm so sorry."

"We all must meet our time in whichever way the good Lord intends, but Evie is determined not to arrive early for the big day. I felt it best to bring her home, rather than irritate her anxieties. Evie is a strong woman, Claire. Or, I should say, she once was. But her temperament was always delicate. She felt things greatly—happy or sad. I think all those years took some toll on her and now…well, now I try to make life as easy going as I might. We are both more at peace that way.

We shall manage her recovery here, I'm sure. We've only the two of us left…it is most important that I be with her, that above all else.

The two women stood quietly for a moment then Claire bent to give Cora a gentle hug. "She's lucky to have you, Cora. And now you both have me. I'm just down the road and I certainly have nothing else I have to be doing. You call me whenever—for whatever. Alright?"

"Oh my," Cora said, touching her fingertips to her lips to hold back what Claire could only imagine were long staunched emotions. "I truly don't want you to feel obligated."

"I don't," Claire said. "I feel *concerned* for my friends. That's kind of a new thing for me lately, but it's an overdue skill, I think." Gwen and Del had taught it to her, she thought. Or maybe, knowing them had cracked a shell and let it out. Either way, she realized it gave her more satisfaction than she would have expected. Claire sighed and turned to the bowls. "Well, let's get this out to Evie before it gets cold."

"I have a little TV tray in the utility closet. I'll retrieve it and follow you with the silverware."

"Sounds like a plan." Claire wondered if she ought to talk with the sisters about other plans as well, but this was a good start.

DEL ZIPPED UP HER PACKED suitcase and straightened the comforter on her bed in Gwen's small guest room. It was little more than a bed and dresser, but it was cozy, and the view from the third floor window, tucked into an eave of Gwen and Andy's old Victorian home, swept over the valley, along the Grande River and up to the mesas beyond.

The view lacked the lush greenery of her home in Blue River, where entire mountainsides of fir trees rose from the shores of the Blue River reservoir and gave way above to snow covered peaks. But Grand Valley, with its wide horizons and views of the flat-topped Grande Mesa, a desert mountain with more scrubland than pine forests, had a beauty of its own, especially in the early morning as the sun cast long, pink-hued shadows across the valley.

Gwen pulled a sheet of sugar-crusted chocolate croissants from the oven just as Del walked into her kitchen, setting her suitcase by the back door.

"Are those what I think they are?" Del poured herself a cup of freshly brewed coffee that smelled like it had started the day as very dark-roasted beans. She breathed in the aroma. "Boy, you are spoiling me."

"It's the least I could do when you come all this way to help me clean up my mess! And then you're practically stuck up in the attic, in that old bedroom. I'm sorry it's the only one besides ours that's really in good enough shape for habitation. We'll be working on this fixer-upper for years to come."

"Even when you get all the bedrooms in shape I still want that one. I don't mind the walk up two flights of stairs, and I don't mind the location. It feels like a fairy-tale room, like I'm hiding at the top of the castle away from the world, just waiting for my Prince Charming."

"So...are you planning on calling Mr. Charming when you get home? Or are you going to continue to avoid him and give your favors to the evil Carl?" Gwen smiled, clearly enjoying dishing up a croissant for Del along with fairy tale metaphors.

"Oh, I'm trying not to think about it. I don't want to spoil the visit. It's been wonderful to spend time with you and Claire. I've missed you both a lot."

"I know, sweetie," Gwen said, joining her friend at the kitchen table that sat beside a small brick fireplace, unlit on this autumn day. "We've missed you too, and I think it was good for all of us to get together."

"We should do it more often."

"I agree. Maybe we can take turns going back and forth, Blue River one time, here another."

"We should try to do it quarterly. Then yearly we should try to do something more...like our beach trip last year." Gwen smiled, remembering the trip they'd all taken to the beach last spring, returning her at last to the sea and the shore and the shells she'd fallen in love with years ago as a child. The trip had been a rejuvenation for all three of them. "We don't have to go to the seashore every time."

"I love the seashore, but we can mix it up. We should ask Claire. She's probably loaded with ideas of places to go, don't you think?" Del licked chocolate from her fingertips and took a sip of her coffee.

"I'll mention it to her. It might be good for her to have something to look forward to-something to plan."

"You're right. Claire needs a reason to get up in the morning. I was the same way after my divorce. Sure, I had the kids, but still...I'd always had the kids. I needed something more. You and Claire helped me with that. Now we need to help her."

"You're right, and I think the trip would be a good goal; something to set her sights on. But Claire needs more, I think. She's used to being a very busy person."

"But being so busy ended up giving her that terrible ulcer and, along with that horrible man who beat her so badly in the attack, it almost killed her. If Claire went back to work, to real estate or anything else, has she learned to set her priorities and draw the line do you think? Would she take care of herself? Or just wear herself down again?"

"She's just never gonna know until she tries." Gwen picked at the crumbs on her plate, then stood and walked over to her sink, washing the last bits from the plate. "And really, I've never seen anyone try so hard. Claire doesn't know how to do anything half-hearted. She's gotten so good at yoga she could practically teach it, and her garden, for all her cluelessness about what to actually do with its bounty, is really over-flowing."

"Don't I know it? She gave me two huge zucchinis to take home."

"Those dang zucchinis, that's how my whole fire got started, baking up cakes with Claire's zucchini."

"Those cakes sure were toast!" Del giggled. "Sorry." she added, seeing the rueful look on her friend's face. "I'm sure you can always get more zucchini from Claire."

"Believe me, the last thing I need is more things to do. My to-do list is turning into an epic. Sometimes I wonder if I've really overdone it this time. When you're young it never occurs to you that you could ever take on too much. But as you get older, well, I get these little freaked-out moments now and then wondering how I'll really handle it all-or if I even can."

"Gwen, you should get more help, and not just out front, but in the kitchen. You don't have to do it all. That's what being the boss means; you get to delegate. If I didn't know that I'd be a terrible director of fund-raising. The bigger the job, the more help you need."

"I know." Gwen topped off her coffee cup and re-joining her friend at the table. "Actually, I just put an ad in the paper for a baker."

"That's great."

"I suppose…"

"What? Why wouldn't it be?" Del patted Gwen's hand.

"You are like a mother hen, Mama Del."

"If I am I learned it from you; you mothered me along a time or two. So tell me why this baker idea isn't a great one."

"I've always done it all, Del. Giving up some of that control, that's gonna be hard. But I like working in the front of the house too. I like getting out of the kitchen. Does that sound bad?"

"Are you kidding me? That sounds like an owner and a good manager. You know what you like, and you also know what needs to be done. You're learning your limits and your needs. I think it's a big step and you need to take it."

"Sounds like Claire and I have more in common than I realized."

"Maybe Claire will learn some things from you about how to be a success without sacrificing your life."

"Yeah, but I have to learn it first!" Gwen laughed. "Let's not get ahead of ourselves."

"You'll be great, I know you will." Del hugged her friend and kissed her cheek.

"Thanks, Mama." Gwen laughed and hugged her back.

DEL'S DRIVE BACK TO BLUE River passed quickly. She'd spent the time imagining all sorts of scenarios for dealing with Jimmy…and Carl. Unfortunately, by the time she arrived home she hadn't been able to come up with any she was comfortable with. Del realized there wasn't going to be any easy way around dealing with the men in her life.

Her neighbor, Mrs. Vogelman, had been kind enough to bring in her mail and set it on the kitchen counter. Del put off unpacking until after the mail was sorted; until she was sure there was nothing from Jimmy.

Of course, there was no reason she should have expected something from him. Still, she was always hoping that he might just write, he might just call... But the only calls she'd had all weekend were from the kids, who were in the Caymans on a last minute get-away that had required Micky to get a little leeway from the school for an exceptionally 'long weekend' with their dad and his latest girlfriend.

He'd pitched it as an opportunity for them to learn more about marine biology and promised their teachers they'd return with written reports and, Del supposed, some sea life souvenirs for their classrooms... and their teachers. Naturally, they agreed. People always agreed with Micky's ideas because he sold them just like he sold a jury on his client's innocence. It had taken Del years to learn what he was selling her, but when she did she'd found her own excellent attorney and, thankfully, Micky accepted the inevitable and cooperated for their children's sake.

Their happy voices, with tales of snorkeling and building sand castles buoyed her spirits, even if she did feel some regret to miss out on sharing the experience with them. That, she knew, was one of the sadder results of a divorce. It made her all the more determined to find special moments with them when they were home.

Del wheeled her suitcase toward her room but stopped at the sight of a large vase, filled with pink roses, pink tulips and white lilies, placed in the center of the large, oak coffee table in her living room. For a fleeting moment Del's heart held still at the possibility that Jimmy had sent them, but even before she read the card she knew they were from Carl. Massive floral displays were not Jimmy's style. She plucked a small pink card from the blooms. Its hand-written message said:

Sorry to leave early after lunch. Call me and maybe we can try dinner this time.
Yours, Carl

Del recognized Carl's handwriting. On the table, beside the vase, Mrs.Vogelman had stuck a small Post-It note that said:

Florist brought these over to my house when you weren't home. Lovely!

"Shit." Del stood for a moment, looking at the flowers and re-reading the card. She knew dinner would mean kicking the relationship up a notch, and she was troubled by the sentiment, *Yours*. It felt rather personal, intimate even. Carl was polite, attractive and certainly thoughtful, if flowers were any measure. But she wondered why a dinner invitation from him didn't have the same effect on her as one from Jimmy always did.

"Maybe I just need to give the man a chance," she said to the card, and herself, leaning down to smell the bouquet's fragrance. "Once I know him better I'll be excited about being with him…I'm sure." She tried to boost her confidence, even though a little voice inside was nagging, with Jimmy I was excited about getting to know him, before we ever went out.

"Every guy's different. That's it, it's just new–*he's* new." If her heart didn't believe it yet she was determined her mind would agree. Jimmy was A.W.O.L. and it was time to move on.

GWEN ARRIVED AT THE BAKERY early enough to get a head start on the day's pastries while her employees manned the front counter. The first of two applicants were coming for an interview after the morning rush and she wanted to have time to spare, though she wasn't certain what the interview would be like.

Gwen had interviewed many employees over the years, but those had been for simpler positions that only required greeting customers, cash register skills, cleaning tables, etc. Even finding someone who could handle barista skills seemed simpler than this challenge. Now, she was looking for someone who could replace her, and she wasn't quite sure how she felt about that.

The morning rush took a little longer to ease up than usual, thanks to a small vintner's convention in town from Friday through Sunday. Becca and Carolyn were cleaning up from the rush. Usually Carolyn took Saturdays off, but Gwen had asked them both to come for the morning, to free up some time for the interviews.

Her eleven o'clock arrived three minutes early, which Gwen thought was a good sign. She looked to be mid-twenties, tall and thin, wearing a floral sundress that was bright beneath her pale complexion and white-blonde hair that cascaded over her shoulders. She looked clean and had no visible piercings or tattoos. Gwen took it as a hopeful sign. Unfortunately she quickly found she was almost clueless in a kitchen and, when asked why she'd applied for the job, discovered she thought it would be fun to learn to bake. Gwen smiled, wrapped up the very brief interview and said she'd be in touch.

The front door swung shut behind her first applicant and Gwen bent over the table at the back of the room, head in her hands rubbing at her temples and wondering if this was going to be a wasted day after all her preparation. The last thing she needed in her kitchen was a student.

Becca tapped her on her shoulder and she looked up. The teen had long blonde hair pulled into two braids with pink rubber bands at the ends to match the rubber bands on her braces. "Gwen, there's a guy over there, came in during your interview." Becca nodded toward one of the chairs near the front door. "He said he was looking for you, but not to bug you. He got a latte and three pastries."

Gwen glanced toward the front where she could see only the man's back. He appeared to be late twenties, early thirties at the most, but even from the back she saw his wavy brown hair was tied in a pony-tail. He wore a t-shirt and cargo shorts, with worn flip-flops, and his attire made it easy to see his right arm was completely tattooed, as was his right leg, from the knee down.

"What did he order?" Gwen asked.

"One croissant, one lemon tart, and one red velvet cupcake," Becca said softly.

"Interesting choice."

"Were you expecting him?"

"Nope. My next interview is another woman."

"Oh, is that some gal named Sandra something?"

"Yes, why?"

"She called during the rush," Becca said. "Sorry, I got so busy I forgot to tell you."

"Tell me what?"

"She can't come, she's sick. She sounded awful, all hoarse and congested and stuff. Said she'd reschedule when she's better."

"Shit."

"Yeah, so, you wanna talk to him?"

"Sure. Send him over."

Carrying his coffee in one hand and the plate of pastries in the other he joined Gwen at her table. He set his cup and plate down, took the seat across from her and leaned forward, reaching out a hand to shake hers.

"Jason Cuselli." He wrapped both hands around Gwen's in a solid but casual greeting before leaning back in his chair and crossing his right leg over the left, resting his ankle on his knee. A tropical jungle of a tattoo crept up the right leg but Gwen noticed that his right arm had something completely different, with a series of Native American symbols from wrist up to where his sleeve met his arm.

He was almost six feet, with a warm complexion that might have a European background. His eyes were nearly chocolate, with generous lips, thick brows, and cheeks that hinted time spent in the high altitude sunshine. "Thanks for seeing me without an appointment. I only noticed your ad last night. I was having dinner at the Peach place."

"Peach City Bistro?"

"The very one. Thought it was an interesting concept, though I gotta say I didn't expect much. They surprised me—totally. I figured they'd corner themselves with that whole peach gig, but they are rockin' it."

"I like it." Gwen smiled at what she thought was actually a pretty spot on review."

"I'm traveling alone and I wasn't in the mood for the bar scene, so I picked up a local paper to pass the time. That's where I saw your ad."

"You're not from around here?"

"Nope. Until last night I figured I was passing through."

"Where to?"

"Not sure. Wherever the map takes me. I hit the road a few weeks back, decided it was time to see America. It's been an awesome ride so far. Not so much about the destination as just getting out of town and finding a new perspective."

"Where did you get out of town from?" Gwen thought that this interview—if that's what it actually was—was certainly following an odd path.

"Big Apple. New York City. Best water on the planet, incredible food and what I decided is probably, excuse my choice of words, the bullshit capital of the culinary world."

"Really? Were you working there? In a restaurant, I mean?"

"Oh, sorry, should have given you this first," Jason said, pulling a neatly folded piece of paper from his back pants pocket. "My résumé."

Gwen unfolded the sheet of light grey vellum and read through a summary that began with a degree from a very impressive East Coast culinary academy with French roots, and ran through several pastry chef positions at increasingly prestigious restaurants, the last, she was pretty sure, possessed Michelin stars. There was even a year spent under the tutelage of a legendary chef in the south of France.

"Wow. I mean, wow. Is this for real?" she asked.

"Yep. It's not that unusual where I came from, but I guess it is more than you usually see."

"More like ever see. What on earth are you doing here?"

"Well, Gwen, I guess I'm applying for a job as your pastry chef. I'm very qualified, if you hadn't noticed."

"I'm absolutely certain I cannot match what you are probably accustomed to being paid."

"You're correct, though it's probably not as much as you'd think. But I'm not looking for a huge paycheck here, I've been in that atmosphere, and believe me, it's not worth it."

"I'm not sure how rewarding it would be. The only perk I could guarantee would be free coffee. We're a pretty simple bakery here."

"All the better. Believe me, I've had my fill of celebrity chefs and restaurant politics. I don't need a place where the guy next to me is looking to climb over my back—after he stabs it—to reach the next rung on the ladder. I bailed on all of that, Gwen. That's why I hit the road. To get my soul back. It's been a good trip, so far."

"So far?"

"I gotta be honest with you; I'm not sure how long I'll stay. I mean, I'll sign a contract, I'll make a commitment, but probably gonna draw the line at 6 months—max. After that, I just have to see. I'm not saying I won't be staying longer. Maybe this is it for me, but I just rolled into town a couple of days ago and, so far, it's looking like a place I'd like to get to know better. It's definitely a good place to find a great glass of wine."

"That it is." Gwen leaned back in her chair to consider his offer. "Honestly, Jason, I wasn't crazy about the idea of hiring someone else to bake anyway. I mean, it's always only been me in the kitchen. It'll be a big change for me, too."

"Like being in control, do you?" He smiled.

"Maybe I do." She smiled back.

"It's a common curse among chefs, I can tell you that. This is not a profession for the retiring type. But sometimes it's more of a mission. Guess I'm feeling lately like doing some missionary work." Jason grinned.

"I'm a realist. I know I can't do it all; I do need some help."

"Well…" he picked up a piece of his tart and nibbled at its sweet caramelized edge, "for what it's worth, I don't think you need help because you don't know what you're doing. This is damn fine. I could probably find you a position as pastry chef at a very nice restaurant in New York. But I kinda think, like me, you've got different priorities."

"On that I will agree. Tell you what, why don't you head back to the kitchen and—"

"Make you something? Like an audition?"

"Exactly. If all goes well, we'll see how we both feel about a six month commitment. Deal?"

"Deal."

Eleven

*T*O: GWEN
    CC: Claire

So…I get home and what do you think I found—flowers from Carl! O.M.G.!! They are really very pretty—roses and such. He wants me to call him so we can go out to dinner. Oh geez…I don't know what to do! And no letter or message from Jimmy. I just feel like hiding in my basement! Help!! Any ideas? Advice? Anything?!?!?

Del :)

To: Del

CC: Claire

Del, you are just going to have to talk with Carl. If you are sure you don't want this to go any further then you had better explain that to him.

Did you expect something from Jimmy?

Gwen

To: Gwen
CC: Claire
No…I didn't expect anything from Jimmy. I just thought maybe he would call or send a letter or something. I mean, how can he be so heartless? Doesn't he know how I feel?

Would it be acceptable to email Carl? Or send him a text?

How are you doing, by the way? I'm sorry I didn't ask sooner. :(

Del :)

To: Del
CC: Claire
From what you told us, Jimmy didn't sound like he was very happy the last time he saw you. And you were with Carl, then, too. Maybe Jimmy thinks you are serious about Carl.

Um, I'm sorry, but I think you should probably speak with Carl in person. After all, you'll still need to work together on the hospital board. I should think it would be very uncomfortable if you don't totally settle the issue in person.

I am fine, thanks. Looks like I might have a new pastry chef. I'll fill you in when we talk.

Gwen

To: Gwen
CC: Claire
Oh, Gwen, I know you are right, but I am not very good

at this sort of thing. I mean, I only ever had one boyfriend before, and I married him! Look how terribly that turned out. I'm so nervous just thinking about it all, I can't imagine how nervous I'll be in person!!! Maybe I should make some note cards and study some talking points. I do that before business presentations. What do you think? That might help!

I am so excited about your new pastry chef!! I can't wait to hear more about him/her!!

Del :)

To: Del

CC: Gwen

Geez, you guys are driving me nuts. Del, what do you expect? You told Jimmy you needed some time apart. You pretty much broke it off with him. Then you show up for lunch in HIS restaurant with Carl. If you were a man I'd say you had some balls!

If you want Jimmy back you're going to have to let him know and that's probably gonna involve some groveling and shit. It might not be pretty but if you are honest with him it might work. If you're nervous have a drink first.

I knew Jimmy for years before I met you and he may hold a grudge sometimes. He wouldn't serve me a dirty martini for almost three months just because I said he should put three olives in instead of two. What can I say, the man is stubborn. If you want him you'll have to learn how to get past that shit, I suppose. Or make him want to get past it. As I see it that's really your only option.

Oh, and tell Carl to take a hike—nicely. Do that first, okay? Or we'll end up doing more email therapy crap.

Got it?
Claire
Ps Gwen, is this new chef a guy? Cute?

To: Claire
CC: Gwen
ok
Del :

Twelve

CLAIRE WAS LATE TO HER yoga class. She'd stopped at the Larson sisters' house on the way, to see if they needed anything from town, and ended up helping Cora ease Evie down the stairs and onto the couch.

"I thought we ordered a hospital bed for the living room. Did that arrive yet?" Claire asked.

"Yes, dear." Cora fluffed up a small pillow to place under Evie's leg where it rested on a worn and cracked, brown leather ottoman. "But honestly, Evie sleeps so much better in her own bed. We told the nice young man not to bother, just take it back. Oh, and don't worry," she had said, leaning conspiratorially toward Claire, "I gave him a crisp dollar bill for his troubles. I thought it was the least I could do," she added, winking.

"I'm sure he appreciated it." Claire could imagine what that nice young man was probably saying to his friends about the sisters.

Claire had departed with a short list of necessities from the grocery store, realizing that she'd probably have to stop by more often now that she knew Cora was inching Evie up and down the stairs daily. That seemed like a recipe for disaster but she didn't know how she could possibly be there all the time.

At least she'd managed to make it for the last thirty minutes of the class. Everyone had since departed but Claire remained, moving slowly from cobra, to downward dog to sun salutation, flowing from one asana, or position, to another.

Claire could feel the tension ease and worked to clear her thoughts as well. Though she'd joined the yoga school initially as a way to fill time—and make Bob stop worrying about her—she'd come to find that she actually enjoyed her yoga practice, even looking forward to it and missing it when she wasn't able to attend. Yoga had become a way to clear her body and mind of stress. She likened herself to a painter, creating a clean canvas every morning on which to paint the day's events.

Her teacher, Calysta, had left her meditation tape for Claire to use. A small fountain tinkled softly in the corner of the studio. Together, the music and water noise masked any last vestiges of the world outside and, once she came to the final minutes, laying on her back, working through rhythmic breaths while relaxing deeper and deeper into an almost trance-like state, Claire could almost imagine a weight lifting off her body, leaving her feeling freer and more at peace than she'd been in a very long time. In fact, she thought, perhaps more at peace in that moment than she'd ever been.

"Claire." Calysta's soft voice whispered from the doorway, pulling her back to reality. "We'll have a class arriving shortly; I thought I'd give you some warning…and time to wind down."

"Wind up is probably more accurate." Claire opened her eyes and rolling slowly to her side to sit up.

"Sorry."

"Hey, no problem. Nothing lasts forever."

She gathered her mat and tote bag, finished off the water in the bottle she'd brought, then crossed the street from the yoga studio and headed for Gwen's bakery. She needed caffeine…and a look at the new pastry chef Gwen had hired the day before.

"Howdy!" Claire swung open the door and heard the jangling of a small wind chime that hung from the handle. She remembered Gwen had had chimes on her door in Blue River. They had clanged loudly on the windy day when Claire had rushed from the bakery to find Del's car wrecked out front. That had been the day they'd all met. It seemed like a very long time ago, but in truth it was just under a year.

"Hi there." Gwen stood behind the counter, arranging a pastry tray in the front display case.

"Where'd you get the chimes?" Claire asked as Gwen handed her a to-go cup apparently in anticipation of Claire's now regular order of a double caramel, skinny latte.

"They're from the old shop. I found them in a box I finally unpacked." Gwen measured out the espresso and went to work.

"You're still unpacking?"

"You'd be surprised what I haven't gotten to yet. Having Jason here has been great. It's only been a day but already I'm getting so much more done. And, I'm enjoying my day." Gwen smiled as she steamed Claire's skim milk.

"I can tell. This Jason must be a miracle worker. And I haven't met him yet—where is he?"

"He's in back. He decided to make some peach pies."

"Oh, competition for Peaches? That's gutsy."

"This town is full of peach pies this time of the year."

"True enough. Of course, they're the best peaches on the planet, so who's complaining?"

"Jason thought we ought to contribute the bakeries *homage* to the local fruit."

"He said *homage?*"

"He did. I guess it's the sort of thing they do in New York."

"My, my, hope I can still afford this place." Claire grinned and took a long sip of her latte.

"Ha, ha. Don't worry, the *homage* label is free of charge. After that he says he's on to fall favorites. Apparently he's already planning something with squashes."

"A pastry?"

"Hmm-mm, with butternut squash, I think." Gwen nodded. He thought they might be good for both breakfast and lunch."

"What do *you* think?" Claire asked.

"I think if he thinks it will be good it will be. Here—" Gwen pulled a dainty plate from the cold cabinet. It held a small assortment of pastries cut into bite-sized pieces. "Try one."

Claire chose what looked like a corner of a strawberry tart and popped it into her mouth. She moaned and murmured around a full mouth, "Oh. My. God."

"I know," Gwen said, nodding and taking a taste for

herself.

"What's in it?"

"This one is a combination of rhubarb and straw-berry, but he's done a strawberry and Cointreau re-duction for the glace'. That's the gel coating. And the crust has toasted macadamia nuts in it. And butter, lots of butter."

"It's incredible! But is it terribly expensive?"

"Not really, only a few cents more than what I made. He's been a great help with re-organizing my ordering system and tweaking several of my recipes to make them more cost effective and just plain better!"

"Oh, sweetie, everything you make is wonderful. Honestly! But this…"

"You won't hurt my feelings. I know what this is, it's the best. This is why insanely wealthy people winter in the south of France. Well, one of the reasons."

"Be sure you get this recipe!" Claire licked her fin-gers before taking another sip of her coffee.

"Absolutely. That's part of his contract. Anything he creates while he's here stays here. Well, the recipe does. He's not allowed to recreate it within one hundred miles. He actually suggested that clause."

"Keeps him from competing with you," said Claire, the realtor in her kicking in. "You forget I know con-tracts."

"That's right. I should have had your help, but we really just sat at the table in back and put it together. He was surprisingly helpful."

"Or you were very trusting?"

"Maybe a little of both, but I did have him whip some goodies up in the kitchen before I committed. That was the clincher, really after I tried those I would have probably agreed to anything to keep him here, aside from ownership!"

"Now you're scaring me. Next time, promise that I help you write it up, okay?"

"Promise. But don't worry, I didn't give away the farm; plenty of warm fuzzies for both of us. I just wish I could have gotten him to commit to a year rather than six months."

"We'll work on that in five and half months, how's that?" Claire asked.

"Agreed."

"So...can I have a looksy at the new cooksy?"

"That's terrible." Gwen smiled and shook her head at her friend.

"I agree. I'm in an odd mood today and I have to head over to check on my charges soon."

"How are the sisters?" Gwen waved for Claire to follow her to the kitchen.

"They think they are fine. I worry one of them will fall down that lovely curved staircase of theirs and land dead in the foyer beneath that gorgeous crystal chandelier."

"Sounds terrible though... rather romantic?" Gwen cast a quizzical look Claire's way.

"Part of me is always marketing any home I see, I guess."

"You think they want to sell?"

"Are you kidding? I think the only one who'll get them out of that house is the undertaker."

"Claire, that's terrible. Really."

"I know. Sorry, I'm kind of joking, but honestly, they are the happiest pair, and so devoted to each other. Still, I think Cora has her hands full taking care of

Evie. And she needs help taking care of that house."

"Can you find them some live-in help, perhaps?" Gwen paused, her hand on the door to the kitchen.

"I'm not sure they can afford it. It's hard to tell if they are hanging by a thread—financially—or just forgetful and overwhelmed."

"My impression, from what I've heard around town, is that they're okay. But I don't know. Is there a family friend you could speak with, perhaps?"

"Hmm…not a bad idea. I'll see what I can find out. But first, stop stalling. Let me see this new pastry chef of yours. He sounds tasty."

"Claire, don't forget about Bob," Gwen said, teasing her friend.

"Believe me, I haven't forgotten Bob, though he's pretty distracted with perky little Terra running around the winery."

"I'm not sure it's what you think it is."

"I'm not even sure what I think it is. But I'm not thinking about it now. Onward!" Claire gave Gwen a gentle push and they both entered the kitchen.

GWEN PULLED THE SHADES ON the bakery's front window, blocking the glare of the early afternoon sun. The lunch rush was just easing up so she passed the reigns of the front desk counter to Becca and went back to the kitchen to see if Claire had decided to live there, and if Jason was getting anything done. Claire seemed to have been instantly smitten with the chef and, try as she might, Gwen had had little luck dislodging her friend from his company.

"Any actual baking going on back here?" Gwen pushed through the kitchen door for the first time in the last hour.

"Plenty of that going on. No worries, Chef." Gwen liked that Jason insisted on calling her Chef. He said it was a sign of respect for her top position in the kitchen.

"Hey, kiddo!" Claire sat at Gwen's kitchen desk writing notes on scraps of paper. "You never told me there was science to cooking. Jason has been explaining everything! We just finished leavening." Claire turned her focus back to the desk, scribbling something on one of the sheets before her.

Gwen looked at Jason, eyebrows raised in a questioning look. Jason simply shrugged his shoulders and continued rolling and folding his current task, which looked like a strudel. "Where is my friend and who is this woman you've replaced her with?" she asked him. Then looking back to Claire, "Since when are you interested in leavening? Heck, since when are you interested in cooking, period?"

"Jason has a wonderful way of explaining things." She smiled over at the man of the hour.

"Don't blame me," Jason said, "she just kept asking me how I did stuff and I kept telling her. It's kinda fun, actually, I feel like I'm teaching a class."

"Jason promised to show me how to do a few things sometime, when he's not too busy."

"What kind of things?" Gwen asked, wondering what her friend and her new chef were up to.

"Baking, Gwen." Claire laughed at the nearly shocked look on Gwen's face. "Really, it's amazing how he does this."

"I've been doing this as long as you've known me

and I don't ever recall you saying anything about it being amazing."

"Because I always thought it was some sort of voo-doo art form. But Jason has made it clear that baking is an extremely logical, scientific-based activity. Anyone who applies themselves and follows the rules can come up with something delicious."

"Like zucchini cake?" Gwen crossed her arms in front of her.

"Exactly." Claire smiled, then, seeing Gwen's expression, tamped her enthusiasm.

"Have you ever even turned on the oven in your house?"

"Well, there was that one very chilly morning…"

"What were you making?" Jason asked.

"She wasn't making anything. She was getting warm."

"Hey, so I found a practical use for it. Sue me. Besides, I've been a one microwave gal for too long. And take out. But Jason is inspiring me."

"To cook?" Gwen couldn't believe what she was hearing. After her conversations with Del about Claire's recovery she was starting to wonder if Claire was losing it.

"Not so much cooking but…" Claire said, waved her hands back and forth in front of herself, searching for the right way to put it. "I like the idea that baking has exactness to it. If you control the ingredients, the portions, the time, there's a guarantee of success. That appeals to me."

"Well, I don't know about guarantees." Jason paused to consider Claire's statement. "You can do it all right and still have it go wrong."

"But, it's a chemical thing, isn't it? If you follow the steps."

"Sure, but there are a lot of things that can screw it up; an oven that's too hot, the type of baking sheet, hell, even the weather."

"True." Gwen said, "Humid days are the worst."

"Some days everything goes to hell for no apparent reason."

"This is complicated, Gwen. You should offer classes. Jason could teach. You could help."

"Gee, thanks." Gwen said, her feelings not too terribly hurt. "I'm still trying to get the basics organized for now, and there's not a lot of room here."

"Maybe eventually." Jason winked at Claire. "I can give you one-on-one lessons in the meantime, if you like."

"Even if it's humid?" Claire asked.

Gwen didn't like the seductive tone in Claire's voice and decided some intervention was called for. "Hey, weren't you supposed to visit the sisters?"

"Oh, shit. You're right. Gotta go." Claire stuffed her notes in her yoga bag. "I'll call," she said to Jason and flew out the kitchen door.

Gwen stood, scowling at Jason.

"Hey, Chef, you sicced her on me, remember?" He grinned.

"I just opened the door so she could meet you."

"Same thing."

"Listen, Claire's been through a lot the last few months."

"Don't sweat it. I'm not after any tail, or any complications. I'm all about the baking. She's great, friendly and attractive as hell, and good company in a lonely kitchen, but she's not my type, so no worries. Really."

"Good, because I can only handle one complete upset in the balance of power at a time and if she dumped Bob for you I'd be in full-out damage control on every front."

"It won't be my fault."

"Stronger men than you have fallen, believe me. I'm counting on your good intentions and strong will."

"I will do my best not to be seduced by your friend."

"Good."

"Glad we got that cleared up." Jason grinned at Gwen, clearly enjoying the turn this conversation had taken.

"Don't let it go to your head." Gwen smiled back.

"What can I say, every bakery needs a Stud Muffin."

Gwen laughed as she returned to the front of the bakery, relieved that Jason really wasn't her problem. But there was that little nagging question. What exactly was going on in Claire's head?

Thirteen

DEL HAD ASKED CARL TO stop by her office on his way to a meeting with the hospital Chief of Staff. She felt relatively safe sitting behind her desk. As long as she kept it between herself and Carl she thought she'd have the nerve to say what she needed to say. At least that was the plan.

She jumped at the sudden brisk knock on her door and didn't have time to answer before the door swung open and Carl strode in, breathless in a way that said he might have taken the stairs two at a time, carrying his suit coat in one hand.

"Just the lovely lady whose help I need." He strolled swiftly around her desk and held out the lapel on his coat. "Look what I did; marinara from lunch, and me with a very important meeting."

"Oh, well…" Del stood and took the coat, looking at the stain and feeling that, if she couldn't succeed in keeping the desk between them, perhaps the coat would be barrier enough. "I'm sure you don't have to impress our Chief of Staff. After all, he's seen worse stains on clothes than pasta sauce." She tried to sound light and at ease, though she was anything but.

"It's not just him, we've got an unhappy customer and I'm the one who gets to make it all better with the guy."

"Unhappy?"

"Apparently the guy's wife had her baby here and she ended up sharing a room with another patient."

"I suppose that happens. Sometimes there are just so many patients that—"

"It doesn't happen to one of your biggest donors, Delly."

Del cringed at the nickname Carl seemed to favor. It made her feel like she was fifteen.

"Well," she pushed on, despite her discomfort, "that ought to make him realize how badly we need the new wing."

"No matter how badly you may need something your top guys can't go without the perks. Even if the rest of the patients suffer they're going to expect five star treatment and they take it personally if they don't get it. Then they take their business and their donations elsewhere and the hospital can't afford to lose a big donor. If you only have one chocolate left in a box they'd expect to get it. But then, if you play your cards right, they'll graciously offer to buy a new box, or in this case, a new pediatric care wing."

"That doesn't seem right. What makes them think they are better than anyone else?"

"They've got the bucks. That's why they expect a board member to take the time to meet with them. And they expect him to look good! Think it's possible to get the sauce out of my jacket?"

"Huh? Oh." Del looked at the lapel. It wasn't a large stain. "Maybe some club soda."

"Great." Carl pulled out his cell. "I'll just wait here, then. I've got a call I need to make anyway." He set the coat firmly in her outstretched arms and plopped into the armchair across the room, dialing, and then listening to the phone ring as he mouthed *thanks babe* to her, adding a thumbs up before turning his attention to his call. "Hey, Jimbo, how ya been…"

Del left the room, suit coat in hand, thinking that in all the variations she'd imagined for their meeting this option had never occurred to her. She searched the fridge in the break room and found a small bottle of club soda. Del didn't know who it belonged to, but she cracked open the top and poured a small amount on the stain, rubbing it with a cloth she'd found in a drawer. After a couple of applications she thought it looked good, though wet.

She placed the half-used bottle back in the fridge atop a small note she'd hastily scribbled on a napkin:

So sorry, it was an emergency-I'll bring you a new one tomorrow!

Then she stopped in the Ladies Room to dry the coat under one of the hand dryers. She thought the results would suffice. If she hadn't known it was stained she never would have noticed.

Del entered her office to find Carl, still on his phone, sitting behind her desk and scribbling on her notepad.

"I'm on top of it, never you mind." Carl nodded briskly to some unknown person on the other end, adding, "talk with you soon," and ended the call. He stood up and tore off the top sheet from her pad. "Had to make a few notes. Hope you don't mind."

Del noticed that he didn't wait for an answer but took the jacket from her.

"How'd it come out?" He fingered the lapel, inspecting her work.

"Pretty well, I think. I doubt anyone will notice."

"I think you're right." He slipped back into the suit coat. "Very nice. You're a life saver."

"Oh, I hardly think—"

"Really, what else would I have done on such short notice?" He paused, an inquiring smile on his face as he looked into her eyes.

"Listen, Carl." Del decided she'd better dive in while she had the nerve. "I needed to talk to you about something very important. I'm really sorry—"

"Me too, Delly!" Carl grasped both her shoulders in his hands. "I felt badly about abandoning you at our lunch last week. Let me make it up to you, okay?"

"What? Oh, don't worry about that, no, I—"

"You are very sweet, but it was not the gentlemanly thing to do to a fine lady such as yourself. No, I won't rest until I make it up to you with a very special evening. As special as you are."

"Oh." Del felt like a deer in the headlights. Again she had not anticipated this turn of the conversation and, flustered, words were failing her.

"I'll take that as a yes. How about I pick you up at seven Saturday night? I checked your calendar while I was using your desk. Hope you don't mind. Saw you're free and it looks like the kids are still with the ex for another week, eh?"

Carl smiled down at her. It was meant to be an intimate smile, but Del couldn't help it when an image from the movie The Lion King flashed into her brain:

the leering Scar as he sent Mustafa to his doom. She shook her head, telling herself she'd been watching too much Disney lately with the kids.

"Really, Carl, you don't have to make anything up to me. I completely understand. Besides, that's not what I wanted to talk to you about. I really needed to tell you—"

"Shit." Carl glanced at the watch on his wrist. "Sorry, excuse the language, just realized I'm gonna be late. Listen, whatever you have to tell me I promise to be a captive audience over dinner. How's that sound? And maybe," he added, his voice lowered to almost a purr, "I can be a captive audience after dinner as well."

The image Carl's voice and words created hung between them for a second, sucking all ability to speak from a dumbfounded Del who could no longer conceive of how this conversation had gotten so far beyond her grasp.

"In fact," Carl's face swept slowly towards hers, "I'll seal that promise with a kiss."

And he did.

CLAIRE LEANED AGAINST THE BACK of her claw-foot tub. Outside the wind was picking up and a soft whistle blew from somewhere up in the eaves of the snug farmhouse. Inside, the only sound was the soft prick-prick-prick of bubbles popping in her bubble bath.

She'd spent the afternoon cleaning out the thinning plants in her garden and harvesting a small bounty of squash, beans and tomatoes. Shortened days and increasingly cooler evenings were taking their toll on the garden's productivity but there was enough to fill two grocery bags, which she'd placed in the trunk of her car.

After a quick stop at Angelo's Market and Deli for meat and cheese she had finally arrived at the Larson's home just in time to make them a basic dinner and leave more than enough behind for the sisters to fix simple meals over the next few days. As Claire suspected, Cora had yet to visit the grocery and there was very little in their refrigerator until she'd arrived. She found them happily nibbling on crackers and cheese from a gift basket that someone had sent, along with best wishes for Evie's speedy recovery.

"There's plenty here, dear, even a salami!" Cora replied to Claire's insistence that that wasn't much of a dinner.

"It even has a small box of shortbread cookies with raspberry centers," Evie added, delightedly pointing out a small box with six, small cookies gloriously displayed in gold foil and cellophane. "And there's a fruit basket in the dining room! It's almost worth the injury for the delicious rewards that follow. Such treats!"

"Don't be foolish, Evie," Cora scolded with a smile. "But yes, it was so thoughtful. Harold and Clarice Partridge are dear old friends."

"Did they bring it earlier?" Claire wondered if she was the only one who seemed to realize that the sisters were slightly in over their heads when it came to meals and maintenance.

"Oh no, the Partridges live in Kentucky! That would be a surprise, wouldn't it, Evie dear?"

"Indeed! A delightful one, but still!"

"Do you have any friends here in town?" Claire was curious where exactly all of their friends must be.

"Well, of course," Cora said.

"So you've had visitors, I'm assuming?"

"Many of our friends are over in Dupont." Cora mentioned the next town west of Grand Valley. "There's a delightful little retirement village there."

"They even have a pond!" Evie added.

"Yes, it's man-made, but there's quite a nice vista over the water looking out on the mesas. We visited with Abigail Mayes, just after her family helped her move there."

"She has a charming little cottage, but they have a main house where all the residents can dine at any meal. It's very comfortable and convenient."

"Really." Claire thought this conversation was taking a very promising turn. Some sort of assisted living environment seemed like just the thing for these two. "Have you considered moving there as well? I mean, with your friends?"

"Oh dear, no, Cora and I are fine here. Maybe someday, when we're older, perhaps."

"Certainly, if we couldn't manage on our own, but we are getting on swimingly. Especially now that we have such a delightful neighbor!" Cora gave Claire's hand a squeeze.

It was clear this was not a battle worth waging at the moment, so Claire took her groceries into the kitchen and put together what she thought was a pleasant alfresco dinner and definitely more well-rounded than cheese and crackers.

It had been late when she finally returned home and, after a night of cooking and general tidying up for the sisters, a bath sounded like the perfect ending for her day.

When she'd first arrived in the valley and toured this little house, the lack of a shower was just one more item on the list of reasons she didn't expect to stay long. But Claire had to admit to herself—though not to Bob—that she looked forward to a bath after a long day. There was something very relaxing and contemplative about a tub full of warm water and bubbles. A shower was a task, but a bath was an experience. Normally she might bring a book to read as she soaked, but tonight the easy whoosh of the wind and the creaks of her home were just the thing to lull frayed nerves.

But were her nerves frayed? Claire had become so accustomed to frayed nerves at the end of a long day showing homes, negotiating deals and plodding through endless paperwork that she almost expected to feel exhausted every night. She was exhausted, but not from stress, she realized, but rather a day's worth of activity. And not all of it had been physically demanding, like her morning yoga or the afternoon in the garden. No, her visit with Jason had been a pleasure; fun, even.

Claire closed her eyes and thought about the young man. He was attractive, and damn, he could bake. What a combination, she thought to herself. Of course, Bob didn't bake, but he did make wine—very good wine. He might not have been as young, but he was terribly attractive and more age-appropriate. Which she had to admit was nice for a change. For instance, it was nice to have things in common to talk about. Events and concerns their generation shared. How often had her relationships ended quickly because there was nothing to say once they left the bedroom. She thought about Bob's dark eyes, and the way his hair felt when he kissed her long and slow and she ran her fingers through the thick, black locks, enjoying the smell of his skin, his hair…him.

Not long ago, Claire knew, she'd have been seriously plotting the conquest of Jason. Yes, it would be a pleasure doing business with him if she could come up with a better use of his talents than Gwen's bakery. Tonight, though, even she had to admit that her interests in him were more business than pleasure. Tonight she realized that, when it came to pleasure, there was only one man she was interested in and suddenly she worried, had she made too much ado about Terra? Or was there something there? Had she found the right man at last only to lose him to her inability to commit?

Claire slid beneath the water, rinsing her hair and trying to hide from her worries beneath the frothy waves. When she slid back up she noticed a new sound, the crunch of tires on gravel, and, reaching for a towel as she climbed from the tub, she hoped it wasn't Cora this time.

Her doorbell rang as she slid into the folds of a creamy satin robe, her damp hair piled high on her head and held with a black enamel comb. She pulled the curtain aside and recognized Bob's truck. For a second Claire felt the skip of a heartbeat that Bob's late night arrivals always lit within her; at least in the past. Now, that flame quickly chilled, replaced with a new and unwelcome anxiety. Why did life have to be so complicated, Claire thought to herself.

She clicked the deadbolt and pulled open the door. Bob stood on her front stoop, bottle of wine in one hand and a single white rose in the other.

"White?" Claire pointed to the rose.

"Truce? " Bob smiled forming on his lips.

"How about the wine?"

"Oh, that's red."

"What's that stand for?"

Bob paused, his smile replaced by a new intensity. "Love."

Claire felt her tension ease and, despite walls her heart seemed intent on building, she felt a warmth she simply could not deny. Claire pushed open the screen door and instantly felt his arm around her waist, his lips on hers and a haze of passion that enveloped her mind and body. So much for holding a grudge.

LATER, WHEN HER HAIR WAS nearly dry and the wine finally uncorked, they lay in a tangle on her bed, the rose sitting on the dresser in a slender water glass enlisted at a moment's notice.

"Hmm…what is this?" Claire inhaled the scent and savored a long, lush sip from her nearly empty glass.

"It's the new Reserve." Bob put down his glass and reached for the bottle. The distinctive Columbine Estates label had been done in a deeper pallet for this special bottle, the pale blue of the columbine now almost azure and a sunset behind it drenched in burgundy and amethyst. "We're going to officially release it at the festival. What do you think?"

"I love it. Will there be posters of the label?"

"Sure, but how about the wine?"

"Oh, that's very good too." She took another sip.

"Really good. In fact, I might want a case of my own."

"I know the owner; I can get you a deal." He kissed her then, a long soft kiss that tasted sweet and salty with a cabernet finish. "You know," his lips moved to her earlobe, then gently down her neck, "instead of getting your own case, you can always share mine... and anything else you find in the cellar at my house."

"I'll keep that in mind." His kisses re-ignited her interests in things other than wine. She moaned softly as he reached her collarbone, and set her glass aside to concentrate on his shoulder. "But a case of my own is much handier. I don't always have Good Samaritans arriving in four wheel drive carriages with bottles of wine late at night."

He slid his arm around her, pulling her body to his, both feeling a new urgency between them. On the dresser the quiet buzz of Bob's cell phone's vibrator hummed against the wood.

"I'll let 'em leave a message, babe," he whispered, his lips grazing hers. "It would be easier to raid my cellar anytime we wanted...if you lived there."

Claire froze, though judging by his activities, Bob didn't seem to notice.

"What?" she asked.

"You wouldn't even have to get dressed; you could raid my stash in the buff!" Bob smiled down at her. "I'd help you, and you know, there's a very comfortable couch in my cellar," he added, referring to the cozy but cave-like room in Bob's home that housed quite an impressive wine collection.

"No, I mean what did you mean about my living there?" She pushed up on one elbow, separating her neck from his lips.

"Ace." He sighed and leaned back on his pillow. "You know I want you to come live with me. I told you that when you came to Grande Valley. It was your idea to live up here, and that's great, but if you lived with me we could see more of each other; especially this time of the year when I'm so busy."

"So you mean my moving in with you would be more convenient for you."

Claire's eyes narrowed, clueing Bob in to the fact that he'd said the wrong thing. "No. I mean, yes, I mean, I want you there. It's not just that it's convenient, but I'd think it *would* be convenient for *both* of us. You keep complaining that we don't see enough of each other these days."

"Complaining?"

"No, no, I don't mean complaining, I mean—" His cell buzzed again and he glanced at the dresser, irritated by the interruption.

"You said complaining. What am I now, a nag? Have to keep the little lady happy so she won't complain?" Claire heard her voice rising and felt her heart pounding. Part of her knew that she might be making more of Bob's innocent words than she should be, but part of her was also remembering Terra's hand on Bob's arm.

"Claire, please, don't pick a fight over this, I only meant—"

"I'm picking a fight now? First I'm a nag, now this? So you're trying to get me to move in with you so I won't be a nagging woman who picks fights?"

"Claire, you know that's not what I meant." Bob reached for her but she pulled away, pulled the sheet between them, pulled her eyes away from his.

"And what would I do all day at your house? Be the

little cleaning lady during the day and at night—what would I do at night?"

"That is not what I said, Claire. That is not what I want."

"Lately all you seem to want is to be at work. It seems like Terra's company is more appealing than mine."

"That's not true." Bob reached for her hand only to have her pull it back, hovering in the air defensively between them. He looked at her hand then met her eyes. There were tears in them, but anger also.

"Then what is true, Bob?" Claire asked slowly, softly, her anger defusing into a sadness she could not understand. Why was she accusing him of something for which she had no proof? This man, who had just made love to her, who had, in fact, expressed his love to her; why was it easier to build this wall than return those words? She pressed the issue. "What's going on with you and Terra?" She made the words come out though she did not want to hear the answer.

"Terra is…a complicated issue, Claire, I—" Bob's cell buzzed again. "Geez, I'd better check that," he said, grabbing it from the dresser. "Bob here," he said, then listening, "shit, yeah, yeah, I know. What time is it?" held his phone out to check the time. "Okay, get it going. I'm on my way." He hung up, reached for his clothes and started dressing. "That was Andy. We've been watching the weather all day for this cold front and it's coming in now."

He paused and they could both here the whistling of the wind around her house and in the trees outside. Like the division between them, it had been building while they talked but neither of them had noticed.

"The merlot is in," he said, referring to the harvest, "but the cab is still out there. We're so close. If the temps drop too fast we'll lose it. Andy and Ter—" He broke off, looked at her, and then continued. "Well, they're deploying the heaters. They've called in everyone they can get hold of. I have to go. I have to."

"That's fine." Claire looked down at the sheet, smoothing out the wrinkles where Bob had been.

"It's not fine." Bob sat down beside her on the bed, tipping her chin up with his fingers until her eyes agreed to meet his. "I don't know how this evening got to this moment, but I can explain and I will, just not now. There's no time and that's a conversation that deserves a lot more of it."

Claire's eye narrowed and she blinked, pushing back tears. I don't cry over this shit, she thought to herself, I'm stronger than this, aren't I? What could she say? What should she say? Maybe there really is nothing left to say, she thought, and looked away.

He stood to pull on his shirt. "Ace, I love you. I told you that and I meant that, and I think you love me too, but that's another thing that's complicated. I promise we'll talk. Soon."

Claire said nothing, deflated by the moment and all her fears and worst nightmares and truths she couldn't accept. He leaned in and kissed her gently on her cheek.

"I'll call soon, I promise."

CLAIRE PULLED ON HER SWEAT pants and a t-shirt. The sound of Bob's truck driving away faded into the distance. She was too tired to sleep and went to the kitchen in search of something to fill the emptiness she reasoned was in her stomach.

In all her care to keep the Larson sisters' refrigerator well stocked Claire had done a miserable job of stocking her own. She decided on a couple of eggs, over easy, and was just preparing to crack them into the melted butter in the frying pan when a flash of light caught her eye. Then another and then the red and white flickering lights reflected on her kitchen window were accompanied by the growing throb and whine of a siren.

Claire flicked off the stove, pushed the egg carton back into the fridge and ran to the front door. A fire truck flew past her house heading west. She followed its path and saw the glow coming from above the trees, coming from the Larson sisters' home.

Fourteen

CLAIRE'S CAR SKIDDED TO A stop on the gravel drive. She jumped out and ran toward the front steps. Flames shot from the side kitchen window and, above, from what she knew was a sitting room adjacent to Cora's bedroom.

"Oh God…" She pressed her fingertips against her mouth, watching as one group of firemen pulled hoses up the front stairs while another attacked the fire from the outside by the kitchen window.

Behind the truck she saw the back of an ambulance, its lights still flashing, and she heard heavy coughing. Claire ran.

She rounded the truck and sprinted into the back of a fireman.

"Whoa there!" he shouted, then coughed hard. He turned toward her, pulling off an oxygen mask. Claire saw a rugged face about her own age, warm brown eyes and a tidy blonde mustache. "You okay, ma'am?" he said between coughs.

"Chief!" a second fireman called from the side of the house. "We need you here."

"On my way." He turned back to Claire. "Sorry,

duty calls, but can I help you first?"

"Stay on that oxygen," a paramedic yelled, lean-ing out from the back of the ambulance and nodding sternly at the chief who clapped the mask back over his mouth.

"I'm looking for the women who live in this house." Claire shouted, trying to be heard above the crackling fire and general mayhem around her.

"Claire? Is that you dear?" A familiar voice came from inside the ambulance.

"Yes!"

"Go to it." The chief nodded toward the ambu-lance, a smile in his eyes that told Claire her greatest fears were not realized.

She looked inside the ambulance's open doors and a wave of anxiety washed away when she realized both sisters were safely within. "Are you alright?" Claire looked at Evie, who sat near the door, her injured foot propped up on a small pail put into service for that purpose. Beyond, Cora lay on the stretcher, coughing sporadically beneath her own oxygen mask, her hand wrapped in a bandage. The paramedic sat beside her, checking vitals.

"I'm fine, but Cora was a hero, I'm afraid, and she almost paid a dear price!"

"What happened?"

"She was sitting up late reading in her bedroom, thank the Lord, and smelled smoked. She ran to the head of the stairs and realized there was a fire below, then swept into my room to rescue me."

"So you came out together?" Claire asked. "Why is she coughing and you're not?"

"She ran back in to call the fire department from

the parlor phone. And of course she had to find Elbie."

"Elbie?"

"Our cat."

"You have a cat? I've never seen a cat in your house." As soon as she said it she remembered the basement door was always left ajar and imagined that must have been where the litter box was. But still, no sign of Elbie.

"He's quite shy, dear. Not a fan of strangers. It's not surprising you've never run into him, but I'm sure he saw you. Didn't you Elbie?" she said.

Evie reached into a cardboard box that sat beside her and scooped up a grey tabby that looked like he had gotten his fair share of the many groceries Claire had delivered of late.

"He was hiding under the davenport. Poor Cora had to crawl on her hands and knees and drag him out. I'm afraid he did not want to come."

She looked at Cora, who coughed and raised her bandaged hand in evidence to Elbie's reluctance, a smile beneath her oxygen mask.

"But once she'd placed the call she braved his claws and the growing smoke to rescue our big boy, isn't that right, Elbie, sweetheart?"

Evie nuzzled his nose and the cat closed its eyes. Claire imagined she would hear purring if it weren't so hectic and noisy all around them.

"Thank God you are both alright. Do you know how the fire started?"

"Hard to say, I'm sure." Evie scratched gently behind one of Elbie's ears.

Cora mumbled something, and then pulled her mask aside. "I am wondering if perhaps our furnace blew. It's seen better days and often made quite a racket when—" she paused to cough, "—mother nature pressed it into service."

"Better keep that mask on, ma'am," said the paramedic beside her.

He was young, Claire noticed, but seemed competent. "Will she be okay?" she asked him.

"Should be, but I think we'll take her in to the ER, just to be sure." His voice was calm amid all the chaos. "I'd actually like to take both you ladies down to Grande Valley General. I think they will probably want to hold you overnight for observation. You want to be on the safe side, you know."

"Oh, no," Evie said. "No sooner do we get out of that dreadful place than we are right back in. I just can't."

Cora pulled aside the mask again. "Young man, I appreciate your caution, but truly, I don't think it's necessary."

"Well," he eyed them with concern, "even if I agreed—which I don't—you can't stay here, ma'am."

"Surely in a day or two…" Evie said.

The paramedic looked at Claire and, catching her eye, nodded his head to indicate the house, then shook it slightly.

"Something tells me it may be a while before you can go back in the house," Claire said slowly, moving closer to talk more intimately with the sisters as the paramedic turned his attention away to organize his equipment.

"Oh no…" Evie held the cat closer.

"Is it that bad?" Cora asked.

Claire looked up at the house, then back at the sisters. "The kitchen is probably a total loss. Most of the rest of the place may be okay, but I'm sure there's smoke damage—and water." She watched the firemen as they aimed their hoses into the house. "Is there someone you could stay with? Somewhere you could go?"

Evie visibly slumped at the bad news and Claire felt compelled to sit beside her, wrapping an arm around her for warmth and strength.

Cora looked to Evie who shook her head so slightly Claire barely noticed.

"We'll find a room somewhere," Cora said at last. "Surely one of our charming local inns can put us up for a night or two!"

"I think it will probably be quite some time before the house is ready to safely occupy," the paramedic said.

"We shall have to call Roger." Cora looked at Evie, who shrugged in response.

"A friend?" Claire asked.

"Of sorts." Cora said, "We will need to find a *room at the Inn* for tonight, all the same. We have no manger to spare here."

"Oh Cora," Evie said, smiling, "I love how you've put that. Surely the good Lord is smiling down on us tonight."

Claire shook her head, only these two could consider their home nearly burning to the ground a blessing; not to mention health concerns for each of them along with the burden of unexpected expenses for temporary lodging. Claire wondered if they even had homeowner's insurance. If they couldn't remember to pay the light bill would they have remembered that? Could they afford it? The two seemed like they were just hanging on and she worried that this could push them into destitution.

"Well, if the Lord is watching," Claire said, "he has a strange way of showing it. Listen, why don't you two stay with me tonight? I don't really have any room, but we can work it out. That way we can at least get you inside and comfortable for now. Maybe I can help you figure out your options tomorrow." Claire pushed aside the little voice in her head that wondered what the hell she was getting herself into and hoped she didn't regret it.

"That is so sweet, Claire." Cora glanced at her sister who nodded firmly this time. "We will be little trouble, we promise." Then, looking at the paramedic she asked, "Is that acceptable to you? Claire is a very responsible person, and we will be just next door. I'm certain if there were any issues she would contact you immediately."

"It's not my preferred solution, ma'am, but if that's what you want I can't make you do differently. You stay put, though, Miss Larson. We'll transport you both over. Make sure you get comfortably settled in. If I didn't at least do that my mother would chew me out good."

"Do I know your mother?"

"Yes, she used to be a Simpson, but married my dad, Terry Henniford."

"Marla, of course—what a wonderful woman you mother is."

Claire listened as the two sisters compared notes on the finer features of the young man's mother. She sometimes forgot what it was like to live in a small town where everyone seemed to know everyone else. Usually that made her uncomfortable, but there was something about this little gossip session in the midst of a near disaster that brought a smile to her face.

"Oh, no!" Evie said suddenly.

"What?" Claire and Cora asked in unison.

"Elbie, what will we do with Elbie?"

"I'm sure the local humane society can find room for him," the paramedic volunteered.

"In a cage?" Evie seemed both offended and frightened by the possibility and something in her body language must have alerted the cat, who sat up and began meowing loudly in protest.

Cora whispered, trying not to cough, "Poor Elbert, he had to have surgery last year and he did not like the overnight accommodations at the vet one bit."

The sisters shared a worried look and then, as if they'd also shared some sort of mental telepathy, turned in unison, to look at Claire, who instantly caught their drift.

"Sure, I guess tonight will be fine, I mean, with both of you there."

"What if we can't find someplace that allows cats?" Evie's concern growing on her face. Again they both looked to Claire.

"I don't know, I don't do pets. Isn't there someone else? Someone who already has cats? How about this Roger guy?"

"Oh...I doubt Roger is Elbie's sort, plus there's Torrence," Evie said.

"Who's Torrence?" Claire asked.

"A very obstinate bull terrier. Quite the trouble maker, I assure you." Evie shook her head. "Elbie is… well, I confess he's been spoiled all his life. He wouldn't do well sharing the spotlight with a dog. But he'd be good for you—I'm sure he would."

"Truly, I think he would behave, Claire," Cora added. "There's an old litter box in the back shed we could use. The extra cat litter is in there too, and if you have some tuna fish, or anything like that, he'll be just fine."

"And fresh water, naturally. No milk, Elbie is watching his waistline, aren't you sweetheart?" Evie snuggled the cat closer, nuzzling nose to nose.

"It will only be a few days, I promise. We will find a place that accepts Elbie or we won't go there," Cora said firmly, followed by a slight cough.

CLAIRE SET UP THE LITTER box in her kitchen and dug out some frozen crabmeat she'd been saving for a dip recipe Del had emailed her. The plan had been to make something special to go with one of Bob's newly released Reserves in celebration of the end of the harvest season. She had foreseen a lovely night with no obligations other than to be together, preferably naked. Of course, after the way things had ended earlier that evening she wasn't sure she'd ever get to use the crabmeat.

"At least someone will enjoy it," she said to the cat that meowed earnestly at her feet, brushing its body against her legs in anticipation of the meal she was thawing in the sink. She picked apart the meat and put the softest pieces into a small bowl that she set beside a water dish already occupying a corner of her kitchen.

"Who needs furniture when you have cat paraphernalia?" she asked Elbie as he gobbled up his post-midnight snack. "That ought to make you feel welcome, huh? Just don't get too cozy."

The paramedic had helped her settle the sisters comfortably into her home for the night. Claire offered her bed to Evie, who had re-aggravated her injured leg in the escape from the house. But Evie insisted Cora have the bed. Evie preferred the sofa, anyway, with its variety of pillows to strategically support her leg.

Both sisters had drifted quickly off to sleep after the stressful night's events. She could hear the soft muffle of Evie's gentle snoring coming from the living room. Claire didn't know who this Roger was, but she'd heard Cora assuring Evie she'd call him first thing in the morning. Apparently he was the answer to their predicament. Maybe he had a large home; Claire imagined the sisters must know everyone in the valley. Maybe this guy owed them a favor. Whatever the answer, it could wait until morning.

Claire left the light on over the stove but flicked off all the other ones. Evie was snuggled beneath Claire's cashmere throw so she grabbed a multi-colored knit afghan her sister, Sally, had sent her as a house warming gift when she'd first arrived in Grande Valley and curled up in her leather chair, pulling the afghan over her.

The Larson sisters were so close that Claire found she missed her own sister, Sally, and Sally's son, Jordan. She hadn't thought of her sister for a long time. Aside from a quick visit back east for Sally's wedding, they hadn't talked much. Claire had spent most of her adult life watching out for her younger sister and nephew. She and her sister had lost their parents when they were both in college and Sally had become pregnant not long after that. Much of Claire's focus had been on ensuring their well-being, but Sally wasn't helpless. She'd become a nurse, found good options for her son, who was mildly autistic, and now was settled down with a wonderful man who loved them both.

While it had been a relief to know Sally's future was comfortable, along with so many other changes of late, adjusting to no longer feeling responsible for her sister's happiness had left her strangely out of touch. For the first time it occurred to Claire that maybe, instead of being a surrogate parent, she could just be Sally's sister.

Watching Cora and Evie made Claire long for the attachment only sisters understood, whether they lived in the same house or half a continent apart. Claire decided tomorrow she would pick up the phone and start a new kind of relationship with Sally. As she, too, drifted off to sleep she barely noticed the soft form that settled, purring, into the crook of her legs.

IT WAS LATE MORNING BY the time Claire stepped out of the shower. The sisters had risen at dawn and she'd awoken to the smell of coffee and the sounds of their puttering in her kitchen.

"We didn't wake you, dear, did we?" Cora had asked when she'd first gotten up.

"No, not at all."

But in truth Claire had lain with her eyes shut, listening to the sister's whispered conversations. Together, they poked through her cupboards looking for whatever they needed. They'd been delighted when they'd finally discovered how to turn on her coffeemaker, giggled as they cracked eggs, about a childhood hen named Pecky (a play on Becky), and even taken a wee taste (according the Evie) from the re-corked bottle of Bob's wine from last night.

Apparently they'd both approved of the vintage, leaving Claire assured that they were not tea-totallers, something that would be hard to pull off in a valley filled with vineyards.

Claire finally rose when the appetizing scents from her kitchen were too much to resist and found herself seated and served at her own table not long after. While the space was tight, the company was a nice change. She'd been alone for so long she sometimes forgot how comfortable it was when her space was filled with the right people. She'd also felt that way on the mornings when Bob was there. Bob had felt more and more like the right people, too...until lately. But she pushed those thoughts from her mind and enjoyed the moment until, at last, she'd excused herself to shower.

Now, drying her hair in the bathroom Claire thought she heard a man's voice in her living room. Thinking perhaps Bob had dropped by, she eased the door open and listened. It was a man, just not the one she'd expected. She threw on her sweats and clipped her hair up before venturing out.

Through the door to her bedroom she spotted Elbie curled up in the middle of her bed with a stomach she knew to be full of crabmeat, plus some chicken she'd picked out of a leftover salad in her refrigerator. Claire planned to stop at the store and get actual cat food later.

She stepped quietly into her living room. From

the kitchen she heard the man's voice and wondered if perhaps the paramedic had stopped to check on the sisters. Walking around the corner she saw an attractive gentleman, his hair with just the right amount of salt and pepper and his chiseled features, only slightly softened with age. He was seated at her table, a cup of coffee and an open briefcase set out in front of him.

He looked up at her and his eyes were an icy blue but the wrinkles around them warmed his face when he smiled. He wore a dark gray suit with a sky blue tie that brought the color out in his eyes.

"Hello, you must be Claire?" he half asked, standing as she entered.

Nice voice, too, Claire thought.

"Yes." Claire looked from Evie, seated beside him, to Cora, standing near the sink, waiting for an explanation.

"Claire, this is Roger Peterson," Cora said.

"Nice to meet you." Claire shook his hand. "You're a…friend?"

"Ah, yes, I'm a friend, too." He cast a look at Cora as if unsure what information to offer.

"It's quite alright, Roger. Claire is a good friend. And for heaven's sake, we're staying in her house! We have no secrets from her. Why, we'd most certainly be far less well off without her attentiveness of late."

"And she's letting Elbie stay, as well," Evie chimed in.

"So, you are a friend," Claire repeated.

"I am, but I am also the Larson family attorney."

"Ah, I see," Claire said with a hint of worry in her voice. "Is everything alright? I mean, aside from the fire, naturally."

"Yes, I'm sure it will be. I've alerted the insurance company and they will be sending over an adjuster today to evaluate what needs to be done."

"That's fast."

"I should think so," his tone inferring that it was most certainly what he'd expect. "In the meantime," he turned to Cora, "I'm hoping to convince my clients that, at least while the work is being done, they might consider staying at Cottonwood Villas, over in Dupont."

"You mean the—"

"Old folks home!" Evie said with a gruff tone, scowling as she turned away to look out the window.

"Now, dear," Cora said, "Roger may have a point." She looked over at Claire. "Roger is only thinking of Evie's well-being."

"I'm taking her rehabilitation into consideration with this suggestion," Roger said. "I believe we can find a temporary villa where they might be quite comfortable and where Evie can easily receive physical therapy as her leg heals."

"How is your leg today?" Claire moved protectively to Evie's side.

"It is sore. I imagine I stepped on it harder than I should have in getting out of the house."

"I'm not surprised." Claire sat down at the table beside her. "Maybe you should see the doctor today, too."

"We definitely intend to." Cora looked at her sister, whose body language practically pouted back at her. "I must admit that the villas do seem like the wisest move. I mean, after all, we can't expect Claire to be at our beck and call. Naturally, it's only temporary, until the repairs are made from the fire. By then Evie will most likely be well and we can move right back in."

"Well, that's one plan," Roger said under his breath, catching Claire's eye. "I think I will check into the particulars and see what our options actually are. I'd better excuse myself, there's quite a lot to do."

"I'll walk you out," Claire said, "then I'll be right back."

She followed Roger out the front door. "Can I talk with you a minute, Mr. Peterson?"

"Call me Roger, please." He opened the door of his black Lexus sedan and tossed his briefcase inside.

"I don't mean to pry, it's only that I'm concerned about the sisters. I'm glad to hear they have insurance on the house. That was my first concern. But with deductibles and moving into the Villas, well, I hear that's a very nice retirement home."

"Assisted living," Roger corrected her. "And they are independent villas—small patio homes, actually. They will still have their sense of home and privacy while having assistance on a daily basis. And of course they are only in the next town up the road, so they will still be in familiar territory."

"That's wonderful." Claire wondered if this guy was always all business. She'd noticed the lack of a wedding ring. "From what I've heard it's very nice—somewhat exclusive, even. I'm just concerned that it might be a little…expensive?"

"Expensive?" he asked, apparently unsure of Claire's point.

"Yes, I mean, can they afford that?"

"Oh, I see your concern. You need not worry on that account."

"I only mean that, if they can't afford it, I might

be in a position to…help, a little, at least. Obviously, my home isn't big enough for all of us to stay in, but I might be able to help with their monthly expenses." Claire was surprised to hear herself volunteering to pitch in. She supposed she could afford to, but really, where had this come from? Generally she kept to herself.

Still, something about Cora and Evie had grown on her. She'd gone from a general concern for her neighbors to actually caring about them. It wasn't as if Claire had a lot of family, and lately, with Bob so busy with work, or whatever, the company of the sisters, though sometimes inconvenient, had become comforting.

Roger stood looking at her, as if debating something. He shut his car door, leaned up against it and crossed his arms, settling in for a conversation.

"You're relatively new to the valley?" he asked.

"Well, yes." Claire wondered why that should matter.

"The Larson sisters are well known and loved in the valley, Claire."

"I'm sure they are. They're a couple of sweeties. In fact, I would think if necessary we could probably put together a fundraiser to help—"

"No, that's not what I mean, though I agree, they are sweet. The sisters are the last remaining members of the Larson family. There are a couple of distant cousins in Missouri, but aside from them, they are the last descendants of Elbert Phineas Larson, one of the original settlers of the valley."

"Elbie." Claire smiled, realizing where the name came from.

"Yes, I find that charming, though the original

holder of that name most likely would not have. He was a serious man; he left behind a…difficult family situation. His widowed mother remarried a man who did not like having a constant reminder of her previous husband living in the house. Apparently he resembled his father greatly.

"Elbert came to this valley in the 1800's. Others came to Colorado for silver, but Elbert was a wise young man who recognized that though there was silver, it would be found by only a few and gone soon enough. Land, however, was forever. He founded Grande Valley—well, he named it too. And he went about buying it up. At one time he owned nearly all the land you can see from the top of the mesa when you follow the valley to the turn in the river."

"Whoa," was all Claire could say. She'd been to the top of the mesa and seen that view. She knew they were talking about tens of thousands of acres, at the very least.

"Whoa, indeed. Of course, over time he sold off parcels, and his only son, Phineas, who went by Fin, sold off more. But he kept a good portion and planted fruit orchards: peaches, cherries, pears and the like on a large portion. The sisters were his only children. As you may know, they never married so there are no heirs. But those two, sweet as they seem, have been savvy business women, particularly in their youth. They ran the orchards quite successfully from the front parlor of their home, the home Elbert built."

"But they seem so…"

"Yes. And to some extent they are. Cora was always the backbone, as you may guess. You might say she was the 'bad cop' to Evie's 'good cop'."

"Hard to think of Cora as bad anything, but I see what you mean."

"Evie was always a little frail and age has only accentuated that. When age and caring for Evie made running the business more than Cora could manage on a day-to-day basis she handed the management off to others. My company oversees everything and they never need worry."

"So, they're not destitute?"

"Oh, no." Roger almost laughed at the thought. "Very much the contrary. However, what they are, is frail and forgetful."

"The bills…and grocery shopping."

"Yes, Cora told me how you've helped out and I do appreciate it."

"Couldn't you get them some live-in help?"

"Believe me, I've tried, but they've resisted. They are a very strong-willed duo."

"That doesn't surprise me, especially Cora."

"Yes, though honestly I think she'd be willing if it weren't for her sister. Evie has a hard time with change. That is why, surprisingly, this latest development might be a blessing after all."

"How so?"

"If I can get them comfortably settled into the Villas and give them a chance to see that it's not such a bad place after all, just maybe…" He let the thought hang in the air between them.

"That's one big maybe, especially with those two. Still, it might work. And I'd worry a lot less about them, that's for sure. What about the house? You'd sell it?"

"I hate to get too far ahead of ourselves, particularly with the Miss Larsons. And it will take a little while to get the repairs completed." He pushed off the car and opened the door again. "Naturally we don't need to wait for the insurance settlement to get to work. The Larsons have more than enough funds for whatever might be necessary. However...I've heard you're a realtor, correct?"

"Yes, but I'm taking a sort of sabbatical."

"Not a problem, but I might like a professional opinion of some of the work that needs to be done. If we can update while we repair, it would put us in a better position should the sisters ever agree to sell. If those improvements come with your suggestions and approval, well, Cora and Evie would probably be more agreeable to the work."

"I don't want to help push them out of their home, if that's what you mean."

"Not at all, Claire. I only want to be sure that an opportunity isn't wasted. Whether they move back in or not, it seems that we'd be smart to keep the big picture in mind. Aside from repairs, it would be safer for them if the place was brought up to code. And someday, that house will have to be sold."

Claire hated to agree with him but she knew he was right. "I suppose it would be better for them, either way, if the house were fixed right, with updated electrical and a new furnace, too. Which reminds me, have you talked with the fire department? Do they have any idea how it started? Was it the old furnace?"

"Nope." He climbed into his car. "Looks like a candle was left burning in the kitchen. Probably burned down, maybe tipped over and caught the tablecloth or the curtains on fire. Perhaps the cat knocked it over. They're still looking into it, but that's where they're leaning."

"Shit." Claire remembered the burning candles she'd blown out in the house and wasn't at all surprised.

"Precisely. We need to get the sisters into a safer environment, Claire. Anything you can do to help will be appreciated."

Claire stood in her drive as Roger pulled away. She hoped Cottonwood Villas was a pretty wonderful place, otherwise this might be the hardest sell of her life.

GWEN STOOD AT THE COUNTER, closing out the cash drawer for the day. The sun was setting earlier now; the long days of summer slipping into fall. She could hear the last sounds of Jason tidying up the kitchen for the night and readying it for the following day. It had been over a week since he joined the bakery but Gwen had fallen into a strangely comfortable new normal.

Carolyn, who had been wiping down the tables and straightening the chairs, stood, arms akimbo, staring at an empty wall in the back room.

"Say, Gwen," she said, not turning from the wall.

"Hmm?" Gwen half responded, mid-way through a computation on her hand-held calculator.

"Any plans for this wall?" When Gwen failed to respond she turned and asked again, "Gwen?"

"Oh, sorry." Gwen set the calculator down and pulled a deposit slip from the cash drawer. "What wall?"

"This one, to the left of the fireplace." Carolyn pointed to a wide, creamy beige wall that was flanked on one side by the fireplace and the other by the door to the kitchen.

"I don't think so." Gwen stared at the wall and wondering what plans she ought to have.

"Would you be interested in a watercolor? Or... perhaps a series of watercolors?"

"Would I? You bet, but I've seen what your pieces sell for. I don't think my bottom line is quite there yet." Gwen smiled and waved the deposit slip for affect.

"Oh no, I'm not angling for a sale. At least not from you." Carolyn tucked her short brown curls behind each ear, allowing two large, coppery hoops to swing free from each lobe. She walked to the counter where Gwen stood. "Actually, I was thinking of a display of my pieces. I have tags I can attach with prices and in-formation, if someone wants to buy them. I think it would make that space feel a little cozier, and of course, it would also be a way to get my name out there a bit more. I'd replace pieces when things sold. It could be a mini gallery of sorts."

"You're looking for clients? Is business hurting?" Carolyn had told Gwen she came to the bakery as a way to get out of her studio more often and hang out with real human beings instead of canvas and paints. She never seemed to be hurting for cash. Her clothing might have been casual but her jeans were designer and her sweaters cashmere.

"Not at all. Whatever I consign at local galleries goes pretty quickly, and I have the occasional commis-sion. But unless you're a serious art lover you probably only want one, maybe two of my pieces, and once you buy it you're done. I depend on new buyers more than repeat ones. You get a steady stream of tourists in here, along with locals, so I thought I could brighten up your wall and find some new art lovers in the process."

"Sounds like a win-win to me," Gwen said. "I used to paint, you know, and I hung the paintings in my old bakery in Blue River."

"You never told me that. What happened to them? Are you still painting?"

"I gave most of them away," Gwen said almost shyly. She didn't add that the theme had been shells, and that each shell represented someone to her; someone whose character was reflected in the shape and utility of that shell. Those were the people who received the paintings…not necessarily ever knowing how they're character influenced the artwork. "I've been so busy since we moved here there's no time to paint."

"Don't you miss it?"

"I do." Gwen realized she hadn't even thought about it until now. How had she gotten so busy?

"You should take it up again, maybe even join me sometime, when I'm in the field painting *en plein air.*"

"What's that?"

"It's French for painting in the open air. I like to set up by a stream, beside a pasture, wherever the mood draws me, and let nature take over my canvas. It's refreshing and inspiring and gets me outside on days so beautiful my lovely studio feels like a stuffy dungeon."

"It sounds wonderful."

"It is. You know, I've been trying to encourage the town council to host a *plein air* festival. It's become popular among artists in recent years. We'd draw artists to a lovely location for several days of painting outside, and we'd draw tourists and art lovers who enjoy watching painters at work. At the end, we could host a gallery event somewhere to display everyone's work and maybe even get some of it sold."

"What a wonderful idea. I'd certainly turn out to encourage the idea if it came up at a council meeting."

"I may take you up on that. But in the meantime, now that Jason is here you can pick up your paint brush again"

"What's this about me and painting?" Jason strode through the swinging kitchen door, his leather jacket slung over his shoulder and wisps of hair falling free from his pony-tail. "I don't do that anymore. But I did make some good money back in college painting houses on the side."

"No way am I pulling you from the kitchen." Gwen said. "We already have customers coming in for your croissants every morning, and I think that attorney on the corner is addicted to your strudel."

It's hard to resist the lure of cinnamon and apples wrapped in a flaky crust."

"Wish I could." Carolyn laughed as she pressed her hands against her stomach. "I'm trying to convince Gwen to let me display some of my paintings on the back wall."

"Hey, I saw that one you did for the wine festival last year. Bank manager has it hanging in his office. Not bad."

"Harvey is a big fan." Carolyn winked, leaving it at that and leaving Gwen to wonder what else Harvey might be that would inspire a wink.

"This joint's great, Gwen, but it would liven up the back wall. Place I worked at in Soho had original art-work from local artists on every wall. Adds character and the neighborhood liked that they supported the arts. Could be good for P.R.."

"True. And I think it would just be nice to look up

and see anything you painted, Carolyn."

"Sounds like a go-for-it to me. You ladies have a good evening, I'm hitting it."

They said good night in return and he left, crossing the street to where his Harley was parked beneath a cottonwood.

"Anything you'd particularly like on that wall?" Carolyn asked.

"It's up to you."

"Okay, I'm on it. Meanwhile, there are other blank walls in here, you know. Maybe you should consider filling them yourself."

Gwen smiled and returned to preparing the day's bank deposit. "Maybe I will." The idea of picking up her brush again actually sounded like fun. She hadn't realized until now how much she actually missed it.

GWEN GRABBED HER KEYS AND was flipping off the last of the lights when she heard a tap-tapping on the front window. Claire leaned against the glass, wrapping her hands around her face to peer in.

"You are still there!" her muffled voice shouted through it.

"Hang on." Gwen unlocked the front door to let herself out. "I'm just closing up."

"I figured. Bob's busy as usual; how about Andy?"

"What do you think?" A smug smile crossed her face. She pulled the door shut behind her and turned the lock.

"Wanna join me at the Boathouse for a drink, maybe dinner?"

"Dinner and a drink sounds perfect. And you can tell me where you've been lately; haven't seen you in days."

"It's an interesting story."

"Why do I feel it involves the Larsons?"

"Because I spend so much time with them I should practically change my name to Larson?"

"Oh yeah, that's it!" Gwen laughed and wrapped her arm in Claire's.

PART DIVE AND PART DECENT restaurant, for nearly two decades the Boathouse had occupied a slice of land along the spot where the Grande River curved out of town and on toward the vineyards. Since it was down the road from the main action of shops and wineries, sitting on its own between the two, it didn't attract much of a tourist clientele. But the locals considered it second only to home.

The front room was filled with a long wooden bar and several high-tops. Turn right past the bar and a cozy back room hosted just enough tables to keep up with the mix of families, singles and post-happy hour crowd that arrived in a steady trickle from the time the doors opened at noon to the Boathouse's official last call at 1am.

In good weather it was a straight shot past the bar to the back patio that fronted the river and was roped off from the shore with a nautical themed post and rope—hence the name. On hot days patrons nursed their microbrews and margaritas while cheering on tubers as they cruised easily down the river, beer in hand, or towing their child's tube.

Claire and Gwen grabbed a seat on the patio, po-sitioning themselves so that the setting sun warmed their backs.

"What'll it be, ladies?" said a twenty-something guy whose nametag identified him as Nik.

"I'm going with a margarita, Nik," Claire said. "On the rocks, no salt."

"Me too," added Gwen, "but keep the salt."

"Will do." Nik jotted their order on his pad. "Menus are there." he pointed to two thin folders stuck be-tween the salt and pepper holder and a small crock holding packets of various sugar options.

"I figure we better enjoy the last drinks of summer before winter demands all those heavy cabs." Claire divvyed up the menus.

"I'm more a pinot noir gal, myself."

"Hey, isn't that your delicious new assistant, Jason?" Claire pointed to the bar where Jason was chatting with someone just out of site, beyond the entrance to the patio.

"It is. He left a little before me. I guess he was anx-ious to make happy hour. And his *food* is delicious. I cannot speak for him personally. And you can't ei-ther…can you?"

"Don't worry, I've only tasted his baked goods. I'm remaining celibate, if that's what you're implying."

"Celibate?"

"Well, maybe not entirely celibate, Bob did stop by one evening recently. It was great until it wasn't."

"You two having trouble? This isn't about—"

"Oh, shit" Claire said under her breath, her eyes on Jason.

"What?"

Gwen started to turn to see the bar when Claire reached out to hold her arm and stop her. "Don't turn around," she whispered.

"Claire, what the heck is going on?"

"It's her."

"Who her?"

"Terra."

"Bob's assistant? Did she just come in?"

"No, that's who Jason is talking with. And they are very animated if you ask me."

Gwen couldn't resist. She nudged her napkin off her lap and bent over to pick it up, taking the opportunity to survey the situation for herself. Sure enough, Terra stood at the bar, chatting with Jason and, apparently, the bartender as well. She laughed at something Jason said and reached out to touch his arm, holding her hand there just a moment longer than Gwen thought was necessary, unless…

"You don't think—"

"Sure I do, that little kitten is playing the field. Poor, dumb Bob can't take his eyes off her when she's around. He thinks every idea she has is pure genius and she bubbles over at his praise. But it looks like he's not the only one she's bubbling over about."

"I don't know, Claire. She stops in a lot for coffee and she always seems so sweet. Somebody spilled their latte the other day and she even grabbed a towel from the counter and helped clean it up. And that was a woman, not a man. The kind of person you describe wouldn't usually give another woman the time of day."

Suddenly, Terra leaned out and hugged Jason. Gwen thought she even saw him blush. Then she gave a tiny wave to him and the bartender as she practically skipped out the door. At this point Claire and Gwen were riveted by the scene and quickly embarrassed when Jason glanced over and saw them both staring.

"Shit." Claire said, as they both turned back to the table.

"Hey, Chef." Jason strolled over, beer in hand, to stand by the table. "Claire," he added, grinning. "Why do you two have that cat with the canary look? Are you spying on me in my rare off hours?"

"Of course not," Gwen said, with far too much enthusiasm. "We were just…just—"

"We were surprised to see you know Terra, that's all," Claire said. "Known her long?"

"Just met her." Jason took an empty seat. "She was talking with Dave, the bartender, about possibly holding some wine event here. The place she works does this every year and they're worried about having a place that's big enough. Guess business is good."

"The place she works?" Claire asked.

"Yeah, um…it's that big winery, the one up the hill after the curve, has a flower on their label."

"Columbine," Claire said.

"That's it. You know it?"

"Oh, yeah. Gwen's husband works there." Claire didn't add her connection and for a moment wondered just how she'd explain her connection.

"Really? Good wine, I've tried a few bottles since I got here. She heard I was baking at Gwen's place and asked me about catering. Of course, I don't have the set up for that, and she's not even sure where they are going to be holding it, so all I said was maybe. That made her happy. Guess you saw."

"We did indeed." Gwen looked at Claire who seemed to clearly be stewing in her own world of suspicion. "Don't they have a caterer all lined up already?"

"They do, but apparently they don't specialize in desserts. She's looking to hire someone separately for that."

"We might be able to do it, if they really need someone. That is, if you'd want to take that on along with the regular bakery duties. We'd do it together, of course."

"Might be something to consider; she gave me her card. I'll give her a call tomorrow and see what's up."

"Jason!" Dave called as he set a small pizza on the bar where Jason had been sitting.

"Dinner calls. I'll leave you ladies to speculate on the very nubile Terra," he added, grinning at Claire whose attention he'd finally retrieved. "Evening."

"I think he thinks you're jealous over him," Gwen said, smiling as they watched him walk away.

"What?" Claire shook off thoughts of Terra and returned to the present. "He should be so lucky."

"Sounds like it was business to me."

"Bet she likes to mix business and pleasure." Nik delivered their drinks and Claire took a healthy sip of her margarita.

"Jason is young and single. He probably wouldn't mind that kind of mixing. But this is really getting to you. *She's* really getting to you, Claire. Do you honestly think something's going on? Or is it all—"

"In my head? Oh, Gwen, you're probably right. Bob has told me over and over nothing is going on."

"Then believe him."

"I try. But then I see him with her and, I don't

know, it feels like something's up. There's a vibe coming from him when she's around."

"Maybe her enthusiasm is catching. She's young and upbeat and she's got that glass-half-full thing going on. You only notice Bob, but maybe everyone is like that around her. Jason seemed very upbeat."

"Maybe. Maybe I'm restless about us, about Bob, because I'm restless about me. About everything. I want to be busy doing something. Anything."

"But you have been busy lately, right?"

"With the sisters?"

Gwen nodded.

"Sure, but that's not a career, I'm only helping them out. Roger, their attorney, has them settled into a temporary unit at the Cottonwood Villas. I actually had a meeting with him. He asked me to oversee the renovations and repairs at the house. Insists on paying me— and he's generous, I have to say. I think he's trying to make up for the inconvenience."

"Inconvenience?"

"The villas allow pets if you live there. But not if you're renting."

"Didn't you tell me they have a cat?"

"They did. Now I do, at least for the time being."

Sixteen

CLAIRE SHUT THE LAP TOP and leaned back in her chair, rubbing the ache in her neck. It was past midnight and she'd spent the last few hours reviewing bids from local electricians, heating contractors and plumbers. She'd given them a day to give her their estimates; short notice, she knew, but this was a rush job. The company she'd hired to clean out the aftermath of the fire and get it ready for remodeling had made quick work of it. Now it was time to get the work started. It felt good to be busy, to have purpose for a change beyond weeding zucchini and mastering chakras.

She added *visit sisters* to her to-do list. It has been a few days since she'd last visited them at the Villas. They seemed comfortable enough, though they missed their own surroundings. Claire assured them she had a restoration company hard at work removing the fire's smoke and soot from their treasured belongings. If Roger could talk them into actually buying a house at the Villas, she thought, she'd have everything ready to make the new place feel like home.

"Mroownnn…." Elbie jumped onto her lap and pressed his side against her chest, eager for attention now that she was free from her laptop.

"You are somewhat demanding, you know," Claire said, running her hand from the top of his head, down his body and pulling softly out to the tip of his tail. Elbie purred and pushed harder. "Greedy little guy, eh? Well, can't blame you, I know how it is when you can't get any attention from someone."

She picked up her phone, checked to be certain it wasn't muted, swiped it on, tapped in her passcode and checked her messages. No Bob. Well, it was probably her fault, right? Maybe, she thought. Maybe. "Shit."

Suddenly her phone buzzed and a message came on the screen.

"You up?"

It was Del.

"Yeah." she tapped in. "W*hat the hell are you doing up??"*

The phone rang and Claire answered it. "Why aren't you asleep dreaming of handsome, well-connected board members—and their members." She smiled at her own joke then added, "Sorry, that was lame. What can I say, it's late."

"I know, and it was, but I can't sleep." Del yawned, despite her words. "I had to talk with someone and I knew Gwen wouldn't be up, but I thought you might be."

"What did what's-his-name do now?" Claire's protective nature—when it came to Del—kicked in automatically.

"Nothing. And his name is Carl. But I just know he wants to do *something*. He keeps asking to take me out to dinner. I told him I was sick last Saturday so he stopped calling for a while, but I know he won't give up. Claire, he had chicken soup delivered to my house."

"Well, that's thoughtful, isn't it?"

"From the Dockside!" Del's voice squeaked into a high pitched but whispered scream, struggling to keep from waking her kids.

"Oh…well, maybe Jimmy didn't see the order come through."

"He did. It was his handwriting on the note that came with it."

"What did it say?"

Claire could hear Del rustling through some papers and then she read it to her:

Delly, wish I were there to warm you up in person.
Hope this soup does the job in the meantime. Yours, Carl

"Oh shit. He must have read that off for Jimmy to write down. Del, your plot sure thickens. Not to mention that smarmy nickname he's given you."

"I know. Imagine what Jimmy must think. And he signs it *'yours'*. He's not my anything but now Jimmy thinks he's my-my—"

"Yep, I think he does. Can't this guy take no for an answer?"

"Well…I haven't exactly told him no."

"Why the hell not, Del? I mean, you can't expect the guy to get the message if you don't give it to him."

"I don't know if I do want to give him the message. I mean, he's so nice and considerate. And Jimmy, well…he's being really mean, Claire."

"Are you sure it's not because his heart is broken?"

"He seems more hard-hearted than heartbroken to me. If he really hates me now, and Carl is seriously interested, I can't help wondering if I'm stupid not to at least give him a chance. Oh, I can't decide what to do and I'm afraid to talk to either of them until I do."

"That's gonna be hard, living in the same town and working on the same board with Carl."

"The good news is Carl has to leave town for a while—quite a while. He has business in the Far East and he's going to be gone for nearly a month."

"Sounds like you have a month to figure it out."

"Or leave town."

Claire smiled. "You'll figure it out, I'm sure."

"I might come up for a little visit. The kids are planning a long weekend with Micky soon. Gwen said I can stay with her anytime."

"I'd say stay with me, but I don't have a lot of room to spare." Elbie turned a circle and curled up in Claire's lap. "And apparently I have a cat now."

"What? I never thought you were the cat type, or any pet, for that matter."

"I'm helping out some friends. It's just for a while." She stroked the thin soft ends of Elbie's ears and closed her eyes as his purr deepened. "I don't have time…. for pets."

"Uh-huh. Well, maybe I'd better go, you sound tired."

"It's friggin' one in the morning, Del."

"Thanks for letting me vent, Claire. Sweet dreams."

"Hmm…," Claire mumbled as the line went dead. When she awoke an hour later she couldn't remember if she'd said good-bye. She scooped up Elbie and transplanted them both into her bed.

CLAIRE HAD THOUGHT THE LARSON sisters would be ensconced in their new villa, knitting afghans and reading books to pass the time. But she was wrong. It took her a while to track them down but finally she found them on a large patio behind the club house participating in a Tai Chi class. Cora swayed easily through the steps. Evie, standing behind a chair, a cane in one hand and her injured foot still in its soft cast, moving as best she could through the poses.

"Claire!" Cora called out. "How delightful to see you. Join in, why don't you?"

Claire set aside the bag of goodies she'd picked up at the deli. She found a spot nearby, thanks to an accommodating elderly gentleman who smiled a little too broadly as he made room for her. She stepped easily into the familiar sequence. Tai Chi had been one more component of her yoga classes and she'd participated often enough to be familiar with the steps.

Between moves she answered the sister's questions about Elbie, leaving them assured their precious pet was being suitably spoiled by Claire.

"Wasn't that invigorating?" Cora enthused later, as they returned to their villa and she began putting away the items Claire had brought.

"I do like it," Evie said, "but I think I'll like it even more once I am fully mobile again!"

"I can't blame you." Claire helped settle Evie on their private patio, propping her foot atop a pillow set on a low table. Cora brought a multi-colored afghan for Evie's lap.

"Nice blanket," Claire said.

"Isn't it lovely?" Evie ran her fingers along the afghan's scalloped edging. "Abigail Sanders gave it to me when we first arrived. So many of the residents have stopped by to offer anything we might need. They heard about the fire, of course. It has been a blessing to be around such thoughtful people. And seeing Abby—how wonderful! We were girls together in school so many years ago, you know."

"Really? What a coincidence."

"Not actually," Evie said, "We have several friends who live here. Abby's family ranched on the mesa when I was young. Much of the acreage has been sold off. She had two daughters, you see, and neither of them cared for ranching. They have vacation homes on the property but they both live in Denver. Abby doesn't care for the city; can't say I blame her. She decided to stay here instead, as she already knew so many friends in the complex."

"We have seen many old faces," Cora voice floated outside from the kitchen.

Claire took a seat beside Evie and cast an appraising realtor's eye on the pleasing view from the shaded patio. Beyond a decorative wrought iron railing that edged the patio, they overlooked a wide lawn sloping down to a large pond edged with cottonwoods.

"It was very sweet of you to bring us a bag from Tonti's, dear." Cora pulled some things from the refrigerator. "But you know the Villas has a shopping service. Evelyn—that's the woman who assists new members—showed us how to place an order with the computer."

"Computer?" Claire asked, not recalling that the

sisters were all that tech savvy. "I didn't know you had one?"

"Oh, no, we don't," Evie said. "But there's this room they have here that has several. All the residents can use them."

"We've had quite a time learning the ropes."

"They even hold classes."

"Quite," Cora confirmed. "It's been most informative."

"And fun." Evie added. "Do you know you can even play games on it? I've gotten rather good at one of the word games. It's like Scrabble and I was always very good at Scrabble. Unfortunately Cora won't play with me anymore, will you dear?"

"No. I've taken more than my fair share of trouncing, I'm afraid. One knows when one has been thoroughly beaten. It's truly Evie's forte."

"I've found many friends at the Villas who love to play it with me. It's quite thrilling. And the best part is that we all sit side by side as we play each other. It's so enjoyable. And you wouldn't believe what else!" Evie picked up her knitting basket from beside her chair and set it on her lap. "We can even play from our home. They've given us these little computer thingies...what are they called, Cora?"

"I-Pads, dear." Cora returned from the kitchen with a tray of refreshments just as Evie pulled her I-Pad out from the knitting basket.

"That's it. And you can do so many other things as well. It's truly amazing." Evie returned the basket to the floor and turned on the veritable symbol of technology which now had her full attention.

"Really?" Claire sat beside Evie, sipping at the lemonade Cora brought her and wondering at how resourceful the Larson sisters were, and how she could ever have worried about them fitting in at the Villas. Which reminded her of the reason she'd come to see them. Claire reached for her quilted yoga bag which, today, carried paperwork and notes regarding the refurbishment of their damaged home.

"I almost forgot. I wanted to go over some things about your house. The kitchen, for instance, is a total loss. And since it needs to be completely redone, I thought there might be some things we could do to modernize it while still keeping with the charm of your home, of course. I've brought along some ideas." She pulled a file from the bag. "And a sketch I made that might be helpful."

"I shouldn't worry about getting our approval," Cora said. "If Roger has entrusted you with overseeing the work that must be done—"

"Which we were so happy to hear!" Evie chirped in, looking up briefly from the I-Pad's screen.

"Yes, very happy, and completely confident with whatever decisions you make. We feel you know us well enough to know what we would like, but that you are also an excellent judge of what would bring our home into the modern age."

"And you're comfortable with that?" Claire was a little anxious about being put in charge of restoring the Larson home without the sister's active input.

"Absolutely," Cora said. "We are not opposed to some modernization. It's simply that we've never had the need to tackle it. Now fortune, and sadly, my apparent poor judgment with regard to the use of candles, has opened the door to the future. We're happy to share our thoughts on colors and other minor items, if needed, but beyond that, we put our home in your hands, Claire, dear."

Claire looked at Cora, who now busied herself plating a lemon bundt cake for them to enjoy, and Evie, who appeared to be winning the battle of words. She sighed heavily, put the paperwork back in her bag and sat back to enjoy a slice of cake. "Well, if you say so, but I promise I will do my very best to make decisions you will love—in the kitchen and in the rest of the house."

"We're sure you will, Claire."

"And I wanted to let you know that the restoration company tells me it will most likely be a couple of weeks before they can return your parlor and bedroom furniture. It did sustain heavy smoke damage, unfortunately. Roger told me the Villas would let you replace some of the furniture that came with the rental with your own things. I know the furnishings in the rental are pretty homogenized—not much character, I'm afraid. Hopefully some of your things will be available soon."

"Oh, that's not a problem at all, is it Evie?"

"What?" Evie looked up from her game to her sister.

"Claire was worrying about the need for us to have our own furniture repaired quickly for our use here. I was saying that's not a problem."

"Not at all." Evie resumed tapping away at the keypad. "Not since Sven and his wife—what was her name?"

"Ingrid."

"That's it. They told us about that *Icky* place."

"Icky?" Claire asked, cautiously.

"Yes." Cora handed her a napkin. "They said we could find everything we needed there and it can all be shipped here. No need to leave the Villas, and there are a couple handymen on the property to assist with setting things up. They do have quite a nice selection. I feel even Papa would love the simplicity of the decor."

"Truly." Evie said. "We've already placed an order for several charming living room pieces and some very colorful accessories, haven't we, Cora?"

"Indeed we have, dearest."

"Here it is." Evie held up the I-Pad at last so that Claire could see the site they'd been shopping from.

Claire looked at the screen. "IKEA?"

Seventeen

GWEN CURLED UP AGAINST ANDY, pressing her back into his chest and pulling his arms closer around her. Andy's late hours had made intimacy difficult to time lately, so she'd risen before dawn and lit a honeysuckle scented candle, its delicate scent filling their bedroom as she climbed back beneath the covers to wake her husband with kisses and caresses. White curtain sheers fluttered gently in the light breeze that blew in through an open window, slowly evaporating the thin veneer of sweat that late summer love-making left behind.

"It's pitiful that I cannot remember the last time we did this," Gwen said.

"I know, babe. I'm sorry, you know I am. And you know how much I love you." Andy pressed his lips against the sensitive skin along her neck sending a little shiver through Gwen, who smiled and sighed in response.

"Honey, it's an easy price to pay to see you working at a job you really love."

"I guess I do love it. All those years in the cab of a truck, pulling loads over the mountains, I'd look out at the view and plenty of times I wished I was out enjoying it, rather than just looking at it. No matter the weather, I can't say I ever complain about working in the vineyards. Have to say it's kinda nice to look in the mirror and see a tanned face looking back, instead of that pallor I used to always have."

"And it hasn't been lost on me what great shape you're in since you got out of that cab." Gwen rolled over, wrapped her leg over his and ran a hand up his taught abdomen and across his newly defined chest, playing with the reddish blonde hairs that graced it. "When you took this job I didn't know there'd be perks for me as well."

"You can have all the perks you want." Andy drew her into a long, deep kiss.

"Maybe after the harvest season I can have more of what I want. Right now, I'm just happy to get any."

"I know. But it's not like it's the whole year. I think our marriage can stand the test, don't you?"

"Of course, though I bet a lot of couples have a hard time with it, don't you?"

"I suppose. I hadn't really thought about it."

"You wouldn't, and that's good." She sighed as she rested her head on his shoulder. "But Andy, I'm a little worried…about Claire and Bob."

"What? You think they're in trouble?"

"Well, every time I see Claire there seems to be a slow boil going on right below the surface. Heck, sometimes it's all over the top as well. I can't figure out if there's really anything to worry about, or if it's more to do with her whole recovery process."

"It can't be easy getting back on your feet after what she went through. I think she's doing really well.

But now that you mention it..."

"What?"

"Well, Bob hasn't really been himself lately either. He's kinda distracted."

"Do you think Terra has anything to do with it?"

"Terra? Why Terra?"

"Claire's got a little jealousy thing going. Or maybe I should say it's a suspicion."

"She thinks he's fooling around with Terra?" Andy's expression was clearly surprised as he lifted his head to look at Gwen.

"I don't know. I don't think there's any solid reason, like proof, that he's doing anything with Terra other than work. But Claire seems to be picking up on something; I don't even think she knows what it is. It's more a feeling, I guess."

"Women and their intuition." Andy leaned his head alongside hers and brushed his cheek against his wife's hair.

"Hey, women's intuition goes a long way. I had a bad feeling about that storm you were in when you were in the accident up on the pass. I was right, wasn't I?"

"Yeah. You know, now that I think about it, Bob does spend a lot of time with Terra. She seems to always be there, whether he's in the office, the tasting room, the barrel room, out in the vineyard. She's handling sales so I'm not sure she *needs* to be all those places, but she is. It's like he's her mentor."

"Do you think Claire's really on to something?"

Andy lay still for a while and Gwen knew, from experience, that he was thinking about his answer. That was something she loved about her husband. When the topic was serious he took time to consider his answer before weighing in, and this was certainly a serious topic.

"Gwen, I wish I could tell you I thought Claire was way off track—and she probably is—but I don't know. What I do know, however, is that up until this conversation I would have been the first one to say that Bob was head over heels for Claire. I'm not happy that I can't say that with complete confidence now."

"Me neither, and it sucks."

"I do agree with you there. But there's one thing I'm not worried about."

"What's that?"

"You and me." And he proceeded to show her why.

DEL HAD ARTFULLY AVOIDED DINNER with Carl but when he spotted her in the back of the hospital's deli/coffee shop she was cornered.

"Hello, Delly!" he called, laughing at his own joke and crossing between the cafe tables to land in the chair beside her, leaving her pinned between a glass wall and him.

"Hello, Carl." She smiled and made her best effort at a light and easy attitude.

"I was worried I wouldn't get to actually see you before I left." He set his leather satchel on top of the table and opened the front flap. "I wanted to give you something." He dug inside the bag.

"What? I mean, uh, I'm sure there was, I mean, you weren't supposed to bring me anything." Del felt like a stammering idiot and, taking a breath, regrouped along a more professional tack. "You've already made a generous contribution to the fundraiser, Carl. I wouldn't dream of asking you to contribute anything more."

"This isn't for the hospital." He unzipped an inside pocket.

"Oh?" Del had an unsettling feeling that whatever was buried deep inside Carl's satchel was of a far more personal nature than she was ready to accept. She gathered her papers and began preparing for a quick exit. Just in case.

"I asked Linda to pick this up for me. Well, for you."

"Oh." Del knew Linda was Carl's executive assistant. She'd spoken with her many times on hospital business.

But Linda sometimes seemed like Carl's *office wife*, arranging personal details as well, from finding a tailor to fit him for suits to picking out Christmas presents for his sister and her family. She'd even mentioned to Del that she'd overseen the interior designer who had decorated his new home in an exclusive development outside of town.

Del was suddenly worried about what else Linda might be in charge of. Did she pick out perfume and jewelry for Carl's lady friends? Did she pick out *lingerie*? Did Carl have many lady friends? He seemed like he might; but then, he also seemed like a busy man with little time to spare for relationships. Del wasn't even sure he'd never been married. Del realized how little she really knew about Carl. Was she being fair to him, assuming what sort of person he was with so little to go on?

"Here it is." Carl pulled out a purple plastic bag. "I know we've had a hard time connecting, what with our schedules, Del. We're both busy people."

"Uh-huh." She nodded, cautiously, taking the bag he handed her.

"I'm hoping this will help while I'm away." Carl waited for her to look inside.

Del reached in and pulled out a cell phone. "I already have a phone, Carl."

"Of course you do, but I had this one set up especially for you, with international service and unlimited minutes and texts. Linda even printed out a little how-to pamphlet for you; it's in there too. That way, if you should ever find yourself with time to spare and want to talk with me, it's as easy as dialing my number. I made myself number one on the speed dial." He reached for her hand. "I hope you don't think it's presumptuous of me to think I could be number one with you, in any way, lovely Del."

Lovely Del was speechless, and even more so when Carl raised her hand to his lips, kissing it softly, lingering just long enough over her fingertips that Del blushed and looked around to be certain no one was watching.

"I've made you blush." He released her hand.

"Well, I, well..." Del simply had no idea what to say to such developments. How did heroines in romantic novels reply to such gentlemanly advances? She was certain she didn't have a clue and not sure she wanted one. How was it that every time she steeled herself against Carl's advances he found a way to disarm her, or at least to take her so completely by surprise?

"Now, Del, don't worry. I do not expect you to call me often. It's only that I wanted you to be able to, if you should want to. I'm going to be gone quite a while. I thought—I hoped you might miss me, if only a little."

"Carl," Del said at last, finally finding her voice, "this is very thoughtful of you. Very. And of course I'll miss you. I mean, well, the hospital board always runs so smoothly with you in attendance—"

"I'm not worried about the board." H placed his hand over hers.

"I know, and I appreciate that thought. And you shouldn't have gone to the expense on my account but I—I do appreciate it. I'm sure there will be times when it will be nice to talk with you." Del didn't add, *about board business*, but only because, considering the circumstances it seemed somewhat rude to think the phone was a business gift when Carl's intentions were clearly very personal.

Might she actually *want* to talk with him? All of this attention from Carl was such a new thing for her. He clearly went out of his way to be thoughtful and he clearly thought about *her* a lot. She didn't think Micky had been this attentive when they'd been dating. Had dating changed? Jimmy had been thoughtful too...but in a different way, in his way.

And how often was a girl likely to come across a man that was clearly so interested in her? Del felt compelled to get past her pre-conceived notions of what to expect from a man and give Carl a chance. Wouldn't she be a fool to cut it off with him before she could make a more well-rounded decision?

Whenever she'd been in charge of choosing the company for her PTO's yearly fundraiser she'd always waited until all the options had been presented and thoroughly considered before making a final decision.

That might have mean eating a lot of different chocolates and tasting every flavored popcorn, but it also meant once she'd made a decision she knew that she was right. Didn't Carl deserve the same opportunity she gave giftwrap? Didn't she?

"I would love to hear your voice anytime you call, sweet Delly." He paused and, slowly, leaned in to kiss her.

Del froze, uncertain how to react. If the hand-kissing thing had been a shock this was downright unreal. For an instant she felt like she might be having one of those out-of-body experiences, until Carl's lips touched hers. She closed her eyes, prepared to steel herself through the moment but was shocked to feel how gentle Carl was, his soft lips lingering just long enough, not intruding, only stating their very tender case.

He sat back, gazing fondly at Del. She couldn't bring herself to say anything, unsure exactly what she might say. What was wrong with her? One minute she was ready to call it quits with the guy and the next minute she was practically swooning over his kiss. Was it possible to feel two totally different things for the same person?

"I'll miss you very much, fair Del."

"When do you leave?" she breathed at last.

"I'm taking my chopper to Denver after I leave here, then I'll catch the red-eye to Tokyo tonight." He gazed a bit longer, then gathered his things and stood.

"Have a good flight." Del mentally kicked herself. What a lame thing to say, she thought, after this man had just kissed her.

"I will. And you take care" He walked away at last,

pausing in the doorway to pantomime holding a phone to his ear and mouthing the words, *call me.*

Del smiled and he was gone. She reached for her own phone.

CLAIRE WAS WALKING THROUGH THE Larson's home with an electrician when her phone rang. She glanced and, seeing Del's name, hit the auto reply for *call you right back.* The progress was moving along very nicely. All the destruction and mess from the fire was gone and all that remained of the kitchen was a shell to be filled. Other parts of the home needed varying amounts of work, but the kitchen, and the bathroom on the second floor that was above it, were the largest projects.

The electrician, Bud Harley, came highly recommended. He looked like he'd given up shaving years ago and probably didn't own anything but blue jeans and short-sleeved plaid shirts. Bud was just old enough to know what he was doing but not so old as to have a superiority complex about it.

He bent over blueprints that Claire had had drawn up by a local architect who knew the sisters and was familiar with the house. He'd worked quickly and made some changes that Claire approved of, updating the graceful structure and bringing it up to code and into the present day while still respecting its origins. Claire liked the changes and hoped the sisters would also.

She pulled a file from her briefcase and showed Bud the specs for the cabinets that had been ordered. Together they discussed the kitchen's needs, as well as the rest of the house.

"I think I've a good idea whacha' need here," he said, rolling up the plans and tucking them under his arm. "I'll take a look-see upstairs and see if there's anythin' specific we'll need, then I'll get cha the bid quick like. Have it for ya by the mornin'. Sound good?"

"Sounds good." She liked this guy.

Bud headed upstairs and Claire reached for her phone just as Gary, the plumber, pulled up in his pickup. Del would have to wait a little longer. Gary was young and energetic and, Claire was happy to find out, the junior to Gary Sr., who had already walked the house before she arrived and sent his son with a game plan and a ballpark bid in mind. Claire sent Gary Jr. off to borrow the plans from Bud.

With no more subs in sight Claire pulled out her phone and called Del back at last.

"Hey, Del, sorry it took so long for me to—"

"Oh Claire, thank goodness you called!"

"Del, what's the matter?" Claire worried that perhaps Del's son or daughter had had an accident. She was prepared for the worst, sitting on the front stoop of the house as Del went into detail about her encounter with Carl.

Claire realized the nature of the problem and smiled to herself. She may not have had many long term relationships in her life, but she did have a great deal of experience with men. She knew Del had married her college sweetheart, who had turned out to be a lying, cheating son-of-a-bitch, and so her recent divorce had put her back into a market for which the innocent and naive Del was wholly unprepared.

"What should I do?" Del wrapped up her story and

finally came up for air.

"I don't know, Del. Frankly, from a third person point of view, this Carl guy seems pretty considerate and attentive."

"What?"

"Think about it. If you'd never met Jimmy and it was just about Carl, how would you feel?"

"Oh." Del fell silent for several beats. "I-I never thought of it like that."

"So, maybe the question isn't, how do you feel about Carl? Maybe it's really, how do you feel about Jimmy?"

DESPITE DEL'S MIXED FEELINGS FOR Carl, or maybe, she thought, because of them, over the next couple of weeks she decided not to discourage him but to go along with the idea of the phone. As a result they'd had several long conversations while he was away. Granted, Del had made an effort to steer the majority of their chats to hospital-related topics, convincing herself that she wasn't leading Carl on by discussing the architect's latest renderings of the future pediatric wing or sharing some innocent hospital board gossip.

Del found she enjoyed their conversations. Carl was intelligent and thoughtful. He'd traveled widely and been involved in many areas of business and politics, not to mention actively participated on the boards of many charities. She was surprised to find that there was much she could learn from him, but she wondered what exactly Carl saw in her that had made him so persistent despite the extremely slow pace she enforced on their relationship.

When he returned home she'd even allowed him to persuade her to join him for a golf tournament that was a fundraiser for another charity on whose board he sat. Del convinced herself that it was merely a fact-finding mission to research a future possible tournament for the hospital.

When she and Micky, her ex-husband, had first been married she'd learned to golf because so many of their vacations were really working vacations with Micky's clients and their wives or girlfriends. They'd joined a local country club and Del discovered she really enjoyed playing with some of the other young wives who had formed an unofficial league that met weekly. But after the kids were born and she eventually started getting busy with their many after-school activities, it was harder to find the time and, gradually, she'd lost touch with those friends.

In truth, while she enjoyed playing golf, she didn't really miss playing with her old ladies group. Her priorities had changed to family and children while theirs still centered on parties and fashions. The women who, like her, also had growing families, seemed to show up more seldom, replaced by younger women without families. She'd found herself feeling more and more out-of-sync with the conversations that invariably filled the time between strokes.

So joining Carl seemed like a fun way to spend a day in spite of her rusty swing and spotty putting. And Carl was surprisingly patient and encouraging, particularly, Del noticed, when others were nearby.

"Take your time, Delly," he'd say as she addressed a

difficult lie. "Don and I can use the time to discuss tax options with his latest charitable gift, isn't that right Don?"

Don didn't seem to mind and Don's girlfriend, Collette, who was young enough to be his daughter, smiled encouragingly and used the time to clean her club heads and make notations on a small notepad. Collette may have been young but apparently she was a very experienced golfer. More than once she'd out driven both Don and Carl.

Afterward, as she, Carl and Don had waited for Collete to return from the ladies' locker room and join them in the grill, she'd discovered that Collette was actually a star on the amateur circuit who was about to turn pro.

"She's the daughter of a friend of my wife's and I like to help out whenever I can getting her time on some of the more competitive courses. Helps hone her skills," he added, then smiling at Carl as the waitress delivered their drinks he added under his breath, "and she's got lots of skills, let me tell you."

Don didn't seem to think Del had heard his comment but she caught Carl's eye afterward and he shrugged, as if to say, *what can you do?* When Collette joined them again it was only to thank them for their company and, when Don stood to say good-bye, she thanked him in particular, giving him a long hug that Del thought was very close and very friendly.

"Collette is very young," she said on the ride home with Carl.

"Yes, but she's very experienced."

"In more ways than one?"

"Well, I don't tell my contacts how to live their

lives, but it does seem like Don is robbing the cradle."

"And cheating on his wife."

"That, too."

"And that doesn't bother you?"

"It does." He reached for her hand. "But like I said, I can't tell them what to do. Listen, I deal with all kinds of people in my business. And I'm working on something new now, which means I need to expand my contacts."

"What are you working on?"

"I'm excited to tell you, but I'm not quite ready to yet...and I might want your help."

"Really?" Del imagined he must be working with a new charitable organization and she wondered if she'd ever heard of it. Would he want her to build houses with him for Habitat for Humanity? No, she couldn't quite see him with a tool belt around his waist, pounding nails into studs. Perhaps it was a water project in a third world country that they could help raise funds for. Del thought she might like the idea of getting more involved in areas where her expertise could help.

"Now you have got to tell me," she said. "You've definitely got my curiosity up."

"Good, but like I said, not just yet."

"Why the wait?"

"It's a big project and I want to be sure before I talk to you about it." He smiled at her and added a wink. "Soon, I promise."

"Okay, but whatever it is, I can promise you one thing, you won't have to worry about my ethics."

"Your good reputation is one of the things I admire the most about you, Del."

"Thank you," she said, but she thought it was an

odd quality for a man to point out to a woman whose intimacy he was trying to win. She was quiet for a few minutes, toying with her thoughts over Carl's project, whatever it may be.

"I understand your concern about the quality of the people I deal with," Carl said at last, breaking the silence and apparently worried that that was what pre-occupied her thoughts. "Honestly, most of them are very honorable. But I'd be lying if I didn't say that there's a certain type of guy who thinks once he's successful at business he can do as he wishes in life. I see it all the time."

"That's sad, don't you think?"

"I guess," he said, distractedly as he reached for his smartphone, scrolling through messages while pulling to a stoplight.

"Carl, you shouldn't be doing things on your phone while you drive. It's not safe, you know."

"Don't worry, sweetie, I only look at stop lights or if I'm stuck..." He paused to text in a quick response to a message, then, glancing at her, completed his thought, "stuck in traffic. You can't be in a business like mine without staying connected. Things are happening all the time. Staying connected is what makes me a success. That, and my persuasive charm." He winked and reached over to give her thigh a little squeeze.

"Oh...well, but still, please be careful." Del wasn't sure if she agreed with Carl's logic, but the brief contact with her thigh had been so unexpected it left her tongue-tied in its wake.

"Of course, Delly. And especially when you are with me." Carl put his phone down. "You're my precious cargo." He slowed the car for another red light and half-turned to face her. "So, want to get a bite to eat tonight? Make it a special evening, just the two of us?"

"I'd love to," Del said, silently scolding herself that in her heart what she loved was that she actually had a valid excuse not to. "But Micky is bringing the kids home tonight. In fact, I still need to go to the grocery after you drop me off. I've got to get some things for dinner."

"Not a problem. We'll carve out some time to ourselves soon enough. I've got to hit the road for Hong Kong soon, but when I get back spending time with my lovely Delly will be top priority. I promise."

Del didn't invite Carl for dinner with her and the kids. Though it had occurred to her to do so, she felt it was far too soon to include Carl in her family life. How could she expect the kids to get to know Carl when she still felt she didn't really know him? Of course, she thought, she only had herself to blame for that. She'd put him off more than led him on. Carl gave her the impression he considered it a chase and he liked the chase. But did she want to be caught?

Despite all their conversations, short meetings over coffee or lunch, and a day on the golf course, who was Carl? He was never rude to her, in fact, he was very polite. He treated her like a lady. But the idea of finally succumbing to that romantic evening together, which Carl so clearly wanted, left a knot in her stomach. How much longer could she put him off? And really, why shouldn't she accept his attentions? He was attractive, after all. Though he'd never done anything she could truly disapprove of, something just didn't feel right, as if a veil between them kept her from seeing the real

Carl.

Even after all their time spent chatting on the phone she didn't feel like she knew the real Carl. Where had he grown up? Who were his role models? Did he have family? She knew he had never married and didn't have children, but what about sisters and brothers, what about his mother, was she even still alive?

Del waved as Carl's car pulled away from her home. She shut the door and walked inside, through the airy living room with its mountain contemporary architecture that made liberal use of stone, glass and wood. Walking down the hallway past Nate and Cara's quiet rooms and into her own, Del laid her purse and jacket on the bed and then sat down beside them. The children had only spent the day with their father but she missed them all the same. They made her feel grounded and that was something she needed lately.

But they couldn't help her figure out her grown-up issues and that made her thankful for Gwen and Claire. Thankful that they'd come into her life just when she needed girlfriends the most; so many of her old friends had fallen away after the divorce. She was hurt at first, but then she realized they just didn't know what to say or do with a divorced friend. That wasn't their reality. Del thought their kids were enough to have in common, but without an official *plus one* they didn't seem to know what to do with her beyond school and PTA.

She'd made new friends now, women who appreciated her struggles, and had even been through some of their own. They didn't judge or exclude her. And her position heading up fundraising for the hospital gave her new purpose, as well. It was the natural extension of all those years as a volunteer. It was what she loved.

So, shouldn't she love someone who shared her love of giving to a good cause? Shouldn't she be falling in love with Carl? Was she?

She ran her hand along the bedspread, smoothing out a wrinkle. The natural progression of her relationship with Carl would lead here, she thought. Here, where she'd lain in Jimmy's arms, content and, she thought, in love. But he clearly didn't love her now and that left Del wondering if she even knew what love looked like. If she'd been wrong about Jimmy, maybe she was wrong to hesitate with Carl. Maybe Carl was the one for her.

Del reached for her purse, pulling out her phone. She could call Gwen and talk with her. Or even Claire. They both knew Jimmy. But they didn't know Carl. Maybe she could find a way to bring her friends and Carl together so that Gwen and Claire would have a better perspective from which to offer advice. But they weren't likely to all be together anytime soon. The next opportunity would be her holiday fundraising affair and, she knew, Carl wasn't likely to wait that long to raise the stakes in *their* affair. She put the phone down. Del was going to have to deal with this herself.

She tried to imagine laying here in Carl's arms. He was a handsome man and Del imagined he was experienced as well. It might be fun, she thought. Would it be love, she wondered? Did it have to be, at first? Either way, she thought, steeling herself for the next step, she couldn't put him off anymore. She had to find out. For better or worse.

Eighteen

GWEN SAT AT A TABLE in the back of the bakery, scrolling through travel sites on her laptop in search of a *girl's getaway* for Claire, Del and herself. She'd appointed herself unofficial organizer, realizing she could use the break as much as anyone. Something in the late fall might work, after the craziness of the harvest and the annual wine festival were past but before the insanity of the holidays set in. So far, however, she hadn't found anything that felt right.

The afternoon crowd had wound down and Becca was wiping off the tables before closing. She'd swapped out the blue rubber bands on her braces for bright yellow ones and had her long blonde hair twisted with a matching scrunchy into a fountain-like display atop her head.

"Want me to start counting out the drawer, Ms. Gwen?" Becca asked, rinsing off her hands in the sink.

"That would be great." Becca might have interesting taste in rubber bands and hair-dos, but she was also in Honor's Math. Counting the drawer hardly began to tap into her brain cells. "Better lock up first and turn the sign to *Closed*. I think we're done for today."

"Will do."

Jason pushed open the kitchen door and headed to Gwen's table. "Got a minute, Chef? I want to run some ideas past you for the Columbine Vineyard's dinner."

"Sure." She moved her laptop to the side. Maybe tomorrow she could try again, with fresher brain cells of her own. Besides, she was curious to see what Jason had come up with.

Gwen had given him the go-ahead to cater the dinner after he told her Terra was leaning toward holding the dinner at the winery and wondered if they could cater it all and not just the dessert portion.

It was a big leap from bakery to caterer but Jason promised to handle the details. Apparently the idea of creating a small satellite catering business with Gwen as his partner was a challenge that got his creative juices flowing. If this worked, Gwen had thought, it might be a way to keep Jason from leaving town.

"Here's the menu I've drawn up. What do you think?" He handed her his computer tablet with a spread sheet showing menu items, ingredients, and expenditures along with charges and projected profit.

"Very impressive." And Gwen truly meant it. She didn't put this much detail into her planning and expenses at the bakery. "Maybe I should put you in charge of the bakery's bottom line, too."

"Baby steps, Chef." Jason grinned at her. "Let's see if we can pull off this production first. This looks good then?"

Jason's menu actually made her hungry just reading it:

Crisped Prosciutto and Parmesan with Artichoke
Bruschetta
Arugula and Heirloom Tomato Salad with Chardonnay
Peach Vinaigrette
Rocky Mountain Grass-Fed Beef Filet Mignon in a
Zinfandel Reduction
Garlic and Herb Mashed Potatoes accompanied by
Seasonal Vegetables
Artisanal Cheeses
Assorted Pastries from Gwen's Bakery
Coffee and Dessert Wines

Below the menu Jason had made notes about which Columbine Vineyard's wine would accompany each course. The choices made sense to Gwen and she particularly liked the direct reference to her bakery. She pointed to it. "Nice touch."

"Cross marketing. We not only want to feed them, we want them to come back for more. In this case, they might want to hire us to cater another event or they might just want to stop in for another one of whatever awesome pastry they chose at this dinner. It's a win-win, Chef, for both of us." He winked to seal the deal on his point.

"Numbers look good, food looks good, cross marketing looks great. Do we have the go-ahead from the winery?"

"I told Terra I'd send it over after I ran it by you, along with our estimated bill for the entire event, of course. She'll run it by Bob and let me know. But I think we have the inside track."

"Why do you think that?"

"Call it a gut feeling." He didn't elaborate and she

didn't ask.

"Okay, let me know what you hear." Gwen handed the tablet back to him. She pulled her laptop back in front of her and Jason glanced at the screen as he stood.

"Planning a trip?"

"Maybe. I'd like to put together a girl's getaway later in the fall for Claire, Del and myself. Beaches seem like the theme for us, but I can't find anything that's really just right."

Jason looked closer at the dates and said, "You know, not all beaches come with *tropical* settings. I know a nice island in New York that has beaches although that time of the year there's no swimming of course, but the waves are awesome. And better yet, there's some great Christmas shopping, shows and restaurants within walking distance."

"Manhattan?" She looked at him and he nodded back. "I hadn't thought of that. I've actually never been there, but I think Claire has."

"I could call a few old friends and get you some amazing dinners if you're interested."

Gwen tapped *New York City* into the search bar and scanned the options that appeared. "Hmm. Let me think about it."

"You know where to find me." Jason nodded toward the kitchen door.

DEL SAT AT THE DESK in her office, reviewing figures and details for the holiday benefit. The specifics were falling together nicely and over the course of the last few days she'd been able to meet with the caterer as well as the committee of volunteers who were organizing a silent auction.

Years of experience organizing committees were paying off and Del felt a real sense of accomplishment that she actually was up to the challenges her new position presented her.

A knock on her door drew her attention. It eased open and Carl looked cautiously inside.

"Hi, sweet Delly. Didn't know if you'd be on the phone. Do you have a minute for me before I leave?"

"Of course." She walked around her desk to greet him halfway. In the last few days they'd only talked a couple of times. Carl had been tied up with some big new deal he was putting together and hadn't shared much about it beyond his growing enthusiasm.

Del had made an effort to express more interest in both Carl and his mysterious deal and Carl, in return, had promised to share the details once things were firmed up. But he'd also alluded to what they might share on a more personal level, once his time freed up.

Del put out her hand to take his but he passed it by, wrapping his arm around her waist and pulling her forward. She kissed him briefly, then pulled playfully away. "What a nice surprise."

"I couldn't leave without stopping in to see you one last time. It's been too long and, well, I needed to put my arms around you before I fly to the other side of the world."

"Hong Kong sounds very exotic. What an adventure to go someplace like that on business."

"Business is business. I don't get much time to see the sites." He took her hand and led her to the small loveseat that sat near her bookcase and to one side of the door. "Maybe the next time I go you could come with me." He patted the cushion and she sat down beside him.

"Oh?" Del didn't know what else to say. Traveling with Carl wasn't a step she'd even imagined yet.

"It gets lonely." His hand swept along her thigh, pulling her body closer. "I get lonely." His hand ran up her back, and he pulled her into a kiss.

Del felt herself falling into his arms and into the kiss. Hadn't she promised herself she'd see where this relationship was going? She hadn't expected it to be going anywhere on her office loveseat, but Carl did have a way with his lips. Soon they were trailing down her neck. As her hand rested on his shoulder she felt an urge she hadn't felt for some time and, running her fingers into his hair, she encouraged his kisses to linger lower and lower until she felt him playing with the buttons of her blouse.

"Carl." She was barely able to muster more than a whisper, "maybe we should save this for a—"

"Baby, you are driving me crazy," Carl breathed against the top of her breast.

She felt his hand change course and ease its way beneath her skirt. "Oh! Carl, really, shouldn't we wait until..." Del knew the timing was bad, but the heat that his advances generated overwhelmed her common sense. What was she, a teenager? Couldn't she control herself? Couldn't she control Carl?

Of course she could, she thought to herself, pulling her head out of the hormone infused cloud that seemed to have engulfed them both. Her hands slid to his chest and eased them apart as she discreetly scooted back a couple inches and crossed her legs.

"Delly," Carl said sadly.

"I know, but not here, like this. Not for the...the first time."

"Yeah, I get that. I'm sorry, I know the ladies like romance and the middle of the day on your office couch probably doesn't qualify."

"Thank you for understanding, Carl." She wondered just how much experience Carl had had with the 'ladies'.

A knock at her door made Del jump. She looked at the door, then to Carl, and for a moment felt like a teenager caught making out behind the bleachers.

"Want me to get the door?" Carl whispered with a conspiratorial smile on his face. "Or we could ignore it and pick up where we left off." The smile turned amorous and he leaned toward her.

"No." Del wiggled her finger at him as if scolding a naughty boy. "I'm sure it's important, and you have a plane to catch, correct?" She stood and hastily buttoned up her blouse as she walked to the door. She pulled it open. "May I help you?" But froze when she realized who was at her door.

"Adele." The easy smile that had been on Jimmy's face faded as he looked her up and down.

Del instinctively reached up to sweep her hand through her hair. Why hadn't she thought to check it? Surely Carl had mussed it and it showed, but she didn't find anything amiss. Was she flushed, she wondered, but resisted the temptation to touch her cheeks.

"Jimmy," she said at last. "It's nice to see you." And she meant it, though perhaps she would have preferred seeing him at her door at any other moment but this one. "Won't you come in?" She opened the door further to admit him to her office but realized too late that Carl was still on the couch, watching their exchange. She glanced his way and could have sworn he was smirking though she couldn't imagine why.

"I can't stay, I was just—" he glanced toward the couch. "Carl."

"Jimmy." Carl jumped off the couch to shake his hand. "To what do we owe the honor of your visit?" He stood beside Del and, wrapping his arm around her, rested his hand lightly on her hip.

Del saw Jimmy's eye look at the hand on her hip and decided that if she were to die right now it would be better than living this moment. But, as her wish remained ungranted, she crossed her arms and tilted slightly away from Carl, her smile now tight and firm.

Jimmy looked back at Carl for a moment, then handed Del an envelope. "One of your volunteers stopped by the Dockside to see if I'd contribute to the silent auction. I had an appointment here and decided to drop it off myself. Clearly my timing's not great."

"Oh no, no time like the present." Del took the envelope and cursed herself for sounding like an idiot on so many levels. She wondered what kind of appointment he'd had, if he was well. But with Carl there she couldn't bring herself to ask. Del wondered if it would even be appropriate for her to ask, all things considered.

"It's a dinner for four. Drinks included. Hope it brings you—the new children's wing, that is, a nice donation."

"That's so kind of you."

"Indeed it is," Carl added. "The hospital is fortunate to have benefactors such as yourself."

All three stood silent for a long moment before Jimmy gave Carl a nod of acknowledgement.

"Well," Carl said, "I've got a plane to catch so I'll get out of your hair and let you two talk."

Before she could respond Carl had pulled her closer, planted a kiss on her lips, patted her bottom, and winked at Jimmy. "I'll call you from Hong Kong, Delly!" Then he strode out the door.

Del was dumbfounded for a second and then, pulling herself together, though certain Jimmy must see the red flush of embarrassment that she now clearly felt in her cheeks, she turned back to him. "Really, Jimmy, that is so kind. I truly appreciate your contribution."

"It's a good cause," he answered curtly.

"Um, would you like to come in?"

"No, I have to get back to the restaurant. And you better fix those buttons, *Delly*." With that he left.

Del glanced down and realized she'd buttoned the buttons into the wrong holes and her blouse looked like a child's first effort. She shut the door and leaned her head against it.

"Oh, God..."

C LAIRE FINALLY SETTLED INTO HER chair with Elbie. He had patiently followed her since her return home, through the bathroom to the closet for a change into yoga pants and a lavender t-shirt, then into the kitchen for a glass of wine and a box of crackers. He'd hopped up and settled himself between her left thigh and the arm of the chair.

"It's all about you, eh, Elbie?" She ran her hand from the top of his head, down along his back, eliciting a slowly building purr and causing his eyes to close and his front paws to stretch and dig into her leg. "Hey, easy fella." His claws retracted and he settled in for a nap.

Claire took of sip of her cab, set the glass on the side table along with the open box of crackers and placed her laptop on the other side of her lap, so as not to disturb the creature whose presence in her life was becoming a given rather than an intrusion.

She'd thought about that earlier, when she remembered to stop at the grocery store on the way home from the job site at the Larson's home to pick up some more canned food for Elbie. She'd decided to add a couple bags of treats that she reasoned a cat might find tempting; if anything really tempted a cat besides catnip, mice and a sunny spot.

Elbie ignored her taps on the keyboard as she typed out an update on the project for Roger. He, along with the sisters, had certainly given her carte blanche—and he'd paid every bill Claire had sent his way—so she assumed everyone was satisfied thus far.

And why shouldn't they be? Claire was doing a great job on the renovations and saving money wherever possible. The electrical and plumbing were just about done and the cabinets had arrived that morning. Soon, it would start looking like a house again. And she had to admit the job was *fun*. It had been a long time since Claire had considered work fun and, even though it felt more like play, she was being paid nicely by Roger—and the sisters' estate.

Email sent, Claire went in search of Columbine Vineyard's Facebook page. She remembered Bob saying something about Terra managing the page as part of their new marketing program. It was a somewhat distant memory since she and Bob hadn't talked for a while. They'd texted and emailed and had a couple of brief conversations when he tried to invite her to dinner but she'd declined due to the overwhelming work load involved in the fast turn-around of the Larson's home. It was true she was very busy, but was she really too busy for dinner with Bob? No. That wasn't true and she knew it. What she was, was avoiding having to deal with what she'd come to think of as the 'Bob situation'.

A picture of the winery's vineyards filled the top of her screen as the Facebook page pulled up. A small photo of a cluster of wine bottles nestled in the bottom left corner of the photo. Claire scrolled down to see Terra's updates. With the start of the harvest there were now many postings with pictures of activity in the vineyards and, once inside, shots of the pulpy *must* of the first grapes fresh from the crusher and ready for a cold soak to enhance their color and flavor before fermentation began.

Another post showed the first young wines in their holding tanks, allowing the dregs of the process to settle prior to pouring the wine into oak barrels to begin the aging process.

Further down, in an earlier post, was another picture taken just before harvest. Claire recognized the core team, standing arm in arm, all smiles, in front of rows of grape-laden vines. Gwen's husband, Andy, grinned on one end, clearly happily settled into his new career.

Bob, she noticed, had his arm looped over Terra's shoulder, pulling her closer in a territorial sort of way.

Terra leaned into him and tipped her head against his shoulder in a way that Claire felt was a little beyond the business relationship Bob repeatedly professed.

Claire studied the shot, examining every nuance of body language, looking for a clue that explained what was going on between Bob and Terra, if anything was, but afraid to find it.

"Shit," she whispered to herself. Elbie looked up at her briefly before pressing deeper against her thigh and resuming his nap. Claire shut the page and closed her laptop, placing it on the floor beside the chair. She took a long, slow sip from her glass, laid back her head and closed her eyes. A frown formed on her lips and creases crept slowly across her brow. A close observer would have had only a moment to see the glisten of tears in the corners of her eyes before Claire quickly wiped them away. She ran her fingers through her hair, then took another, longer sip of wine.

"Shit."

ANDY WAS PULLING ANOTHER LATE shift at the winery. Gwen was getting used to the routine of the harvest season, which really meant she'd gotten used to being alone. When Andy had driven the big rigs she'd spent many nights alone, but she'd also worried about things like weather and traffic and the unknown of the dark road and the late night phone call that she never wanted to get. This kind of alone she could handle.

Once she'd cleaned up her dinner dishes she turned on the TV and scanned the channels, looking for something to pass the time. But nothing grabbed her attention so she turned on some music instead and squatted in front of a low bookcase, scanning for a title she hadn't read or might want to read again. She could re-read Austen or Cather, always good friends in a pinch, but tonight was different because of something Carolyn had said.

Gwen glanced in the corner and noticed her watercolor case, a small easel and a pad of paper tucked behind a large stone crock that held afghans. She hadn't painted since she'd come to the valley. She'd been too busy, she had told herself, but she knew it was something else.

In Blue River, Gwen had painted sea shells, memories of a brief trip to the sea when she was young that haunted her for years until lately, when she'd returned along with her new girlfriends, and faced down old demons and started fresh.

It seemed to Gwen that she'd painted more than enough shells, but she hadn't found something new to inspire her and, in the meantime, her paint case gathered dust in the corner.

Gwen pulled it out and, moving it to a small table near the front window, she opened it up revealing her paint palette lined with semi-moist, multi-hued strips of pan-colors, and empty white pots, awaiting water and color. She set the small easel on the table and laid a sheet of heavy, white, cold-pressed watercolor paper on it.

A slender blue vase on the broad windowsill held a cluster of wildflowers that Andy had brought her from the vineyard. Gwen clutched the flowers in one hand as she poured out a small amount of water from the vase into one of the larger white pots. She picked up one brush and then another, but set them down again, not sure where to start or what to start with.

Then she looked back at the wildflowers. Three sky-blue Rocky Mountain columbines extended from long, willowy stems. Each one dipped in a separate direction, the petals all gracefully spilling out from creamy white-blue centers filled with long, yellow tipped stamens.

"Perfect," Gwen whispered to herself. The symbol of the winery that had brought her and Andy to the valley, and the symbol of new life every springtime in the mountains was the perfect symbol for Gwen, 2.0.

Time passed quickly once she turned herself to her new subject. She'd lost track of everything around her until movement outside the window caught her eye and she looked up to see Del, small suitcase pulled behind her, approaching her door. Del paused at the doorbell, her hand hesitating in mid-air, and then she noticed Gwen through the window. Del smiled and shrugged her shoulders and Gwen rose to open the door.

"Hi," Del whispered, unable to say more before bursting into tears.

"Del," Gwen said softly, pulling her inside and shutting the door behind them. She set Del's suitcase near the stairs, then led her to the couch where they both sat, Del struggling to shake off her tears and finally, after several large breaths, gaining her composure. Gwen sat beside her the whole time, rubbing her back and whispering comforting words, "It's okay...that's right...take your time..." Finally, when Del had calmed enough, Gwen crossed the room for a box of tissues and, offering them asked, "Wine?" Del nodded.

Two generous glasses of Columbine Estates Pinot Grigio were poured and Del took a large and lingering sip before Gwen finally got around to asking, "So... what's up?"

Del almost started crying again but Gwen's steadying gaze and another sip of Pinot pulled her back together. She thought for a long moment and then seemed to finally get down to her point.

"Men."

"All of them?"

They both laughed and Del relaxed into the couch beside her friend.

"No, not all, but it seems like most of them; at least most of the ones in my life." She took another sip from her glass and launched into a re-telling of the events that had taken place earlier in the day in her office. She signed heavily when she got to the part about the buttons, then, finishing off her glass of wine, she held it out to Gwen.

"I'm so sorry, Del. You must have wanted to crawl under a rock. I would have." She filled Del's glass halfway then set the bottle aside.

"What is wrong with me, Gwen? Why can't I have a nice, normal relationship with a man? Like you and Andy?"

"Well, remember, Andy was my second try. I didn't do so well the first time around. Except of course, for Jeff. He's the only good part of that failed marriage. But I thought you had a good relationship with Jimmy before."

"Before I screwed it up, that's what you're trying so nicely not to say."

"No, I can't say what either of you did or didn't

do. Certainly I have to think that it takes two to break up as much as it takes two to get together. I mean, if Jimmy really wanted you back, I guess he'd be working toward that goal. Is he?"

"Not that I can tell, but then I guess from his point of view I'm not really encouraging it. Especially after today."

"Do you want to encourage it?"

"Part of me does, but part of me is a little...afraid."

"Of Jimmy?" Gwen asked. "Granted, I don't know him *that* well, but he never seemed scary to me. Did he...do something?"

"Oh no. I mean, he was always a perfect gentleman, and so caring." Del blushed slightly then recovered. "It's only, since we separated or broke-up or whatever this is, he seems, well, harder. Does that make sense?"

"Like he doesn't care?"

"It's more like he wants to hurt me, not physically, but my feelings. I can feel the wall when I'm near him, when we talk, and he never lets me see anything kind, it always feels hurtful. Always."

"Hmm..." Gwen sat silently for a long moment, watching her wine as she swirled it in the glass. "You know, I'm no expert, Del, but I wonder, is it possible that, rather than trying to hurt you, he's trying not to get hurt himself?"

"Like it's a defense?"

"Exactly. Plus, he sees you with Carl and he's got to be thinking you've moved on. It can't be easy for him, if he still has feelings for you, that is."

"I worried about that at first, but he seemed so un-kind the last time I saw him. I don't know how to get past it. I don't know if I can."

"Well, I could see where you wouldn't want an un-comfortable relationship with Jimmy. You're bound to run into him around town, after all. But you don't want to give him the wrong impression. You don't want to have more than just a friendly relationship, do you? And what about Carl? Haven't you two been spending more time together?"

Del hung her head, closing her eyes and rubbing at the corners with the fingers of her free hand. She'd had a long day working on the hospital's fundraiser. It had been many weeks of long days and, though exhausted and exhilarated from her work, as far as her personal life went, she wasn't any closer to figuring herself out than when it all began. "Shit."

"Something tells me we aren't going to figure this out tonight. Let's get you in bed."

Gwen reached over, taking Del's glass from her and setting it on the coffee table in front of them. Then she picked up Del's suitcase and led her to what Del had come to think of as her little room in the attic. The perfect place to hide, for now.

Nineteen

CLAIRE'S CAR MADE THE EASY turn away from the river front and into the Columbine Estates parking lot, avoiding the section of the lot occupied by a large dumpster and heavy equipment being angled into position for the installation of new fermentation tanks. Bob had been particularly busy lately with the expansion and updating of the winery equipment. Claire couldn't fault the man for being committed to the success of a business he clearly loved. But she couldn't help wondering if that feeling extended to one of his employees.

She pulled into the shade beneath a large cottonwood and, turning off the car, reached for her cell to check messages.

She'd decided last night that it was time to confront Bob about Terra—about everything. In the morning Claire decided that *confront* might not be the right word. It sounded like the sort of tactic she had used *Before*, as she'd come to think of her life before the assault, before she'd moved to Grande Valley and, lately, before she'd met the Larson sisters—particularly Cora.

Throughout the remodel Claire had found herself

wondering, more and more, how would Cora handle this? Would she lose her cool? Would she make demands? No, that wasn't Cora's style.

Clearly, Cora had been a successful business woman in her day. Under her guidance and, with Evie's help, they had managed the orchards and their land for many years. They'd created their own little empire and now, in their golden years, others watched over it and, clearly, had great respect for the sisters.

No, Cora's style had been easier; Claire was sure of it. She'd seen how she watched out for her sister. She'd taken charge when necessary and deferred to others where possible. Cora seemed to have found a way of making things work without drama. Claire couldn't think of a better role model.

Cora would not confront, but she wouldn't evade an issue either. She'd address it, discuss it, and resolve it. Yes, Claire thought, that's what she would do too.

Claire put her phone back in her purse, grabbed her lipstick and pulled down the visor, flipping open the mirror on the back while swiping a fresh layer of Desert Plum across her lips. She smudged her lips together and reached up to wipe away where the color had slipped over an edge when the reflection of movement in the mirror caught her eye.

She paused a moment, the tip of her ring finger against her lip, and watched as Terra and Bob walked out of the building and onto the side patio, discussing something as they stepped into the shade of a clematis-covered pergola that enclosed several tables.

Terra was showing an iPad to Bob, and he was nodding as she pointed and gestured. She was smiling, bubbly, and Bob nodded with a smile on his face, clearly satisfied with whatever she was sharing. Something having to do with her job, Claire thought, what's unusual about that?

"Nothing, that's what," she said to herself and reached for her purse, putting the lipstick away and stepping out of the car. She looked up again, just in time to see Bob pull Terra into his arms. Terra tipped her head up, smiling at him and he leaned down, gently placing a kiss on her forehead. Claire's hand chose that moment to firmly slam her door shut.

Bob looked over at her. "Claire, I-I didn't know you were coming," he called from across the short distance of the parking lot. His arms fell away from Terra who smiled at Claire and then, seeing the look on her face, stepped away from Bob.

Terra said something to Bob, gesturing to the iPad and added, louder, "Hi, Claire," before slipping back into the building.

Claire crossed the lot slowly at first, watching the door shut behind Terra and trying to remain calm; trying not to think about that kiss. Trying to suppress the urge to confront and, instead, channel her inner Cora. But the closer she got to Bob the closer a multitude of conflicted inner feelings bubbled to the surface.

"We have to talk," she said, finally.

"Honey." Bob reached for her only to have Claire stop short of his grasp.

"Don't *honey* me," Claire heard herself say, unable to stop the emotions building inside.

"Hey, Ace,"

"Don't *Ace* me either, Bob. I saw that. I saw you holding Terra and—and kissing her. What kind of a boss are you, anyway?" For a moment Claire thought she'd take the righteous path and defend Terra, but Terra, she thought, didn't seem to mind and so that direction quickly fell away, leaving Claire uncertain where she wanted this conversation to go.

"Baby—" Bob caught himself and quickly reverting to, "Claire, it is not what you think—whatever that might be." He waved his arms before her and then nodding toward the direction Terra had exited.

"What might I be thinking, Bob?" Claire said his name with extra emphasis and crossed her arms, raising her chin just enough to accentuate the question.

"Well, I don't know, I mean, I'm sure it's not, I mean—it's not what you might be thinking. It's nothing *serious*, I mean, it's not like *that* kind of serious."

Bob stumbled over his words and Claire let him until her growing frustration got the best of her.

"What the hell are you talking about? What kind of serious is the kind I wouldn't be upset to find the man I love involved in?"

Bob stopped and looked at her. He opened his mouth to speak, then shut it, then, a smile coming to his face, said softly, "You love me, Claire?"

Claire took a step back, looked away and then, re-focusing, took aim. "This isn't about me, this is about you, Bob. Why do I keep finding you in—in physical contact with Terra? What the hell is going on with you and Terra?"

"Not what you think," he said, quietly, "and while we're on the subject," he added, reaching out to take her hands tentatively in his, "I love you, too, Ace."

"I said, don't *Ace* me," Claire said softly, allowing Bob to pull her into his arms, despite her best efforts to despise him.

Bob kissed her gently and then led her over to sit at one of the shaded tables. He held onto her hands, their knees touching as they sat on the bench. "I need to explain about Terra."

Claire looked at him, eyes narrowing, a black feeling trying to fill her soul, but she fought it, thinking of Cora and struggling to remain calm, to hear him out. If this was the end of their relationship, Claire was determined to be present for the moment and not let anger cloud her clarity. But she had to get it out there, get past the unknown.

"You and Terra are lovers," she said at last, prepared to face it all head on.

"What? No! No, no, no! That is not what Terra and I are, *absolutely* not!"

"Huh?" Claire felt a huge weight fall away but still she was confused. "Then what the hell?"

"She's not my lover, Claire. She's my daughter."

Had she heard him right? Not a lover, good...but a daughter? "What? Since when? Where did a daughter come from? Are you sure?"

"Someone I knew long ago. Her mother and I, well, we weren't together that long but obviously it was long enough."

"And she never told you?"

He shook his head. "I was a different person back then, Babe. I've told you that before. She didn't want to be in my life and she didn't want me in hers. But she wanted Terra. She never planned to tell her about me, but as Terra got older, she pushed her more and more until she had to tell her and then, once she knew, and once she was out of college and ready to make her own decisions, she decided to find me."

"But how do you know for sure?"

"Know it's true? When Terra told me I knew it was possible, and I called and talked with her mom, then I knew it was, but still, we did a DNA test because, well, it seemed best to be certain."

"So, how long have you known?"

"Since not too long after I met you."

"That long? You've known that long and you haven't said a word to me?"

"At first, you and I were just getting to know each other and then, well, after the attack...after you were hurt and you had your recovery ahead and, everything, well, I couldn't add to that, Claire."

Claire nodded slowly, sorting through the facts. "So you couldn't tell me one of the biggest things to happen to you in your whole friggin' life? You have a daughter. And you couldn't share that with *me*?" Claire could feel Cora's Zen slipping away amid growing confusion.

"It's not that I didn't want to or that I didn't plan to, it's just I didn't think you were ready, I didn't think you could handle one more—"

"That's not your decision. Something this big you should have told me right away. I should have been a part of this, a part of you figuring this out."

"I can see that now."

"Instead, watching you with Terra has just made things worse; I couldn't figure it out. I couldn't figure *you* out."

"There's nothing to figure out with me, Babe. I'm always here, you can always have faith in me. You don't have to worry about me; what you see is what you get."

"No it's not. Now I see a father, and that's not what I thought I was getting, that's not..."

"Claire, honey, listen to me, this doesn't change *us*, I'm still me and I still love you and you still love me, right?"

"I don't know...I..." She stood, pulling her hands from his. Though she knew what he said was true she couldn't help feeling...what, she thought, betrayed? Maybe, or maybe that something was missing that she'd always thought was there. Like a sin of omission, for whatever reason, because he hadn't told her before, had been living this little alternate reality alongside their blossoming relationship. It left her feeling that she didn't really know him; at least, not all of him. Claire was used to being in control of her men but Bob had thrown that all over from the start and now, now what?

"I have to go."

"Claire."

"Not now." She backed up and held the palms of her hands out toward him, as if to push Bob and the air he inhabited away.

"Honey, please."

But Claire was striding toward her car, shaking her head and pushing still at the air around her, as if she could slip from the atmosphere and escape reality.

She drove quickly away from the winery—too quickly. Still in a haze of frustration and confusion over Terra's new identity, she missed a stop sign and saw the pick-up truck only seconds before she and it swerved to miraculously miss each other. Regaining control of her car, she pulled to the side of road, her heart racing and tears welling in her eyes.

"Hey! Hey!"

Claire heard someone outside her car and looked out the passenger side window, to see the faded green pick-up pulled to the side of the cross road. Its owner, an older gentleman with a few days growth of graying stubble and a red baseball cap pulled snugly over equally unkempt hair, was hanging out the driver's side window, waving at her across the empty road that separated them.

"Oh great," Claire said to herself, unbuckling her seatbelt and scooting over to roll down the window. She fully expected an expletive infused rant as she crossed her arms on the ledge of the open window and yelled over, "I'm very sorry about that!"

"You okay, missy?" the man asked.

"What?" Claire wasn't prepared for concern from the man she'd almost t-boned.

"You okay over there? That was a close one, alright. Took my breath away, I'll tell ya. You weren't doing that texting thing, now were ya, young lady? Because if you was, I hope this served as a good lesson to ya."

"Um...no, no texting. I'm really sorry, just having a bad day, wasn't paying attention. It was totally my fault, I'm very sorry if I scared you, sir." Claire had learned long ago that in circumstances like this it paid to simply say you're sorry and move on. But she had to admit, she really was sorry. Not to mention shocked that this guy wasn't stomping across the lot to tell her what he *really* thought about her driving.

"Oh, I weren't scared, only startled, that's all. You're the one should light a candle at evening mass and say a prayer of thanks. This truck of mine may have seen better days but it's built like a tank. Your pretty little city car wouldn't have stood a chance if you'd hit me.

I'd barely feel it, but your car would be in a world of hurt—you too, most likely. Ya catch your breath before ya take off, and say your thanks, little lady."

"I will, and thank you! Really, thank you for being so...understanding."

"We're all in this world together, missy. Gots to look out for each other."

"Never thought of it that way." Claire felt her entire body sigh, releasing tension she hadn't realized she was carrying. "Thank you, again!"

"You betcha." he tipped the brim of the well-worn baseball cap at her before driving away.

Claire slumped, resting her forehead against her crossed arms, and sat in the silence. No cars passed. A breeze blew against her hair and she could hear mourning doves cooing back and forth from the near-by cottonwoods that lined the river; the faint murmur of its water, skipping against rocks and lapping at the shore on its voyage downstream. For the first time in a long time, she cried.

Even after the assault that had put her in the hospital she hadn't cried. She'd been strong and proud of it. From that point on she'd been fighting a battle to get her life back to normal but now, in this moment and this place, she felt like she was wandering in a wilderness of her own making.

What progress had she made in all that time, she wondered through her tears. What did she have to show for it? A temporary home, a temporary job and now, she worried, was her relationship with Bob also temporary? She'd barely figured out her feelings for Bob and now there was a daughter. A daughter he hadn't told her about.

Yes, deep inside, she understood his reasons for holding back. She even appreciated that he cared so deeply, that he'd worry about compounding her recovery with new stress. Still, knowing that Bob had been carrying this around for most of their relationship made her feel she had to reassess every moment in a new light. As if it wasn't totally real. As if she had to start again. Again.

Her phone buzzed beside her, alerting her to a text and pulling her out of her thoughts. Claire leaned back into her seat, wiping the wet away from her face and reached for her phone. It was from Roger.

The Larson sisters wish to speak with you regarding a new concern. Please contact them at your earliest convenience.

What now? Claire wondered. She'd tried to share the details of the remodel with Cora and Evie but they'd shown no interest, putting it all in her hands. She'd already ordered new cabinets and appliances, and that morning she'd okayed the electrician's and plumber's bids, giving them the go-ahead to start work. She'd planned to visit the job site next, fully expecting the contractors would both be there, already hard at work. But now what? What changes had the sisters decided upon and what changes would she need to make?

She might as well find out right away, she decided. Though truly, she was thankful for the distraction from everything *Bob*. Was he right and she'd been too pig-headed to realize it? But didn't she have a right to be upset about his lack of total disclosure. Still, Terra wasn't a clause in a contract, and neither was all she'd gone through in the last few months. If Bob loved her and cared about her, wasn't it only natural for him to want to protect her from anything that might cause her more stress and interfere with her recovery?

But he'd known all along and said nothing, not even when he should have realized Terra was causing a rift in their relationship. Or, at least, the lack of understanding about Terra.

"Shit." Yes, she was thankful to put this all aside for a moment and worry about the sisters. After all, Bob wasn't going anywhere.

Twenty

A FTER A MODEST AMOUNT OF repair work to her make-up, Claire drove over to the retirement village in DuPont. She'd decided there was no point in going to the house until she knew what changes the sisters might have come up with. And when it came to the sisters Claire had learned it was always better to see them in person.

Cora told her once that she found it 'off putting' to do business over the phone. Claire could imagine Cora, in her prime, dealing face-to-face with her orchard employees as well as the markets where she sold her fruit. She could easily imagine Cora as a force to be reckoned with. A kind and gentle one, but a force all the same.

Despite her hesitation about what was basically a 'royal summons' sent via Roger, Claire could feel her spirits lift as she approached their unit. It had been decades since her parents died tragically in a small airplane crash and she had few memories of her grandparents. But something inside Claire told her that her growing feelings for these sisters, who had no children or grandchildren of their own, were so much like those she might have felt in the presence of her own grandparents.

"Claire, dear!" Cora greeted Claire, ushering her through their door. The main room was packed with boxes marked IKEA and Claire maneuvered through them toward the kitchen, where Evie was busy dicing cooked chicken breasts.

"How delightful." Evie set down her knife to give Claire a snug embrace. "You are just in time to join us for lunch. We're having chicken salad sandwiches. We always love company with our meals, don't we Cora?"

"Yes, dear. It's always a nice surprise."

"Well," Claire said, "maybe not so much of a surprise, since Roger told me you needed to talk with me as soon as possible." She took a seat at the breakfast bar to observe Evie at work, realizing that for nearly the entire time she'd known her, Evie had been recovering from her fall and Claire had always seen her being waited upon by her sister. This was a more industrious version of Evie, though she still wore her walking cast.

"Oh, Roger." Cora gathered plates and condiments for her sister. "He is so Johnny-on-the-spot', isn't he Evie?"

"Indeed! We'd only just spoken with him this morning and already he has delivered you to our doorstep."

"I brought all the plans and some additional information on lighting fixtures I found for the kitchen, if you were wanting an update on the project."

"Goodness, no, we have every faith in your ability to handle the details, dear," Cora said. "That wasn't what we'd hoped to speak with you about. But first, and more importantly—"

"—how is our sweet Elbie?" Evie finished her sister's sentence. They both looked expectantly toward Claire, clearly hoping for a good report.

"He's fine. He's great, actually."

"He's eating well?" Evie's brow creased with concern.

"Very well. And, I have to admit, I might have added some goodies here and there...some tuna, or leftover chicken."

"Elbie loves that, doesn't he, Cora?"

"He does. So, he's not been a distraction for you? Not making any mischief?"

"Not at all. In fact, he's really been good company; better than I would have expected."

The sisters smiled at Claire, and then each other. Claire could have sworn something went unsaid between them and, not for the first time, wondered if they shared some sibling mental telepathy.

"Well, it's very nice to hear he's getting on well. I'm sure you will miss him." Cora glanced at her sister. "But we will be so happy to have him back home with us."

"And at the rate things are moving, that shouldn't be long."

"Actually," Cora said, "that was what we wanted to speak with you about. But we had to discuss it with Roger first because—"

"—we were afraid he might not approve, but he did!"

"Yes, he did. With great enthusiasm, I must say. Roger is ever the good soul when we throw him what Father called a '*curve ball*'."

"He didn't see this one coming, did he, Cora?"

Evie actually giggled as she stirred the chopped

chicken, celery, apples and mayonnaise together in a large red, ceramic bowl. "I don't believe so, dearest. And in fact, how could he, we never did."

Claire watched this exchange with curiosity, wondering what the sisters were up to now. She eyed the boxes in the living room and wondered if they intended to move back into the house before it was finished, bringing new furniture in tow.

"What is this new development? And what's up with all the boxes? Why did you get this stuff already? Isn't it a little early for new furniture? You'll be living with boxes for a while until we can get you back into the house and put it all together. It's really not livable quite yet, and your furniture is in storage, except for a few pieces still being cleaned, what with the smoke and soot from the fire." She hoped to put off any premature plans they might be plotting.

"Mr. Trsander, the handyman, had to drive to Denver yesterday and he was ever so kind to pick up our order while he was there. He's actually planning on stopping by a little later to start unpacking everything, isn't he, Cora?"

"Yes, he is. I don't know what we'd do without him!"

"But where will you put it all?" Claire asked, mystified at the plan. "This place is already full of furniture."

"That," Cora said, "is why we wanted to speak with you."

"Indeed, we have wonderful and—"

"—surprising news," Cora finished.

"Okay," Claire braced for what could be next. "Out with it."

They stood side-by-side and in unison said, "We've

decided to stay." Then both sisters giggled like school girls as Evie pulled bread from a bag and Cora took a pitcher of lemonade from the refrigerator.

"But I-I thought there weren't any available units in the village." Inside Claire was delighted to hear their decision, particularly as they both seemed to be flourishing since they'd arrived. But outside, she was a woman of details and she needed to get some things straight.

"Indeed, there were not," Cora said soberly. "But unfortunately, in the village, a vacancy is both a sad and happy event."

"Somebody died?" The words slipped from Claire's mind to her mouth before she'd had a chance to run them through a sensitivity filter. "I'm sorry! I didn't mean to be, you know..."

"No reason to apologize, dear," Evie said. "It is the cycle of life and it is an occasional sad but true fact of life in the Village. But with the bad, comes the good, and there will now be a lovely unit available just down the walkway from where we are now. In fact, its view is even more delightful, if that's possible."

Cora placed the sliced sandwiches on plates and set one before Claire. "The gentleman passed just after we arrived. Naturally, we didn't even consider the unit at the time, as we had no intention of staying. But we must admit, we've come to enjoy the company of our new friends—"

"—and all the delightful activities. I do believe we'd miss everything if we left now. Don't you think so, Cora?"

"Yes, dear."

Claire jumped at the sound of the doorbell's buzzer.

"I hate that buzzer, Cora. We absolutely must get a nice bell in our new home."

"I agree, dear." Cora opened the door. "Mr. Trsander. You are just in time for lunch. Evie, can you make a sandwich for Mr. Trsander as well?"

"Indeed!"

"Thank you, Miss Cora," said a familiar voice.

Claire turned just as an older gentleman, with a few days' growth of graying stubble and a red baseball cap snugly pulled over unkempt hair, entered the room. The same gentleman she'd almost t-boned on her way over.

"It's you," she said.

"Why, hello there, missy, I didn't expect to see you again. You know these fine ladies?"

"You two know each other?" Cora asked.

"Yes..." Claire said, "I kind of, well, I—"

"She nearly ran straight into the Hulk and I on our way over." He winked at Claire. "Always been a fan of the comics, ya know. Thought it were a fitting name for my trusty truck. It's generally mild-mannered, but sometimes it does get surly."

"Oh, dear." Evie looked from him to Claire. "No one was hurt, correct?"

"All's fine and dandy." Mr. Trsander tipped his baseball cap in confirmation.

"Good. Claire here is the friend we told you about. The one who's fixing up our home after the fire." Evie set a sandwich down for their new guest.

"That's awful kind of you." He picked up a sandwich half and took it along as he surveyed the boxes. "The Misses Larson have told me how much they appreciate your help. Speaking of help, I think I'll get to work on these boxes if that's ok. I hear the painters are packing up at your new unit so it's lookin' as we can start moving things in later today—mornin' at the latest."

"That's wonderful news," Cora said. "You just do what needs to be done, we'll take our lunch out onto the patio, along with Claire. We have some business that needs doing today."

"Thank you, Mr. Trsander." Evie took her plate and headed for the patio door.

The handyman, taking a large bit of his sandwich, tipped his hat again but didn't glance up. He was already in deep contemplation of a lengthy set of instructions.

"OK," SAID CLAIRE, ONCE THEY'D seated themselves outside, "what's wrong?"

"Wrong?" Evie reached out to pat Claire's arm. "Why nothing's wrong. In fact, I think everything will be just right, don't you, Cora?"

"Yes, dear. But let's explain everything to Claire before her worry overtakes her appetite. Eat, Claire. It's really very simple. Since we have now decided to live here, we no longer need Papa's home, as we've always referred to our house."

"You want to sell it?" Claire asked, worrying that they wanted to hire her as their realtor. She hadn't decided if that was what she still wanted to be, but she'd have a hard time turning the sisters down in their hour of need.

"Oh, no," Evie said. "We could never allow a

stranger to move in. At least...not in our lifetimes." She looked over at Cora, wistfully, adding, "that just wouldn't be right."

"No, Evie is right. It holds too many dear memories for us to part with it in such a harsh manner. But we feel naturally foolish keeping it empty so we've come up with a perfect solution."

"We're giving it to you!" Evie blurted out.

"Wh-what?" Claire almost choked on her sandwich.

"Well, in a manner of speaking," Cora clarified. "We would like you to take over management of the house. If you agree you may do what you like with it. We will pay for all the current repairs, of course, and we will supply a reasonable stipend to cover basic expenses. But beyond that it's entirely up to you. If you wish to do further upgrades, that is fine with us. You may rent it out, if you wish, though we were hoping that you might consider living in it yourself."

"It's far more spacious than the caretaker's house you're in now."

"Yes, that's true. And it might feel like something more...grounded. Evie and I feel that perhaps, if you intend to stay in Grande Valley, you'd like more of a sense of place."

"Of *home*." Evie added reached over to give Claire's hand a squeeze.

"Indeed, of course, we appreciate that you might not want to do this or might not be sure. If you are dead-set against the idea, we will seriously consider the option of selling, as much as it pains us. But if you are even just a little bit tempted, we'd like you consider giving it a go. We have no immediate relatives, as you may know. Our intention is that, once the Lord takes us home and our estate is settled out, that the home will go to you, along with an acre or so around it. The orchards are already intended to be gifted to friends who currently tend them in our stead."

"And if you decide you don't want the house after all..." Evie said softly.

"Then Roger, as the executor of our estate, shall sell the home and reimburse you for any amount you may have put into it out of your own pocket. So do be sure to keep records, going forward."

Claire sat silent, staring at both the sisters, her sandwich forgotten.

"What do you think, Claire?" Evie asked, an expectant look on her face.

What did she think? Was she ready to be a homeowner in Grande Valley? After the scene that she'd just played out with Bob, did Claire even want to be in Grande Valley anymore? And even if she did, living in that house couldn't be her reason for living. After all this time trying to get her head on straight Claire felt as if she were losing her mind.

"Oh shit." She ran her hands through her hair, then let them fall into her lap, all the while shaking her head back and forth.

"Claire, dear!" Cora came immediately to her side, wrapping her arms around her as Evie stooped in front of her, taking Claire's hands in her own.

"What is wrong? Have we done something wrong?" Evie asked.

"No...no..." Claire moaned.

"Tell us." Cora rubbed her hand soothingly along one of Claire's arms.

Claire took a small sip from the lemonade Evie offered her, wishing it were a vodka and tonic instead. She shared her tale of woe about Bob, herself, and Terra, ending with the near collision with Mr. Trsander.

She reached up to brush away a tear and stopped, looking at the moisture on her fingertips. "What the hell? Since when do I cry at over stuff like this? Since when do I *have* stuff like this? Oh, it might have been better if he'd hit me!" Claire said finally.

"No." Cora said, "Don't you see, it's a wake-up call from the Lord."

"Well, I don't know about that." Claire eyed Cora hesitantly.

"Oh, no, Claire. Cora is right," Evie insisted. "All of life is a path we take that brings us, if we are patient, both mercy and grace. Naturally, you don't see it that way, you're not a believer. If you were you'd see that you have to have faith. Faith that there's a reason you didn't T-bone poor Mr. Trsander."

"And perhaps, faith that Bob meant what he said," Cora added.

"Have you two been conspiring with Bob? He said I should have faith in him, too."

"Well, there you go then." Evie sat back, slapping her palms against her thighs as if it had all been settled.

"I'm not sure that settles it." Cora read her sister's body language.

"It ought to at least give you pause to consider, shouldn't it, Claire?"

"I suppose." Claire wanted to believe in Bob and she wanted to be excited about the house, but it all came so fast. She needed time to sort it out. "I'm just a little—"

"—overwhelmed," Cora concluded Claire's thought. "And my, you have every right to be, Claire dear. We most certainly didn't mean to add more to your plate."

"We would never want to hurt you," Evie said. "You've become very dear to us. So many of our friends have already gone to be with the Lord and, well, their families have concerns of their own. They are kind to us, of course, but we are not their responsibility and they are not ours."

"Evie is right. We have felt a growing isolation these last few years. But in a very short time, and in spite of great adversity of your own, you have sweetly taken us under your regard. It has not been lost on us, Claire. Your kindness has most certainly endeared you to us."

"Oh, yes." Evie nodded in agreement. "And we never would have considered settling in the Village if we hadn't known Papa's house would be in your very capable hands. Your kindness helped us in our hour of need and now that we have found such a lovely new home and wonderful friends, we want to help you. Please accept our home as yours, Claire. It would make us both very happy."

Claire stood, too restless to stay put, and stretched her arms over her head, joined hands and stretched side to side, as if warming up for a yoga session, ending up with her hands, clasped, resting on top of her head as she contemplated the view from the patio along with her life.

Was it really such a bad idea after all? And even if she wasn't exactly certain about what this new development with Bob would mean for their relationship, how could she possibly know if taking the sisters up on their offer would be for the best, no matter what happened with Bob? Claire felt like her whole life was up in the air. How could she make a decision with any certainty at that moment? Maybe, for once, the best decision was indecision. She dropped her hands to her side, letting out a long sigh as she did.

"Okay, first," she said, turning to face the sisters' expectant faces, "let me say how very grateful I am for the offer and well, for everything. You two have been more than kind to me in return; you definitely don't owe me anything."

"Oh, but we do, dear," Evie said.

"Shush, Evie," Cora interrupted, "let Claire have her say."

They both settled back into their chairs, resting their hands in their lap. It was not lost on Claire that Cora's left hand rested on her right, her head tipped to the right, and Evie's right hand rested on her left, her head tipped to her left. Like paired-dolls, each a mirror image of the other.

"Thank you," Claire continued. "Clearly, all my efforts to get my act together over the course of the summer have not turned out well."

Claire could see that Evie wanted to say something but Cora shut her down firmly with her eyes. Claire resisted laughing at the sight. It was comical but touching and it made her realize how much she loved these two women.

"I understand your reasoning and appreciate what you're trying to do but—"

Claire saw Evie's mouth open and a pained look crossed her face, but she glanced at her sister and held her tongue."

"Oh, shit, I'll think about it," Claire said at last.

"That's wonderful!" the sisters said in unison, rising to share an impromptu group hug.

Claire couldn't resist hugging back.

"I'll tell you what," Claire said once they'd separated, "I'll keep up with the repairs and you continue working with Mr. Trsander to move you into your new home. Meantime, I'll give it all some thought. It's a lot to process, you know?" The sisters nodded, smiling at each other. "Don't get overly excited," she added. The sisters shook their heads in unison.

"Now," Evie said, "the first thing you need to do—"

"—is sit back down and finish your sandwich." Cora smiled.

Twenty-One

DEL SPRINKLED CINNAMON ATOP THE neatly piled froth of a cappuccino and handed it to her customer. "Thanks for stopping in."

"Nicely done." Gwen slid a sheet of éclairs into the bakery case.

"It's fun, and a lot easier than I thought it would be."

"Then I guess I'm grateful you showed up on the day Caroline had jury duty. If I'm lucky she won't be tied up all day."

"Well, if not, I'll be here."

"I appreciate that, I really do, but don't you have work of your own to do?" Gwen nodded toward Del's laptop, open on one of the back tables, a notepad and pen beside it.

"I'm fortunate that my emotional crises occurred at that magical moment when all my *worker bees* are busy with their tasks and won't require my assistance for at least another week. And no meetings scheduled; no deadlines either. Anything that needs doing can be done remotely for at least the next week.

"Micky was delighted to have the kids stay with

him. Ever since he bought a second home in Blue River, so he could see more of the kids during the school year, he's been bugging me to let them stay more often. And of course, they love it because he takes them to his country club."

"Won't it be getting too cold for golf pretty soon?

"Yep. That's why the club has an indoor fitness center complete with pool, gym and climbing wall. Like an indoor activity Disneyland. It's the new thing for families."

"Families with bucks to spend."

"Exactly. I'd have to choose between paying my club dues or my utilities."

"Easy choice."

"It is. And I don't really mind. It means the kids enjoy being with Micky. For a long time before the divorce he was always too busy for them. It's good for them to spend time with their dad. He owns his own law firm so if he wants to work from home nobody will complain."

"And if you want to get out of town..."

"It's a win-win I guess."

"You guess?"

"It's not that I'm jealous that their father can afford to do things like this with them, it's just that, well..."

"You miss being a part of it."

"Exactly."

"I get that." Gwen took two broken cookies from the case and, breaking them into smaller pieces, set them on a sample plate on the counter. "I remember the first time Jeff went to visit his dad. His father isn't very 'hands-on", so he didn't really know what to do with him. As a result, they ended up doing almost everything you do with a child over the summer."

"That's cool."

"In two weeks."

"Whew!"

"Yeah, I think Jeff slept most of the first day after he got home. He was exhausted. And I was glad he'd had so much fun but, a part of me was also sorry I didn't get to be a part of it. See the expression on his face when the gorilla came up to the glass at the zoo, see his first super heroes' movie with him, take him to the beach for the first time."

"I totally get that. I tell myself they're going to have more and more experiences that I won't be a part of as they grow up, and that's normal."

"But it starts sooner when you're divorced."

Del could only nod, her eyes tearing up.

Gwen pulled her into a tight hug. "And that is why we need our friends at times like this. To remind us it's okay for those kids to have fun with their dads. It's a good thing to have that happy relationship. And it's an even better thing when they come home, with a smile on their faces, and tell us all about it. Then ask what's for dinner and could we help them finish that school project they were supposed to be working on over spring break."

Gwen released Del as they both laughed.

"Isn't that the truth? Then you spend a late night, heads together over the kitchen table gluing strings and glitter onto the solar system."

"I've been there." Gwen smiled. "So you are right, it is a win-win."

"It is." Del grabbed a rag and went to work wiping down the espresso machine. "Plus, I'm getting pretty good at this coffee machiney thingie you have here. I was a little intimidated at first, but it's actually pretty user-friendly."

"That's the idea. I have enough complications in my life. I don't need my espresso machine to be one of them. It looks like the lunch rush is winding down so if you want to get some work done I'll man the front. Jason took off a little bit ago to run to the winery. He's finalizing the details for the dinner with Terra and checking out the space."

"It's wonderful that you're going to cater Columbine's annual wine festival dinner. That's a new sort of venture for you, isn't it?"

"Yes, it is. I'm nervous about it...but kind of excited too. I never thought I'd be doing something like this. I mean, adding in the coffee shop to the bakery seemed like a big leap to me. Now I'm dipping my toe into catering and, really, I'm also considering making this some sort of partnership with Jason; at least the catering end. I never thought I'd do anything like that and it's happening so fast."

"What does Andy think about it?" Del knew that, due to his new job, Andy hadn't been able to be as helpful with Gwen's new bakery as he had been with the one in Blue River, and worried how Gwen felt about that.

"He's all for anything that makes me happy. I think he still feels a little guilty about bringing me here; since the move was due to his taking the job at the winery. And also since he's been so busy I barely see him lately."

"But you're happy about the move, aren't you?"

"Oh yes, very, but it has been a big change and then,

with the fire and all."

"But if you hadn't had the fire you probably wouldn't have hired Jason, right?"

"Funny how things work out sometimes, isn't it?"

So true, Del thought. If she hadn't found the clues to Micky's infidelity in his pockets while doing laundry she might still be married to him. She'd never have met Gwen and Claire. She wouldn't be working at St. Francis, she wouldn't have met Carl...and she wouldn't have fallen in love with Jimmy.

The chime that hung from the front door of the bakery shook her free from of her thoughts and drew their attention. Bob leaned halfway into the bakery as if hesitant to come all the way inside.

"Hello ladies," he said somewhat meekly. "I'm looking for Claire."

"Not here," Gwen said.

Del noticed the concerned look on Bob's face. "Everything okay?"

Bob stepped a little farther through the doorway, ran a hand through his hair, his eyes cast down as if looking for the answer to Gwen's question in the knots and cracks of the store's aged hardwood floors. "I don't know...I think I blew it." He looked back up at them. "I need to talk with her."

Gwen and Del shared a look of concern. Gwen walked over to Bob, took him by the arm and led him to an empty chair where Del joined them in the quiet of the post-lunchtime lull.

"What happened?" Del got right to the point.

"I should have told her sooner," Bob started in. "It's just that I wanted to protect her and, geez! I know how it looked. I get why she's pissed but...I mean, I love her." He looked to them both with imploring eyes that met their confused expressions.

"Start at the beginning," Gwen directed him and Bob laid out the facts regarding Terra and the details of his earlier encounter with Claire.

"Oh my," Del said at last. "Poor Claire must be very upset."

"Poor Claire must be very pissed," Gwen added.

"She is," Bob said. "But she has to understand that I was waiting for a time when it wouldn't be one more big thing for her to handle. I wanted to have her get to know Terra and, once they struck up a friendship and Claire was feeling more at ease with her new life here, then I thought I'd—"

"Spring it on her." Del understood how fragile her friend still was. Bob had been a rock for her to cling to as she found her own new footings. Now, she knew, that rock shook underneath her.

"Claire likes to be in control," Gwen added, "and this news, coming completely out of the blue must have made her feel even more out of control than ever."

"I know," Bob agreed. "I get that now. I should have realized it before and I know I blew it. But damn it!" Bob banged his fist against the arm of the chair, "I love her and I'm not going to lose her over this—misunderstanding!" He looked up at them with a clearly pained expression.

Gwen touched Bob's arm to calm him. "We understand what you intended," she said, nodding to Del who smiled and nodded back at him. "But knowing Claire, she thinks you deceived her."

"Which, yeah...I guess I did."

"Exactly. Give her a little time, Bob. And let us talk

to her."

"Yes," Del said, "she needs to talk it out and we can help her to see you only had the best of intentions."

"But from now on," Gwen looked him hard in the eyes, "no matter what, don't keep anything from Claire. She's an all-cards-on-the-table kind of gal."

They sent him off with a promise that they would keep an eye out for Claire, but it was barely half an hour later before the front door banged open, jarring the chimes and the peace of the store.

"What a crazy, shitty, amazing day I am having." Claire plopped her purse on the counter and adding, "What do you have that's alcoholic? I'll take cooking wine if I have to."

DEL WAS HAPPY TO TURN the reins of the counter over to Caroline, who had returned early from jury duty. So fifteen minutes later, the three women were huddled around a corner table at the Boathouse.

"You ladies gonna become my new regulars?" Nik asked, coming from behind the bar to take their orders. "What's it gonna be, late lunch or early dinner?"

"Wine. Red." Claire sat back in her chair, arms folded across her chest, her eyebrows lifted in a way that silently added *make it snappy* to her order.

"O-kay," Nik drew out the words as he took a step back. "You other ladies?"

"I'll have an iced tea," Gwen said, smiling kindly at him in an effort to lighten the dark mood Claire was casting.

"Me, too," Del added, "and how about some nachos

for..." she looked at Claire, "filler."

"You got it." He quickly retreated.

Finally alone Claire looked up at her friends. "I don't know where to begin."

"I do," Del said, "let's start with Terra being Bob's daughter."

"You know?" Claire shot an equally surprised and suspicious look at them both.

"Bob came looking for you at the bakery," Gwen said. "He told us everything and we completely agree that he should have told you right away."

"We understand *why* he didn't, sweetie. He had the best of intentions, you know. But we agree he blew it."

"*Did* he!" Claire leaned over to accept the wine glass Nik delivered with great haste before setting down the iced teas and retreating. Claire took a hearty sip from the glass, swallowed and sipped again. "It just makes me want to, to—"

"Leave?" Gwen asked hesitantly, afraid of the answer.

"That was my first instinct, I guess. You know this relationship stuff is new to me and, having been burned in the past I wasn't so sure I wanted to go there again. But Bob was so, well, so Bob."

Gwen noticed Claire couldn't help smiling in spite of her anger and hoped that was a good sign.

"He is a pretty nice guy." Del reached out to gently rub Claire's arm.

"Dammit, he is. I guess I'll have to forgive him... eventually."

"Eventually?" Gwen asked.

"Well, we can't let him set a precedent of deceiving me. Even for the best of reasons. A short period of atonement may be called for. There should be gifts as well." She laughed again and even smiled at Nik when he delivered the nachos. He smiled back, hesitantly.

"I am glad to hear you aren't leaving because of this," Gwen said.

"I can't leave anyway. Not now that it looks like I'm pretty much going to be a homeowner."

"*What?*" Gwen almost choked on her iced tea.

"You're buying a house?" Del asked excitedly.

"Not exactly." Claire explained the Larson sisters' plan.

"That's amazing. Isn't it?" Del looked to Gwen for confirmation.

"So, you've committed to it?" Gwen thought this was a good development in her friend's life, but worried it might be too much additional commitment, coming on the heels of the news about Terra.

"I told them I'd consider it. I told them not to get all excited."

"But they did, right?" Gwen could only imagine their enthusiasm at the prospect.

"They were like two bottles of champagne on the verge of popping."

"But, if you stay, what will you do? I mean, well, for a living? If you have to, that is." Del stammered.

"It's cool, kiddo. You can ask if I *have* to work. I've done pretty well over the years so I suppose if I didn't want to I could get by."

"And there's Bob... right?" Del asked.

"If you mean that someday, maybe, if Bob and I were, well..."

"Married?" Gwen smiled.

"Yeah, shit, he's just old-fashioned enough to

want to make it official; and probably the kind of guy who'd be more than happy to keep me in the lap of wine-country luxury."

"Or at least permanently stocked with cabernet." Gwen toasted Claire with her iced-tea and Claire took another generous sip of her wine.

"True, I doubt I'd have to worry about making a living but there's no way I'm sitting around eating bon-bons all day. I'd go nuts."

"You could do charitable work." Her friends knew Del's years as a volunteer had been the résumé that led to her current position heading up fund-raising for St. Francis Hospital's new pediatric wing.

"And I would never disparage volunteer work, sweetie, but I need something I can sink my teeth into. Something with more potential for, oh..."

"Profit?" Gwen asked. As much as Gwen loved to bake they both knew she'd struggled with the bot-tom-line over the years. She appreciated the satisfaction of financial rewards as well as personal.

"I do like a healthy paycheck. But I don't know that my heart is really in real estate anymore."

"There are so many things you could do, Claire," Gwen reached for her purse. "I've got a pad of paper in here. We can brainstorm and come up with some options."

"You might include in those options where Bob and I are going to live, if and when I do finally agree to co-habitate. We'll have two houses to choose from."

Nik stopped at the table, apparently drawn by Claire's improved demeanor. "You got everything you need, ladies?"

"I think so," Gwen said, looking at Claire. "You

want another glass of wine?"

"No, I think I'd better stay clear-headed. I have a feeling I'm going to be having a serious chat with Bob later. A statement like that used to make me gringe, but I think I'm actually looking forward to it. And I think I'll need to have a little talk with Terra at some point, too."

From outside, the slow, growing wail of a siren pierced the air. All three women knew it came from the fire station down the street, alerting the town's volunteer force that there was a call. Two men sprinted past the restaurant's front window, then another and another.

"Sorry, ladies, duty calls," Nik said, setting his tray and order pad on the bar. He pushed open the door to the kitchen and called out, "Hey Jerry! I'm heading out, can you take over here?"

A disembodied voice called back, "Will do!"

Nik winked at the women and did his own sprint out the door and down the street.

"I think it's kind of quaint that Grande Valley has volunteer fire fighters." Del nibbled on her nachos.

"They have a full-time force, too." Gwen reached for a chip. "But it's small. If they blow the siren that means they need additional help."

"I wonder what it is," Claire said just as Gwen's cell phone rang.

Gwen looked at the screen. "It's Andy. Hi, Honey," she said into the phone. "What's up? What? Oh..." Gwen looked at Claire as Andy answered her question. She knew she couldn't hide the concern washing across her face.

"What?" Claire looked back at her friend, their eyes

meeting. "Shit, what?"

Only a moment earlier Claire's world had been a hopeful one. Gwen knew it had been a long time since her friend had felt that way. A knot grew in her stomach as she realized she had to answer Claire and the answer might change everything.

GWEN INCHED HER CAR UP as far as she could, then pulled to the side of the road. The road had grown more congested as they neared the winery.

"We can park here and walk up to the winery, it's not far."

"Looks like a lot of folks have come out to see... what's happened." Del pointed at the growing crowd in the street ahead.

"Probably family members." Gwen caught Del's eye before looking over to Claire who sat silently in the front beside Gwen.

When Andy had called to tell Gwen about the accident, and that he was fine, he'd added that he hadn't been able to find Bob yet. Since then Claire had tried several times to call him, finally giving up after she'd been sent once again to his voicemail. She held her phone limply in her hand and gazed down the road, lost in her thoughts.

"Claire." Gwen rested her hand on Claire's arm. "We'll have to walk from here. It's not far. You ready?" she added, when Claire didn't move.

Finally, Claire took a long, ragged breath and turned

to her friends, her eyes brimming, the slightest quiver in her bottom lip. "What if—" She gasped before biting that lip to still it.

"Claire, darling," Del said, reaching out to take her friend's hand, her voice soft as if consoling a child. "We won't buy trouble today, trouble finds us whether we seek it or not so we'll be prepared, but for now, let's expect the best. Okay?"

Claire turned and looked at her friend, "Since when did you get so wise, kiddo?"

"Since I met you and Gwen."

"Thank you." Claire barely a whisper.

They all sat for a heartbeat or two before Claire finally opened the door. "Let's go."

They walked on either side of her, a phalanx of support as they approached the winery. The parking lot was filled with emergency vehicles. Firemen and police hurried about their tasks barely pausing to tell concerned onlookers that there was nothing to report yet. They just didn't know.

Beyond, it was clear what the source of the emergency was. A huge crane that Claire had seen earlier, preparing to lift the new grape press through a small hole in the roof and into its place in the winery had lost its footing and tipped over smashing into and through the roof.

Indeed, nearly half the roof was gone, replaced by a gaping hole where it had torn down one corner of the building. The crane itself must have snapped in two in the fall. The new press was lying on its side on the patio where she and Bob had stood earlier, their relationship falling apart around her as now the winery itself was.

Just a short time ago she'd been sitting with her friends, realizing how much she wanted that relationship, how much she wanted Bob. How much she wanted to tell him how she felt and get on with their future, whatever their future was, but now...

"Where is he? Do you see him?" Claire's voice choked.

"There's Andy!" Del said, and they turned to see Andy running toward them, his shoulders, wiry gold hair and boot tops spattered with a skim of fine dust.

Gwen wrapped her arms around her husband's neck and held him close, murmuring how glad she was that he was okay before releasing him so he could speak.

He pointed toward the roof, a bewildered look on his face. "The crane snapped just as it started to lower the press through the roof. No idea why, but it happened so fast we barely had time to get out." He held Gwen around the waist, giving her a slight hug against him as he caught his breath before looking at Claire.

"We were all in the there watching the progress, with Bob up front directing the action, as usual. All I remember is him yelling to get out and he shoved Terra, who was standing near him, into my arms. I grabbed her and ran. Jason joined us and the three of us got out just as the roof came down."

"Where are they?" Del asked.

"With the paramedics; they're okay but something hit Jason's shoulder. It's bloody but they say it's not serious. They're patching him up before they run him down to the emergency room just to be sure."

"And Bob?" Claire looked toward the building, afraid of the answer.

Andy released Gwen and walked over to Claire,

reaching out to gently touch her shoulder as she pulled her attention from the wrecked building to meet his eyes.

"We don't know, Claire. There's a lot of debris the firefighters have to dig through just to get in there. But they'll find him, I know they will. Bob knows this building inside out so if there was any way to take cover I'm sure he did. They just have to get to him. But it could take a while."

"I just wish we knew more." Claire said, weakly. "Isn't there anyone in charge we can talk with?"

"Hang on." Andy sprinted away, coming back a few minutes later with a firefighter in tow.

Claire recognized him from the Larson sister's fire. His rugged face was smudged with dust and rivulets of sweat under the large brimmed helmet bearing the words *Chief* across its brim. His mouth, beneath a mustache the color of straw, was set in a grim line.

"This is the Fire Chief," Andy said as they approached the women.

"Chief O'Brian, ladies." He nodded his head toward the small group. Then seeing Claire, he added, "I'm thinking I've seen you too much lately, ma'am?"

"Claire." She reached out to shake his hand. Bob is my—" she paused, unable to fill in the rest of the sentence.

"He's her *Significant Other*." Del squeezed her other hand.

"What?" Claire looked at Del.

"Well he is, whether you're mad at him or not you know he's *significant*. And that's what they call it now."

"I—I..." Again, words failed Claire.

"Why don't we just call him Bob, for now," Gwen

interjected. "Any progress, Chief?"

"We have a pretty good idea of where they might be. We're missing two men, if you weren't aware."

"Oh, no." Gwen looked to Andy, wondering who else could be trapped in there but before she could ask the radio strapped the chief's shoulder crackled and he turned away to answer the voice on the other end before turning back to the group.

"I need to go, but don't get ahead of yourself with worry, Claire. We've got a good team and we are doing our best to find your... *Significant Other.*"

He paused and smiled at Del, who smiled back and may have actually blushed.

"I will update you as soon as we know more. It's hard, I know. But try to hang in there."

"Thank you."

"Sweetie." Gwen reached for Claire's hand. "Why don't we find someplace to wait and get out of the way of these guys?" Gwen nodded to a group of firemen who were breaking out axes and picks from a compartment on the side of a truck. One of them looked over at their group and Gwen recognized Nik, their server at the restaurant, now head-to- toe in his gear.

"Didn't think I'd run into you ladies here." Nik grabbed an ax before walking quickly over to them. "You know someone who works here?"

"Several someones." Del greeted Nik halfway to protect a little bubble of privacy for Claire. "Is it bad in there?" She asked almost in a whisper?

Nik glanced over Del's shoulder towards where Claire stood, a dazed expression on her face, and must have realized that his words were better shared just with Del. "It's a mess, I won't lie to you. But that doesn't mean there aren't survivors."

Del nodded, her hands fisted against her chest as she processed what might be.

"Hey." Nik rested a heavily gloved hand over her fists. "You'd be surprised the things people can survive. I'm not saying they always do, but I wouldn't write anyone off just yet. Who's she looking for?" He nodded toward Claire.

"Bob. He's the owner. Sounds like he pushed everyone out ahead of him."

"And they all made it, huh? He's a hero, that's for sure. We'll do everything we can to save him."

"Let's go Nik!" A voice called as the crew started running toward the building.

"Gotta go!"

"Stay safe."

"I always try."

ANDY LED THEM TO THE ambulance where Jason sat on a makeshift gurney, being treated by a paramedic. Terra sat beside him, worry clearly consuming her. She looked back and forth from the collapsed structure to where the paramedic was applying gauze and bandages to Jason's bloody shoulder.

Claire stared at the blood, then looked slowly over toward the building and considered all the possibilities the scene before her held to change her life for better or worse. "Oh God..." she breathed.

All the energy drained from her body and she thought she'd collapse but, thankfully, Gwen chose that moment to wrap an arm around her friend's waist.

"Why don't you sit down." Gwen eased her toward a spot beside Terra. "How are you?" she asked Jason.

"I'll live." He glanced at Claire. "I mean, I'm cool, just a scratch."

"And you?" Gwen asked Terra.

"I'm okay, but..." She glanced at Claire. "I don't know where my—Bob is."

"It's okay, sweetie," Del said, "we all know he's your dad. Where did you see him last?"

"We were inside, watching the crane lower the new press and there was this loud bang."

"I think a cable or something snapped on the crane." Jason watched the paramedic tape off the edges of the gauze.

"One second everything was fine and Dad, Bob, was joking around with Tim, the rep from the equipment company. He's a young guy and he was telling us about stopping at one of the local pot shops, since it's legal in Colorado, and Dad was ribbing him that it would be better for his business if he bought a bottle of wine instead."

"One second everybody was laughing," Jason said, "the next the building was falling down around us."

"Dad shoved me toward Jason and Andy and we all ran for the door. I thought he was right behind us but then when I looked back..."

Jason reached for her hand, lacing his fingers through hers. Their eyes met and she tipped her head against his free shoulder, tears slipping quietly from the corners of her eyes and sliding down each cheek in slow streams.

"The door was just gone. It was crazy, man. Never seen anything like it. We called and called for Bob and

Tim, we picked around in the rubble but the deeper in we went, things would move—we didn't want to make it worse." Jason glanced at Terra. "Then the firemen arrived and here we are."

"They say it's possible they're trapped in some kind of space or pocket, that they're okay," Terra's voice cracked.

Claire watched the girl whose very existence only hours earlier had torn her world apart. Now they shared a common bond, a common worry and any anger she'd held was washed away by Terra's tears. She reached out and swept away a lose strand of Terra's hair that fell across her face.

"Don't you worry," Claire said, finding the inner strength that only minutes before had eluded her. "Your dad can be a pretty tough S.O.B. when he wants to be. I know he's alive, I don't know how but I just do, if that makes any sense."

"Me, too," Terra whispered. "I feel that way too, but I worry maybe, you know, it's just me. I can't imagine finally finding my dad and then, well, I can't imagine he's not...alive."

"I know." Claire sat quietly beside Terra as the paramedic finished up with Jason's shoulder. She was so busy watching the firemen and taking in the entire scene, so busy trying to will Bob alive that she didn't notice her cell phone ringing in her jacket pocket.

"Sweetie, I think your phone is ringing," Del said. "Do you want me to answer it for you?"

"No...just let it go to voicemail, it's just—" That's when Claire came out of her fog and realized whose personalized ring tone her phone was chiming. "Bob!" she yelled and tore her phone from her pocket, swiping the screen to answer the call. "Bob, is that you? Are you okay?" She heard breathing and hit the speaker so they all could hear.

"I'm here, babe" Bob said, his voice weak.

"Dad?" Terra said, sitting up and yelling into Claire's phone. "Where are you?"

"Terra...okay? Everyone else?"

"Hey, boss," Andy said, leaning toward the phone while waving toward the firemen as Del ran to get someone.

"We got Jason and Terra out and everyone else is accounted for except you and Tim. Do you know where you are?"

"I think I'm under one of the fermenters. I can feel the flat bottom above me but it's dark. I-I don't remember getting here. I don't remember...much, might have been out...my head's killing me and—" he paused, coughing, then a moan followed by a long moment of breathing and, "Did the roof fall in? What happened? Is-is everyone okay? Terra?"

Claire looked at Terra and they all paused a moment, realizing Bob might not have been as lucid as he sounded.

"Yeah, Terra's fine, Bob," Andy said. "Looks like the crane lost its footing and tipped, snapping the arm, took out a lot of the roof and wall. Where are you? Do you see Tim?"

Claire held her breath waiting for Bob's answer but all they heard was breathing, then nothing for a moment, then a scrape as if metal were moving against concrete.

"Here! Listen!" Del yelled as she ran over to them, pulling Nik along.

"What?" Nik asked.

"It's Bob," Jason said, gesturing toward the phone.

Nik reached for the phone. "Bob? Can you hear me? This is one of the firefighters. We're trying to reach you but we need your help. Can you describe your location? Can you make some noise without moving anything?"

Nik walked quickly away, phone in hand, continuing to talk with Bob while waving at his crew.

Claire watched Nik leave with her phone, relieved that there was hope, relieved to hear Bob's voice but also realizing she hadn't said what was important before the phone was gone. She realized she hadn't told Bob she loved him.

The paramedic was packing up and looked over at Jason. "Why don't we get you to the hospital? I think you ought to have a doc check you out, just to be sure."

Jason shook his head then and looked at Terra. "No thanks man, I'm staying right here until we know for sure what's up in there."

"Just promise me you'll stop by the hospital later, okay?"

"Something tells me we'll all be at the hospital later." Jason glanced at Terra and Claire.

"I'll make sure he sees someone before the day is out," Terra said. "I promise."

"Good enough by me. Now, we've got another ambulance on route, but if you'll excuse me, I'm gonna help my partner get some things ready. I'm real hopeful I'll have passengers soon and I want to get a move-on, a-sap. You," he added, looking at Jason, "stay put here. I don't want you walking around unless and until you're up to it."

With that he disappeared inside the vehicle leaving the friends sitting in silence as the minutes ticked by.

Suddenly, shouts erupted from within the collapsed structure and a moment later the paramedic and his partner jumped out, a large gear box in hand and chatter coming from a walkie-talkie strapped to his shoulder. "Sounds like they found somebody." He sprinted toward the building.

"Thank God." Del said.

Claire stood, taking a few steps forward, then stopped.

Del reached for her hand. "I remember, when I was little and my Aunt Kay was very ill, Father Condon, our pastor, came by the hospital to comfort the family. Everyone felt so helpless. It was one of those wait-and-see kind of things. Father said when all else fails put it in the Lord's hands. That's probably advice I should remember more often."

"You mean...instead of late night texting your friends?" Claire smiled weakly.

"Maybe I could do both." Del squeezed Claire's hand. "But, in the meantime, what do you think about...saying a prayer?"

Gwen joined them and took Claire's other hand. "Good idea," she said. The three friends stood, hand-in-hand, heads tipped as Del spoke.

"Lord, I know you've got a lot on your plate, but we could really use your help here today. We ask you to be with Bob and Tim, and with the firefighters as they work to rescue them. We ask for your grace...and your mercy. Please bless them and all of those who wait here beside us. Amen."

"Amen," Gwen and Claire said together, and heard

it echoed behind them by Andy, Terra and Jason.

"That's all we can do for now," Gwen said. "Now we wait."

Later, Claire couldn't have said how long they waited. Time seemed frozen one second, speeding the next, then at last they heard shouts and, finally, Tim was carried out on a rolling gurney, unconscious. They all cleared the way to the ambulance and watched as the paramedics attended him. Another ambulance pulled up several feet away, waiting for its occupant to be rescued.

"He's alive," Nik yelled over at them when he saw their silent concern. "Bob's alive too. He'll be coming out next."

"How—" Claire started to ask but found her voice choked off with worry.

"How are they?" Gwen asked for her.

"Both of 'em are pretty beat up. But they're alive."

Claire felt the vise of worry and dread release some of its pressure.

"It's a start," Gwen said quietly.

"He'll be okay." Claire turned toward where Terra sat beside Jason, "He'll be okay."

Terra nodded back, trying for a smile though barely succeeding.

When, at last, they carried Bob from the rubble, Claire reached for Terra's hand and together they walked tentatively toward the other ambulance. From outside they could see Bob's eyes were barely open above an oxygen mask and the women stood back, not wanting to interfere with all the activity around him as he was hooked up to an IV and his vitals assessed. Bob's neck was immobilized with a brace and his body, covered in dust and small bits of debris, lay still.

A female paramedic looked out at them as she tore open packets and strung tubing in the process. "Any family here?"

"Me!" Terra called anxiously. "I'm his daughter. And this is his..."

"Significant Other." Del winked at Claire.

"You okay with that?" Terra smiled meekly at Claire, lowering her voice so only she could hear. "I know Bob will want you with him and I figure well, you know, if you're official they have to, like, include you, you know?"

"I'm feeling pretty insignificant right now, but whatever works." Claire just wanted to be with Bob. She looked up at the paramedic. "Can we see him? Can we ride with him?"

"He's holding his own for now. It's cramped quarters in here right now, ma'am, but we're transporting him to Valley General momentarily. You two can follow us there–just don't try to keep up. Wouldn't want another call to come get you, understood?"

"Sure." Terra said. "Want to come with me, Claire?" Terra looked over her shoulder toward Jason. "You come too, babe. They can check you out. I don't want two people I—" she paused and looked shyly at Claire, then, moving to join Jason. "Well, I want to be sure you're okay, you know?"

Claire looked away, smiling to herself as she realized that her potential new boy-toy had found an extremely age-appropriate love interest. Her smile faded though when she looked up at Bob and felt an almost overwhelming anxiety for his well-being. Bob had to be okay. She couldn't occupy a world where he wasn't and no matter what, she'd do everything in her power to be sure he was.

"I'm gonna get my car keys. Luckily I stowed my purse under the bar in the tasting room and it's on the other side of the building. I'll be right back for you both."

Terra ran off and Claire looked up at the paramedic. "Sounds like we'll be right behind you." She frowned down at her. "Or as behind as we can be and obey the speed limit."

"Sounds good." She returned her attention to her patient.

Claire watched, her eyes resting on Bob's hand, lying limply along the edge of the stretcher.

"Can I talk to him?" she asked. "Before you leave, I mean, if there's time?"

"Just," the woman said, stowing gear in a side cabinet. She reached out to give Claire a lift up beside her. "But only a moment, okay?"

"Yes. Thank you."

Claire stooped beside Bob. His eyes were closed and she could see where blood clung to his hair and had pooled at the base of his neck. His face and nose were covered with an oxygen mask and Claire knew that was a good sign. He was breathing on his own, thank God. One pant leg was torn, and Claire saw they'd immobilized and bandaged the leg. Something was wrong there though she couldn't tell anything more from a glance.

"Ace?" Bob's voice was weak and his eyes shut.

"I'm here, Bob," she whispered close to his face, running her fingers lightly along his cheek.

"I know...I smelled your...perfume." His eyes remained shut but a smile inched along his lips.

"Terra and I are following you over, honey. We'll be right behind you, I promise." She leaned in and softly kissed his temple and whispered, "I love you."

"Don't have to tell me—" he paused for a long breath, "—what I already know." Then an alarm rang out behind her.

"Vitals are dropping!" the paramedic yelled, "hop out ma'am, we're rolling!"

Stunned, Claire jumped out and watched, speechless, as the doors slammed shut, sirens wailed and the ambulance pulled away, quickly gaining speed once it exited the parking lot.

Gwen and Del were instantly beside her but her strength was gone and she crumpled, unable to hold back the fear and grief she'd fought against for so long on so many fronts. Bob wasn't just a *front*, he was her life.

Twenty-Three

CLAIRE HAD SPENT WAY TOO much time in hospitals over the last year. First her own recovery after the attack in Blue River, then the Larson sisters and now Bob. She'd had too many long days and longer nights, too much bland hospital food and stale coffee, too many out-dated magazines and far too many anxious minutes dragging into hours of dread and worry. The waiting, whether for herself or for others, was the worst. And now she sat in the sterile confines of yet another generically appointed hospital space, waiting for news about Bob.

Terra was on a beige couch across from her, busily texting to God-knew-who. Jason had already seen a doctor and been pronounced fine though bruised and banged up. They'd given him something for the discomfort, which he'd taken before laying his weary self down along the couch beside Terra, resting his head in her lap. Claire could hear his soft and steady breathing, in and out, in and out, as he slept.

Gwen sat beside her, reading a dog-eared copy of a home and garden magazine that, Claire thought, had gone out of business over a year ago. Del had stepped out to take a call from her office.

Terra's taps on her screen, Jason's breathing, the flip of pages of Gwen's magazine and a somewhat obnoxious smooth-jazz rendition of Stairway to Heaven that was softly wafting in via some unseen speakers were the only sounds in the otherwise silent room.

Claire clenched and unclenched her hands, took deep breaths and counted the tiles across the floor. Anything to pass the time and push away the suffocating image of Bob's bloodied body on the stretcher, entangled in tubes and poked with needles.

The doctor had met with her and Terra before surgery, explaining to them that he'd clearly taken a hard hit to the head, leaving a nasty gash and undoubtedly a concussion. But by far the most serious injury was a fracture to his femoral shaft. Apparently Bob's legs hadn't made it under the fermenter and the firefighters had had to dig them out from under debris—including a steel beam—before they could get to him. That beam had landed on his upper leg leaving him immobilized and in great pain. That, combined with the concussion, had most likely caused him to lose consciousness for a while.

They'd found Tim, crammed in where Bob had shoved him before diving in after him. Tim's shoulder had taken a beating but he was otherwise in pretty good shape. It was Tim who had nudged and nudged at Bob, waking him up and encouraging him to reach for his ringing phone despite the pain. He'd finally managed to dig it out of his pants pocket and hit the speed dial to return Claire's multiple calls.

About damn time, Claire had thought when told the story, remembering the flood of relief combined with fear when she'd heard his ringtone on her cell.

Claire jumped at the click and whoosh as the door opened, revealing Bob's surgeon and, behind him, the hallway leading to the surgical suites. Dr. Jenware was tall and fit for his forty-some years. His expression was somber, giving Claire pause as she nervously stood to greet him. He was balding on top, and she couldn't help a little smile at the sight of his neon green clogs beneath his pale blue scrubs. She'd heard he was one of the best orthopedic surgeons in the west so she'd expected more of a curmudgeon and somehow those clogs told her this was a man she could talk with, rather than be lectured by.

"How'd he do?" she asked, as she met him halfway.

"Pretty well. That beam did a job on his femur, but we put him back together and, with time and barring complications, he should be just fine."

"He'll be okay?" Del walked into the room.

"Looks that way." Gwen stood beside Claire.

Terra jumped from the couch, smiling, and gave Claire a hug before she even knew what hit her. "He's gonna be okay!" she said brightly to Jason who sat up on the couch, clearly still in a groggy semi-conscious, pain killer induced state.

"That's great, babe." His eyes fluttered briefly open before he crossed his arms and slumped back into dreamland.

"Can we see him?" Terra asked.

"What sort of complications?" Claire asked, cutting right to the point of the doctor's comments.

"With any surgery we naturally have to be alert to anything from infection to blood clots. He made a mess of that bone, and he's patched together with plates and pins."

Claire saw the pale expression on Terra's face and wrapped her arm tightly around her shoulder. "So what you're saying is we shouldn't expect he's going to be back on his feet tomorrow."

"We'll probably have him up and about pretty quickly, with crutches of course. But total recovery is going to take a few months, and he'll need therapy to keep his muscles strong and get his strength back in the leg. Plus he took a nasty hit to the head. He's got a concussion so we're going to want to keep an eye on him. I want him in the hospital for a few days but once he goes home, I'd prefer he not be alone, at least in the early stages. Does he...live with anyone?"

The doctor looked from Claire to Terra, clearly unsure of exactly what his patient's personal living arrangements might be.

"I'll stay with him," Claire said. "That's not a problem."

"I'll help," Terra added.

"We'll all help," Gwen said, and Del nodded agreement.

Despite the difficulties of the moment, Claire felt her tensions ease and even managed a small smile. "So, Doc, can we see him?"

"Sure," he said, looking from Claire to Terra. "He's in recovery and not conscious yet and likely won't be for a while. And even when he is, he's got some great meds coursing through his veins so don't expect him to be too talkative. But you two ladies can come with me, if you like. You can sit with him until they're ready to take him up to a room. How's that sound?"

Claire gave Terra's shoulder a squeeze. "Sounds perfect."

GWEN AND DEL VOLUNTEERED TO take Jason home on the way back to Gwen's house. The two women left him curled up in a deep sleep in his own bed. By the time they sat at Gwen's kitchen table nursing hot cups of tea, it was well past midnight.

"Sure you don't want a glass of wine?" Gwen wondered if the day's events called for something stronger .

"No, this is good. I'm feeling kind of empty after the day we've all had. Tea is more comforting right now."

"Sounds good to me. Andy sent me a text a little while ago that he'd be home soon. He's had a long day and night trying to get the winery harvest-ready despite all the destruction."

"It's been a long day all around." Del added cream and sugar to her cup. "I thought Claire really stepped up and put her feelings for Terra aside tonight."

"I have a feeling it's more than that."

"That would be nice; for Terra and Bob."

"And for Claire. Terra has been a big stumbling block for her."

"This morning I would have said that Terra would be the end of Claire and Bob."

"This morning I would have said Claire was prepared to use her as an excuse to put an end to her relationship with Bob—and Grande Valley." Gwen didn't add how anxious she'd been that she would. She'd grown accustomed to Claire's proximity and hated the idea of losing her closest friend in the valley.

"Why would she do that?"

"She's afraid. It's odd but now that I think about it, this whole summer has been about Claire getting over being afraid. She was afraid for her safety and her health after the attack."

"And afraid to go back to real estate but afraid to do anything else."

"And afraid to commit to Bob even though—"

"He's the sweetest guy!"

"He is the sweetest guy. Well, after Andy, of course."

"Of course."

Gwen glanced outside, wondering how much longer before Andy came home. The day's events had left her with a desire to just be near him, see him across from her, know she could reach out and touch him at any moment. Funny, she thought, how it took a near tragedy to remind her how grateful she was for him. How much she loved him. She realized Claire was experiencing similar feelings, maybe for the first time in her life.

"Bob's been so committed to Claire despite her misgivings." Gwen held her cup in her hands, comforted by the warmth of the china against her skin. "I don't think she's ever had anyone like that in her life. It should have been wonderful and I think it was at first. But the longer it went on the more serious she knew Bob was. That had to be scary for someone like Claire."

"It was hard for her to get used to the idea of having friends when we all first met, remember? I think that was scary for her, too. But she got over it and look, now she has two awesome best friends."

"She does. We are awesome, aren't we?" Gwen agreed, laughing with Del.

"We are. So she should look at how well that friendship stuff worked out and have a little faith in Bob."

"It's easy to say but not always easy to do."

The two women sat in silence for a while. Del cradled the cup in her hands. Gwen noticed her friend's silence.

"I'd say a penny for your thoughts but I've got some day-old cookies from the bakery; how about those instead of pennies?"

"Sure." Del set her cup down. "My thoughts may not be worth day-old pastry or even pennies. I'm feeling, well...it's silly."

"Silly how?" Gwen opened a bakery box between them revealing a dozen small, sugar-sprinkled cookies.

"Here I am saying Claire shouldn't be afraid but then, well, here I am hiding out in Grande Valley because I'm afraid to face Carl."

"And Jimmy?"

"Yeah, him too. Maybe even more."

"You know you are always welcome to visit, even if you're hiding out." Gwen handed a cookie to Del. "Have some sugar therapy."

"My favorite kind of therapy. Sigmund Freud would have gotten a lot further with his female patients if he'd offered them tea and cookies, don't you think?"

"Definitely."

"Gwen, I don't really know how I feel about Carl or Jimmy, but I do have to stop hiding from them. That much I've figure out."

"Does that mean you're heading home?"

"I think so. But not tomorrow, I want to stay one more day just to be sure Bob is out of the woods and Claire is okay."

"Sounds like a good plan to me."

Car lights swept along the side of the house, and Andy's car pulled into the garage out back. Gwen felt the release of built up tension between her shoulders. She hadn't even realized it was there, but it felt easier to breathe now, as well. She stood and flipped on the outdoor light and opened the screen door.

"Hi, honey." She said as he stepped inside, clearly beat after a very long day. He gave her a kiss, holding it a heartbeat longer than usual before he noticed Del sitting at the table. "You girls solve the worries of the world?"

"We wish," Gwen said.

"First we have to solve our own problems, I guess," Del added.

"Well, I've got another one for you, if you can handle it."

"Oh, no. Now what?" Gwen returned to her seat and patted the chair next to her.

Andy sat beside Gwen, resting his arms on the table, hands clasped. He sagged as if steam had been released from inside him.

"I've got a contractor coming in the morning but I've been going over the space with the Fire Chief and an insurance adjuster. Half the warehouse is either completely totaled or, at the least, in for a major overhaul. It's gonna be a while before we are completely back up and running and it couldn't come at a worse time, with harvest in full swing."

"Oh, Andy, we've been so worried about Bob we didn't think about the winery. And how's Tim? We heard he was in surgery too, but nothing else."

"I stopped by the hospital on the way home. Tim's

gonna be fine. His wife is there and they had to patch up his shoulder. He'll probably be heading home in a day or two. They're newly-weds, you know."

"How sweet," Del said. "And thank goodness he's alright. Imagine finding someone only to lose them so soon."

"Probably kind of how Claire was feeling; and Terra too, for that matter. Did you stop in and check on Bob?" Gwen rested her hand on top of Andy's, grateful that she could, grateful that he wasn't in the hospital too. Or worse.

"Yep, they've got him all settled in his room. Terra was just leaving to go check on Jason."

"We left him sound asleep in bed and he's probably still there," Gwen said. "Whatever they gave him for pain knocked him out."

"I didn't realize Terra and Jason were so...you know." Del reached for another cookie.

"Hey, I'll take one of those." Andy picked a couple cookies from the pastry box.

"Honey, I didn't think. Are you hungry? Want me to make you a sandwich? Want a cup of tea?"

"A sandwich would be great, but I could sure use a beer."

"I'll grab you a bottle." Gwen stood and planted a kiss on top of his head. "So, what were we talking about?"

"Terra and Jason," Del said. "What's going on there?"

"I know." Gwen placed a chilled glass in front of a grateful Andy and set a bottle from a local microbrew beside it. "I think they've been spending a lot of time together working on the festival dinner for the winery.

And I saw them together a couple of times when it seemed like more than business."

"Too bad Claire didn't notice that, she might have reconsidered her worries about Bob and Terra."

"Worries about Bob and Terra? His daughter?" Andy asked.

"You knew?" Gwen stopped and stared at him. "And you didn't say anything?"

"Bob only just told me yesterday—he asked me not to say anything, honey. He knows how close you gals are and you'd be tempted to say something."

Andy looked at Gwen, who only scowled as she put mayonnaise on bread and plopped thick slices of chicken breast on top.

"He was looking for the right time to tell Claire but he wanted me to understand why he was giving so much responsibility to a fairly inexperienced young girl. He'd noticed some of the employees were giving him looks and he wasn't too worried about them, but he didn't want to lose my, well, I guess respect is the best way to put it.

"A lot of those younger guys around the winery would probably envy this old guy with a cute thing like Terra, but Bob knew I wasn't one of them. Claire is friends with my wife. Hey, she's friends with me, so he didn't want me to think less of him."

"Were you shocked?" Del asked.

"Kinda, but hey, I get how that sort of thing could happen to a guy with a past. He is making it right with her and she's a bright kid, hard worker too."

Gwen set Andy's sandwich slowly in front of him as she sat beside him, "So, what I'm hearing is that you knew Terra was Bob's daughter but you never said anything to me. I know we've both been busy, but that's a big secret to keep, and I thought we didn't keep secrets from each other."

"Sweetie, I'm sorry." He wrapped his hand in hers and lifted it to his lips, gently kissing the back of it. "I hated having a secret from you and in my defense, he only told me yesterday…which still seems like today. I guess something happened with Claire that made him put it all together—the impression he might be giving others, I mean. I was planning on asking Bob if it was okay to tell you. I figured he'd be telling Claire soon, anyway." He kissed her hand again and, his lips still against her skin, murmured, "Forgive me?"

Gwen fought her smile. She wanted to be hurt, but in truth, she knew her husband too well. He valued honesty as much as she did and she could only imagine how much being asked to keep a secret like this one had bothered him. She actually felt sorry for him. "Yes, but don't do it again. Now, eat your sandwich."

"Thanks, honey."

"So, it looks like your new catering business has brought together a couple of love-birds, Gwen," Del said. "That's probably a good sign that Jason isn't leaving town anytime soon."

"Well, not at least before his contract is up. But I think I'll definitely be accommodating if he wants extra time to pow-wow with Terra about the dinner."

"Oh, shit." Andy put down his sandwich and reached for his beer, taking a swig as he swallowed.

"What?" both women said together.

"I completely forgot about the dinner, babe. I've been so busy worrying about getting the building fixed and what we're gonna do about harvest. We didn't lose everything so we can still handle a lot of it, and we've been hearing all night from other wineries that are willing to pitch in and give us some space for our grapes. We'll figure it out. But we don't have a place to host the dinner anymore. I mean, it was supposed to be inside *that* space, with tables set up all around the tanks."

"Could you do it outside?" Del asked.

"That's always an option." Gwen reached for Andy's beer and took a sip for herself.

"I've seen lots of pictures of pretty tables set up under the stars at the California vineyards. It's very charming. Why couldn't you do that here?"

"We could, but this is Colorado, not California" Andy retrieved his beer and took a sip of his own. "The odds of a chilly or even wet evening in late September are more likely here. Hell, it could snow. We'd need a tent, at least. Just in case. And even if that worked, it's gonna be a construction site out there for a while. I'm not sure how charming that would be."

"I hadn't thought about that," Gwen said.

"Well, if Terra hasn't thought of it by now I'm sure she will by morning. Poor kid's had a lot more serious stuff to worry about than festival dinners. I'll talk with her about it in the morning." Andy took the last bite of his sandwich and then downed the rest of his beer. "I'm calling it a night, ladies. Gonna be an early morning and I need some shut-eye."

"Guess we'd better call it a night too." Del took her tea cup to the sink. "We should get over to the hospital early, in case Claire needs us."

"Good idea," Gwen said. "Shoot."

"What?"

"I just realized my baker is probably not going to be in any condition to work tomorrow. I'm sorry Del, but I'll have to go in early and get everything ready to open. I can come by the hospital later, after the morning rush."

"No problem, sweetie, I can handle it."

DEL LAY IN HER BED but sleep eluded her. She watched the night sky through the gabled window, stars bright against their dark pallet. A small town like Grande Valley didn't put out enough light pollution to compete with the Milky Way.

She remembered an evening months earlier when she'd braved the bitter cold of a winter night to sneak an elicit cigarette and contemplate where life had brought her. That night she'd watched the starry sky, hoping for a sign. And in fact, she'd found one then, but tonight?

Despite her cozy perch in Gwen's attic room, despite the knowledge, thanks to a late night phone chat with her kids, that all she loved and counted dear was safe and sound and tucked into their own beds at their dad's home, tonight she still felt a restless anticipation. It wasn't so much that she expected anything in particular, only that she felt if there was anything worth anticipating in her future the only way she was going to find out was by taking control of the situation. But that new found self-knowledge was keeping her up.

Something buzzed and she realized the phone Carl had given her was turned on in her suitcase. She zipped open the side and pulled it out. He was calling. She let it ring. It had been a long day and she wasn't sure there was enough room left in it for Carl.

She remembered a time when a day like this would have led to a late night conversation with Jimmy. He'd been so good at helping her sort out her feelings, or simply listening. Jimmy was a good listener. She'd become the listener in her relationship with Carl.

Carl was the talker, the do-er. If there was a problem he took charge to fix it. Like the phone that had stopped buzzing. It was Carl's solution to their communication problem, but did it fix the right thing, she wondered. The display told her it was the fourth time he'd called. There was one message. She hit the voice-mail button and listened.

"Hey Delly, Carl here. Well, I guess you know it's me since I'm the only one who has the number to this satellite phone I gave you. Thought it would make a great little hot line for us to have, you…you know, late night chats when I'm on the other side of the world," his voice grew deeper and lower when he said *late night. "But, I don't seem to be able to get a hold of you. I called earlier and didn't reach you."* Del thought he seemed a little downhearted but he quickly recovered.

"Call me."

With that he hung up, no added *miss you* or *wish you were here.* Del noted that the message had been left early that morning; probably while she was showering. Two more calls came shortly after that and nothing more until now. He had probably been in meetings all day and into the night. She expected there would be another call in the morning and left the phone out, beside her phone on the nightstand, plugging it in to recharge.

Her phone; Carl had given her this phone to be her own, but in reality, it was Carl's and it represented Carl's claim on her, or at least his attempts to claim her. She noted he hadn't tried to call her own phone and wondered why not.

Ping!

Del jumped at the sudden sound of a text coming over her phone. It was Claire.

r u planning to stop by hospital in morning?

Del tapped in her answer.

Of course. How is he? How are you?
Bob's good, sleeping. I'm beat. Can u pick up some stuff at my house?
Yes!! What do you need?

Claire typed in a short list of items along with their locations. Del pulled a note pad out of her purse and started scribbling down the list. Halfway through she realized the list wasn't going anywhere—it was on her phone; she could easily pull it up in the morning and didn't need to transcribe it on paper.

Ping!

Del picked up her phone and read Claire's text.

u r writing that down aren't u?
yes...
lol!
I know, I'm a dork when it comes to technology!
but a lovable one. Thx kiddo!
u'r welcome
nice try, see u in the morning
:)
;)

Twenty-Four

*D*EL SAT IN HER CAR *waiting for the kids to get out of school. She was picking Cara up today instead of letting her take the bus. Cara, who had just turned eleven, was starting a new jazz tap class soon and needed new tap shoes so Del had promised to take her shopping right after school.*

Nate was going home with a friend to work on a science project. She couldn't believe he was almost thirteen and high school was coming on fast.

How had her babies grown up so quickly? Only a few more years and Nate would be off to college with Cara not far behind. What would she do when her children weren't there every morning? She loved her job, but her kids made her feel like she mattered.

If she disappeared tomorrow the hospital would fill her time soon enough. But children needed their mother...until they grew up. Then they became independent. Of course they'd still be close, but it wouldn't be the same. Who would care if she didn't get up in the morning? Who would notice if she wasn't quite herself?

That's what empty nesting was about, being all alone in the nest. Married couples had partners, but she didn't... anymore.

The school bell rang and she watched, but children didn't come out. The bell kept ringing and she wondered why nothing was happening. She looked around and then she looked at her purse and realized it wasn't the school bell, it was her phone.

Del's eyes flew open as she instantly realized it wasn't a dream, it was Carl calling. She jumped out of bed and grabbed the phone just as the ringing stopped. The phone sat silently in her hand as the seconds passed... ping...a message.

Delly, I'm starting to wonder if you are avoiding me. Or maybe you lost your phone. I'm heading out for a breakfast meeting. If I don't hear from you I'll try you later.

There was a pause and then:

Miss you.

Del felt guilty. Honestly, she didn't miss him. Had she given Carl a real chance or had her lingering feelings for Jimmy gotten in the way? Was that fair to Carl? Was it fair to her? She'd never know if she didn't try so Del decided to at least give it some effort and started to text.

Sorry I missed your call. I was in the shower. I'll look forward to hearing from you after your meeting.

She tapped send and waited to see if he wrote back. A full minute passed before she put down the phone and actually got in the shower. She'd tried, and she wouldn't miss his call the next time. At least, she wouldn't *try* to miss it.

DEL TAPPED ON THE DOOR to Bob's room and slowly pushed it open. "Hello?"

"Hey, there." Claire jumped up from a chair by the window to greet her. "Thank you so much for bringing this stuff." She took the bag Del offer. "You're a life saver, I'm dying to take a shower and change clothes."

"No problem." Del noticed the empty bed. "Where's Bob?"

"Oh, they took him for some X-rays, or CAT scan or something, just to be sure everything is good, which I'm sure it is. You just missed him."

"How's he doing?"

"Really well. He's a little out of it with pain killers but the doc says he should be able to get off of the strongest of those before he goes home."

"How long till he can?"

"Not long, a few days at the most."

"That's fast."

"Tell me about it." Claire dug through the bag and pulled out a make-up case. "Hey, if you can wait a few minutes for me freshen up do you wanna join me for coffee in the cafeteria? I hear they have a killer cinnamon roll."

Del agreed and soon the two friends were sipping lattes as they shared one very oversized cinnamon roll.

"These are huge." Del pulled off another chunk.

"I know, and they're really good. Don't tell Gwen."

"Oh, I doubt the hospital is competition for the bakery."

"I wouldn't count on it. One of the nurses told me their bakery here churns out hundreds of these every week, in addition to what they make for the hospital, just to fill special orders for meetings, parties and other events outside of the hospital. Can you believe it?"

"Ah cn," Del said around a mouthful of cinnamon

roll.

"Apparently they're a real money maker. And profits from the sales go to the pediatrics wing."

Del swallowed and took a long sip of her coffee. "What a great idea. But that's a lot of roll for one person."

"One female person, you mean. I bet men love these things."

"They are man-sized." Del took another sip, deep in thought for the moment.

"What's going on in there?" Claire tapped on her own head then pointed toward Del's.

"I was just thinking that a box of these rolls might be a very nice way to say thank you to the fire fighters who saved Bob and Tim yesterday."

"Are you thinking about taking that box by the firehouse personally?"

"Maybe..."

"I'm sure they would appreciate them, especially Chief O'Brian." Claire grinned and bobbled her eyebrows up and down suggestively.

"What? No, don't be silly. It's just a nice gesture. That's all." Del felt a slight flush in her cheeks and hoped Claire didn't noticed.

"I saw the way the chief looked at you yesterday. There was a little chemistry going on there for a few seconds. Even in my shocked state I caught that."

"I hardly think, I mean, well, Carl is pursuing me, you know."

"And you are doing an excellent job of being pursued and staying just beyond his clutches."

"Oh Claire, I don't know what to do about Carl." Del reached for her coffee and sat back in her chair.

She held the cup to her chest with both hands, like a little girl clutching a beloved stuffed animal for comfort, but her heart still ached, not with love but with anxiety.

"Not enjoying the pursuit?"

"Oh, the pursuit is flattering, I have to admit that. I just don't know if I really want to be caught."

"By Carl."

"Exactly."

"Well, seems to me that's your answer." Claire reached over and gave her friend's arm a squeeze followed by a gentle rub. "Generally, getting caught is the best part, don't you think? And you appear to be having too much fun hiding out and playing *bakery* at Gwen's place."

"It is fun helping at the bakery. Although I probably put on a few pounds every time I visit." She paused a moment, then added, "Do you think we should tell Gwen?"

"That you're putting on weight?"

"No, silly, about these awesome cinnamon rolls."

"Ah. No, I don't think so. They've been making these for years, long before Gwen came to town. Why make her worry? Clearly people like a little variety or her business wouldn't be doing so well."

"I suppose you're right. She has enough on her mind as it is. Andy told us last night they may have to cancel the festival dinner now that the winery is going to be a construction site."

"What about putting up a huge tent outside?"

"Apparently that's only an option if you have a safe indoor space to run to if it storms. There are only so many indoor spaces available for something like that and by now they are probably all taken by other wineries."

"That stinks." Claire traced a finger thoughtfully through the cinnamon sugar remnants of her half of the roll.

"What?"

"What what?"

"You got quiet. You have an idea?"

"About?"

"The festival dinner."

"No…I'm sure Terra will figure something out."

"You've definitely changed your tune about her."

"I guess I have. It's clear she cares about Bob…her dad. Her *dad*. That's a freaky thing for me to hear myself say, Del."

"I know." It was Del's turn to set her coffee down and reach out to rub her friend's arm in comfort. "It definitely adds a twist to your relationship with Bob. But you know it's not like there's a little baby that suddenly needs its diapers changed or even a kid who needs to be car-pooled to school. Terra's a grown woman. She's self-sufficient. Really all she's asking for is a chance to get to know you and to be a part of her dad's life."

"You're right, I know."

"It's not like she did anything wrong. She was born. She had no control over that, and she had no control over a mother who didn't tell her the truth about her father until she was grown. And that father didn't know either. Seems to me Bob was trying to do the right thing once he did know. But he kinda blew it when it came to telling you. Still, his heart was in the right place. He didn't want to burden you anymore than you already were."

"I agree. I may have been a little hard on him."

"A little?"

"Yeah, I was a bitch, wasn't I?" Claire smiled.

"I suppose you had reasons to be that way. After all, how were you to know she was his daughter? That's not the most likely thing to suppose when you see an older, attractive man who is supposedly not a family man giving lots of attention to a cute young woman."

"Exactly, but I've had a lot of time to think while I've been sitting in this dang hospital. And when I went back over it all in my head, I realized there were times that Bob tried to tell me, or at least tried to tell me there was a reasonable explanation and he planned to tell me soon. I guess he was trying to find the right moment but to me it felt like he was avoiding that moment. When I wondered why he'd avoid it, well, naturally, I imagined the worst possible reason."

"Even when he kept telling you he loved you?"

"Yeah...even then. We both made a mess of it but now that it's all out in the open I'm moving on."

"Does that mean you're leaving?" Del looked up with concern from a particularly tempting chunk of cinnamon roll she'd been about to nibble on.

"No, no, it means I'm going to take it for granted that the man who says he loves me really does love me. And I need to start thinking about what I'm going to do now that my little garden has given up its last zucchini for the season. I came, I planted and now I need to reap. And I mean more than vegetables."

"Like what?"

"Well, to begin with, I'm moving in with Bob."

"That's wonderful!"

"Let's not go all gushy, kiddo. He obviously can't live alone for a while so it only makes sense that I stay with him while he gets back on his feet."

"Can you call that moving in?"

"I can. Okay, maybe it's more like a test run. But if he gets back on his feet and things are working out then I'll move all my things from the little house as well. It's time to see what this next chapter in my saga is going to look like."

"Looks like Bob to me." Del grinned, teasing her friend.

"Very clever, but the next chapter can't be just about Bob. I need to have a life, too. I need to figure out what I'm going to do with myself."

"Are you enjoying fixing up the sisters' house? Maybe that's something you could do." Del's own search for a new career hadn't been so long ago that she didn't remember how adrift and without purpose she'd felt. It made her want to help Claire find her new anchor all the more.

"The remodeling does feel good. It's creative. Real estate was great, but it was sales. In the end I had a pay check, but with this the final product is something I can touch and I do like things that feel nice to the touch." It was Claire's turn to grin.

"And you can live in the house, right? The sisters want you to."

"Well, yes, but then what? And what about Bob? If Bob and I stay together I'm not sure he'd want to live in the Larson's house. He has a lovely home already."

Del crumpled up her napkin and stuffed it into her empty paper cup. "That will give you and Bob some-thing to talk about on those long evenings living together."

"Speaking of Bob, I'd better get back to the room. He'll probably be back by now. What are you doing with the rest of your day?"

"To begin with, I think I'll buy a dozen cinnamon rolls," Del said, smiling mischievously. True, she'd made a personal commitment to give Carl a chance...but that didn't mean she couldn't explore other options as well, did it?

As she waved good-bye to Claire Del found herself wondering if that's what 'playing the field' meant. She'd have to ask Claire, next time they talked, but she was pretty sure it did. A little voice in one ear asked if she should feel guilty at the idea. A little voice in her other ear was already giddy at the thought.

CLAIRE HURRIED DOWN THE HALL, worried that Bob might have returned to his room and was alone. But as she pushed open his door she heard familiar and surprising voices.

"Oh, Claire dear." Cora Larson rose to give Claire a hug and kiss her on her cheek; a ritual the sisters had taken to more and more lately.

Evie was right behind her but paused after kissing Claire's cheek to whisper in her ear, "Your young man is quite handsome." She giggled while pulling her into a hug.

Bob was propped up in bed looking far less tired than Claire expected.

"The ladies heard about my accident and came looking for you. They found me, instead."

"I had an appointment with my doctor," Evie explained. "Delia Saunders was just leaving his office—her back, you know—and mentioned that Adam and Carol Childe—who just took the feed store over from his father—were in the maternity wing with their new little girl, Ada. Can you believe the name Ada is making a come-back? Cora and I had a friend named Ada years ago." She paused and shared a grim look with Cora that told Claire Ada's story had not gone well.

"And Adam," Evie continued, "who is a volunteer with the fire department, told us about the accident at the winery. Helen Trsander—Mr. Trsander's granddaughter—is a nurse on that floor and she told us—when we asked—that Bob was here. We thought you might be with him and we were worried so we came looking and found Bob, all alone. But we've been having a delightful visit." Evie smiled conspiratorially at Bob.

"You have, have you?" Claire leaned over to give Bob a kiss and then sat gently on the side of his bed where she could hold his hand and, if need be, fend off whatever it was the sisters were up to.

"Never fear," Cora said, "we've made Bob comfortable. Evie found an extra pillow to prop under his leg."

Claire noticed the pillow and looked inquiringly at Bob.

"Feels a lot better." He smiled an amused smile.

"And Cora put some refreshing iced water in his sippy cup," Evie said.

Bob reached over and took a sip from the large sports bottle sitting on his bedside table. "*Very* refreshing."

Claire rolled her eyes in return. "I think you may be

spoiling him."

"After what I went through with *my* leg I have to say that the patient probably appreciates it." Evie reached out and gave the toes of Bob's good leg a tiny little tweak. "We patients have to stick together, right?"

"That's right, Evie." Bob winked at her.

"We are happy to see Bob is coming along so nicely." Cora stood, took Claire's free hand and held it in both of hers. "And you dear, you must get some rest. It's quite clear you have been burning the candle at both ends. I'm sure the progress on the house can wait while you nurse Bob back to health."

"Thank you for your concern, Cora, but I'll be just as refreshed as Bob is once I get a good night's sleep."

"Don't overdo, now." Evie stood beside her sister. "And you will let us know if there is anything we can do to help."

"Naturally."

"Good." Cora looped the straps of her purse over her arm. "We must be flying. Mr. Trsander is picking us up shortly to return us to the villas. Claire dear, you must bring Bob over for a visit as soon as he's up to it."

"Oh, what a wonderful idea, Cora." Evie clapped her hands together like an excited schoolgirl. "You do promise, don't you Claire?"

"I promise. As soon as he's up to it and you two are settled into your new villa."

"It won't be long now, will it Evie? Mr. Trsander is such a go-getter. We'll be all moved in in no time."

"Good, I'm glad to hear it."

"Me, too," Bob added.

"Then get well fast." Cora wagged her finger at Bob, giving instruction to the patient.

"Yes, ma'am."

"And call us if we can help with anything, Claire dear."

Cora turned to leave but Evie looked at Bob and added, nodding, "And don't forget what we talked about."

"I won't." Bob said. Claire looked from Evie to Bob but all she got from him was a Cheshire cat smile. "It's a secret."

DEL PULLED INTO A PARKING spot on the side of the fire station and, going around to the other side of her car, took out a large, flat box bearing twelve luscious cinnamon rolls. The hospital actually sold her a *baker's dozen* of thirteen but Del had had them pack the thirteenth roll separately. She'd decided that perhaps Gwen hadn't heard of these rolls but, either way, maybe Jason would want to see the competition.

Once Del had made the decision to bring the cinnamon rolls over to the fire station she'd also decided that, for once, she wasn't going to second guess herself. She wasn't going to remind herself about feelings that still lingered for Jimmy. She wasn't going to reprimand herself for ulterior motives regarding the chief when, technically, she was still seeing Carl. In fact, she had Carl's phone in her purse...set on mute. No, Del decided that for once she was going to act on impulse and not overthink things. What could it hurt to bring Chief O'Brian and the other firemen some cinnamon rolls? Ever since she'd had the idea she hadn't stopped smiling.

Twenty-Five

"WHAT ARE YOU DOING HERE?" Gwen asked when Jason walked into the bakery kitchen in the early afternoon. "I sent you a text to take the day off."

"Got tired of sleeping; I'm just sore, not really hurt. I needed to get moving." He hung his backpack on a hook and set his motorcycle helmet on the bench beneath it. "Resting makes me nuts. Give me something to do." He looked over at her scolding gaze. "Please."

Gwen's expression softened. She pointed to a table where two sizeable bricks of butter had been laid out beside a large bowl that was draped with a towel. "I was just about to tackle your strudel after disappointing several customers who came looking for it. I guess your timing is perfect, you can take care of that for me."

"Yes, Chef." Jason took down his white chef's jacket from where it hung near his backpack. He worked his way quickly up the side row of buttons, and then turned up each sleeve before stopping at the sink to wash his hands. He turned back toward Gwen. "Thank you, Chef."

Gwen smiled and nodded before returning to rolling out pastry for raspberry tarts. She understood about keeping busy. If Terra and Jason were growing as close as she thought, he was no doubt taking on her worries along with his own. As if he heard her thoughts he turned around and looked at her.

"I talked with Terra earlier. She said they may have to cancel the festival dinner. They obviously can't hold it at the winery now and all the other decent spots are taken by other wineries."

"I know, Andy mentioned it to me last night. So there's no other option?"

"So far no, but she hasn't given up looking into it yet. I told her just let it go for this year. Everyone's gonna understand, after all. But that girl..." He smiled and shook his head. "She does not give up easy. Feisty, if you know what I mean." He winked at Gwen then turned back to his station.

Gwen wondered if whatever was happening between Jason and Terra would be enough to keep him in town beyond his six-month contract. Columbine Vineyard's festival dinner was going to be the first big test of their budding new catering concept. True, she found it a scary new venture, but it was exciting, too. If this event fell through, could they find another one soon enough to keep that spark of an idea alive, she wondered?

"Hey, there." Del pushed open the kitchen door and set a white sack down in front of Jason. "I wondered if you'd be here today." She looked over at Gwen. "Shouldn't he be home resting?"

"Baking is good therapy, apparently."

"Indeed it is." Jason reached for the bag.

"Well I brought you a little something to investigate."

"Really?" Jason opened the sack and took out a very large cinnamon roll, placing it on the work surface beside the strudel dough. "Shopping the competition?"

"Is that from the hospital?" Gwen dusted her hands on her apron as she joined them.

"So you've never had one?" Del asked.

"Never even seen one, though I've certainly heard about them. When I first opened I got a lot of requests for *cinnamon rolls like the ones at the hospital.*" She air-quoted for emphasis. "I never really did cinnamon rolls. Guess that's odd for a bakery, but it wasn't my thing. And from everything I'd heard the hospital's bakery has a corner on them in this town."

"They sure have nailed it." Jason chewed a small chunk he'd torn from the end. "Flavors and texture are very good. And putting it all together in one very big package, I can see why they are in demand."

"Don't they use them for fundraising?" Gwen asked Del.

"That's what Claire said. We went to coffee and shared one of these. I know you probably don't want to compete with a good cause...but I thought you'd like to see the competition."

"Absolutely," Jason said, "and maybe we could come up with a version of our own."

Gwen shook her head. "I wouldn't feel good taking business from a hospital fundraiser."

"No worries, Chef. I'm not thinking of cloning these beasts. It's just getting my creative juices flowing. I don't want to take their customers, but if one of them wanders into our establishment with the yen for a cinnamon roll, maybe we can do a riff on this one that would satisfy them. I'm thinking a similar taste and size, but maybe slim and with the flakey crunch of a palmier, or we could layer slices with hazelnut mascarpone cream...I wonder..."

Jason wandered to a shelf of cookbooks, apparently lost in his own world of culinary creation.

"Where'd he go?" Del whispered.

"That's what he does when he gets an idea. I find it's best to leave him be. Pretty soon he'll pop back out, full of energy and on a mission to bake something new and delectable."

"Interesting."

"Yes," Gwen whispered back, "and since we may not have the festival dinner to keep his interest, maybe cinnamon rolls will do the trick until we can find another event to keep our catering dreams alive."

"And keep Jason in town?"

"You read my thoughts." Gwen looked at the now neglected strudel, "But I guess that means I'll have to pick up where he left off."

"Oh." Del followed her gaze. "I'd better get out of your hair."

"You heading home?"

"I think so. Claire is doing well. She's moving in with Bob."

"Really? She told you that?"

"Yes, over cinnamon rolls. But she says not to get too excited, that she's only doing it to take care of him while he heals. Then, if it works out..."

"It'll work out. Bob will make it work out. You watch."

"I hope so."

"How about you and Carl? Or is it Jimmy?"

"I honestly can't say, but I've decided it's time to figure it out."

"Good for you."

"And it's not like they are my only options, you know."

"Oh, really?" Gwen led Del through the kitchen door and out to a quiet table in the back. "Spill, please."

"Well, I—I didn't just buy one cinnamon roll."

"Do I have to worry about losing one of my best customers?"

"I don't think you're making much on me. I love helping out and you insist on paying me in pastries. I feel compelled to mop the floors when I'm here just to keep up with the calories."

"The floors are always shiny when you're here." Gwen looked around the bakery. "So what are you doing with those extra rolls? That's a lot of calories."

"I dropped them off at the fire station on my way here. To say thank you for everything they did at the winery."

"The fire station. Did you get to talk with anyone in particular while you were there?" Gwen smiled.

"Is it that obvious?"

"Only to those who noticed the chief paying a little extra attention to an attractive citizen."

"I'm not from Grande Valley."

"He doesn't know that. Or did you tell him?"

"I didn't say anything to him. He wasn't there. Actually, he's in Blue River."

"Back in your town? What's he doing there?"

"It was your town, too, until a few month ago. One

of the other firemen said he goes there every month for a meeting with chiefs from other mountain divisions. And he used to live there before he moved here."

"The plot of this new romance sure does thicken."

"Don't be silly." Del reached for her cell, absentmindedly checking for messages.

"Did you leave your number for him?"

Del smiled shyly and rolled her eyes. "Maybe..."

Gwen laughed and reached over to give Del a hug. "Good for you. Monogamy is for the married and you are definitely not married anymore!"

"That's what I thought. I may be again someday, but in the meantime I might as well consider all my options."

"The chief's a nice option if you ask me. Good for you. I can't wait to find out what happens next. Married ladies live vicariously through their single friends."

"If all marriages were like yours you wouldn't have any single friends."

Del left a little later, fresh latte in hand and a box of cookies Gwen had packed for her kids. Gwen couldn't help but wonder what would happen next with Del and all her options. It was fun to be an observer, she decided, but it made her all the happier to have found Andy. It also reminded her of how close she could have come to losing him when the winery roof fell in. If he ever got a long enough break from damage control she planned to show him just how grateful she was.

*C*LAIRE STOOD ON THE BLUFF *overlooking Grande Valley. The river wound through the town and valley*

like a thread sewing up the fragments of her life. She turned at the sound of propellers winding down, holding her hand up to block the last moments of daylight, its gilded umber rays heavy with the humidity left behind from thunderstorms.

The rain brought moisture to the vineyards and swelled the banks of the river. Lightening had cracked open the damp atmosphere releasing the late afternoon squalls that were so common this time of the year. The valley welcomed it, soaking up every drop.

In her memory a similar storm had overwhelmed her parents' small aircraft, leaving their family fractured beyond repair; leaving her sister, Susan, and herself, though they were young women, alone and orphaned.

Across the high mesa she saw the small plane land, its doors open and two people, a couple, climb out, pulling luggage and packages behind them. Even at this distance she heard the woman's laughter following some comment from her mate. She replied, her words indecipherable to Claire's ears, but their tone obviously teasing and light. Then they both laughed and he came around the front and wrapped an arm about her waist, speaking again to her, a murmur from Claire's past, followed by a gentle lingering kiss.

"Mom! Daddy!" Claire called out though they were oblivious to her existence; their world was only in each other's arms now. But then the woman looked up and across the plain toward where Claire stood, hands clasped at her heart.

"Momma…" she whispered, and the woman pressed her finger tips to her lips and blew her daughter a kiss. Though it was too far to clearly see, Claire knew the gentle smile that crossed those lips, the same she'd seen every night at bed time when her mother turned out the lights, blew her a kiss and shut the door, leaving her alone in the dark. But the memory of the kiss lingered and made the dark warm, welcoming and

restful, lulling her to sleep.

The woman turned to gather up her things and followed him away from the plane, away from Claire.

"Momma!" Claire called out again but they were too far. Should she run after them, she wondered.

"Ace, where you going?" Bob was beside her, taking her hand in his, meeting her tear-filled eyes with his own loving regard. "They're gone, baby. You can't go back to them. Come on, come back to me."

Claire's feet felt heavy as lead, impossible to lift, leaving her unable go either direction.

"Claire." Bob gently tugged her hand as he walked toward the valley, his fingers falling away from her outstretched hand as he walked on. "Come with me, Claire," he said again. "Claire!"

"Claire." Bob's voice broke through the haze of sleep, rousing her. "Baby, you okay?"

"What?" She shook off the dream at last, pushing up to sit on the side of the cot she'd been napping on. Bob leaned off the side of his bed, a crutch propped under his arm as if he were about to stand. "You shouldn't stand without someone beside you, Bob. Not yet."

"I know, but you were mumbling in your sleep and then I heard you crying out. It was very clear, you called out *Momma*. Were you dreaming about your parents' accident again?"

Claire had shared with him the story of her parents' death and that she'd dreamed often about the accident when she was younger. She hadn't told him that lately the dreams had returned but changed; that she still saw them in her dreams but the violence of the crash was gone, replaced with easy moments like this dream.

Her father was always distant, which wasn't far removed from reality. He'd been a busy man. He loved his family but he was building his business empire and that preoccupied him. But her mother always knew her. In little glances, waves, good night kisses...her mother always showed her she knew she was there. And somewhere inside Claire felt her tangible presence.

No, Claire hadn't told Bob that part. Did she want to? That feeling was a slender thread that led back to a happier place and telling someone might cut the thread. It anchored her in hard times. If she told him, would the dreams stop? Could she move on if she never dreamt of her mother again?

"Yes, just bits and pieces." Claire wasn't quite ready to share it all and risk losing her mother forever.

"Baby, are you sure?" He hobbled over to join her on the cot. "You were dreaming for a long time. I was lying in bed watching your face." He reached out and brushed back her hair where it fell across her cheek. "You were so peaceful and then suddenly you weren't. I called out to you and I'd swear you reacted in your dream. Do you remember your dream?"

Her first instinct was to say no, but Bob's face radiated concern. And love. How could she tell him any less than the full truth, that she worried that if she was ever truly happy it would mean she'd let go of the past and, in the process, she would lose her dearest memory.

She felt tears fill her eyes and she blinked them away, looking up and around the room and anywhere but his face.

"Hey," he whispered, "don't do that. Come on, come back to me."

"What?" She looked at him, shocked to hear him echo his words from the dream. "What did you say?"

"I know you too well, Ace. Classic Claire avoidance of the big issues in life is to look away and focus on something else. I think we've wasted too much time doing that, don't you? I get it that big issues are hard, but they can be great too. I want us to tackle them together. I've got a daughter. You've got a past that haunts you."

She scowled, starting to shake her head.

"Yes it does. You can't lie to me. I know you well. But we can handle it, honey. Together. We're a team now, okay?"

Claire couldn't hold back the smile that played with the taut corners of her lips. She couldn't help feel a layer of tension slide from her shoulders as his words fell over her. Maybe letting go would be better, not worse. The decisive business woman in her took over and made the call. She leaned over and gently kissed his lips, then smiled. "Okay."

CLAIRE TAPPED AT THE BAKERY'S front window. Most of the lights were turned off but she saw a glow from the door to the kitchen and thought she'd give it a try.

After a moment it swung open and Gwen spotted her outside.

"Sorry." Claire waited as Gwen opened the door to her. "I have a bad habit of showing up just as you are closing."

"I'm in no rush. Andy's working late, as usual."

"I just left Bob at the hospital. I'm going home to start packing a few things to take over to his house.

The doc says he can go home in a couple days and I've decided to go with him. For now, at least."

"And for later?"

"We'll see." Usually this sort of conversation made Claire ill at ease, but not tonight. Tonight it was just a fact, not an uncomfortable one. "But I need caffeine. It's been a long day and I have a lot left to do. Is it too late?"

"Never, come on in. I'll bag up something for you to eat, too. Jason made some mini-quiches that have been big sellers. I've probably got a couple you could pop into the microwave for dinner."

"That would be friggin' awesome."

"Hey." Gwen stopped to look at Claire.

"What?"

"There's the Claire I know and love. I've missed her."

"She's been pre-occupied with a lot of shit. But she might finally be getting it back together."

"I'm glad."

A pan rattled against a counter top in the kitchen, catching Claire's attention. "Jason's still here?"

"Yes, he's working on a new creation. I told him it could wait but he said Terra is working late at the winery too so he might was well put his free time to use. Frankly, I'm grateful he has something to occupy him. What with the festival dinner falling through I've been worried I'll lose him if we don't find another event to keep the idea of a catering company alive."

"The dinner is canceled?"

"You didn't know? I just assumed Bob would have said something."

"When Bob isn't in physical therapy or getting tests

done he's sleeping. It's exhausting and even when he calls Andy to find out what's going on, all that Andy will tell him is that he's got everything under control and Bob just needs to take care of Bob for a while. I don't know how long that strategy will work, but for now he's too exhausted to put up a fight."

"Tell Bob that Andy really is taking charge. I'm sure he doesn't have anything to worry about, aside for the roof collapsing and his injuries and farming out grapes to other wineries who are pitching in to fill the void created when that crane fell through the roof."

"He'll be glad to know it—and here I thought they had a near disaster on their hands." Claire smiled, then, frowning, added, "I guess I should have realized about the dinner. Obviously there's no way they can hold it there. And there aren't any other venues available at this point?"

Gwen shook her head in confirmation as she placed two small quiches into a pastry box along with a lemon tart.

"I'll have to call Terra and see what's up. The dinner is her baby, maybe she's got some ideas we haven't heard about."

"I hope so." Gwen tied a string tightly around the box, snipped off the ends and handed it to Claire along with a large vanilla latte. "Half-caff for you, it's getting late."

"Thank you, Mother. What do I owe you?"

"It's my treat—the least I could do. Just get some rest. You look worn out."

"That's funny, because for the first time in a long time I feel like I could pull an all-nighter."

"I always hated those." Gwen unlocked the front

door to let Claire out. "Try to get some sleep all the same." She hugged her friend and sent her on her way with a feeling of her own, that even though the winery was in pieces, maybe Claire was finally putting all of hers back together.

CLAIRE ARRIVED AT THE JOB site early the next morning to survey the progress. Her sub-contractors had made quick work of their jobs, just as they'd promised her. She'd expected to have to nag a little more but, all told, she'd only 'played mother' once so far with a tile layer she'd found enjoying a beer on his lunch hour.

She'd chewed him out just enough and he hadn't disappointed her since. In fact, she thought to herself as she assessed the new tile floors in the kitchen and baths, he did very good work. If she ever renovated another house, she'd use him. Claire caught herself at that thought. Was she really ready to do something like this again? Would she want to do it for a living, taking needy homes and turning them into something special that a new owner would love? Maybe.

But for now, she was on a mission that had occurred to her during a late night chat with Terra. The festival dinner really was doomed for cancellation. Terra hadn't found another venue in Grande Valley that would work. That's when Claire realized the Larson sisters' home might be the perfect solution, if she could get it done in time.

The sisters had told her the home was hers to use as she wanted, and she felt certain they'd approve of the plan, though she would definitely run it by them all the same. Could it be ready in time, she wondered, as she walked through the house? A few minor items might not be complete, but the kitchen would be, the bathrooms too. And she could have the main floor hardwoods refinished and gleaming in time for tables to be set throughout the house, and even a few on the expansive porch that wrapped nearly half way around the house. A large tent out front could host more tables, leaving Terra with both outdoor and indoor options no matter the weather.

Hosting the festival dinner might open up a whole new life for the sisters' proud old home. Each room she walked through added another layer of opportunity. Whether or not she chose to live in this house, she could revive its welcoming charm and turn it into a home for a variety of events. The options began to tumble through her mind and she sat on the stairs, suddenly giddy at the possibilities and the delightful challenges each one would bring.

She remembered the first time she'd sat on these steps, waiting for someone to restore the power that dark night Cora had arrived at her door in search of help for the injured Evie. It wasn't all that long ago, Claire realized, but in terms of how far she'd come since then, it seemed a lifetime.

Claire really was making a new life this time. She was on the cusp of something that made her happier than anything had in...how long, she wondered to herself. Then she realized she was happier than, well, ever. In fact, if this were the last time she started over it would be just fine with her. She finally felt at home.

G WEN TAPPED AT THE KEYS on her laptop, oblivious to the morning rush that filled the bakery and surrounded her with happy activity. Jason was in the kitchen, whipping up a second batch of his latest creation, cinnamon croissant buns. In the end he'd taken classic croissant dough, generously spiked with cinnamon, swirled it into a bun and dusted the top with sanding sugar that retained its lovely sparkle and inviting crunch with each bite.

Carolyn came in early to work, fresh from having met the dawn up on the mesa so that she could paint the sunrise out in the fresh air—en plein. She'd cut several buns into bite-sized pieces for patrons to sample and, one thing leading to another, the first batch of five dozen was gone, and several orders had been placed for pick-up the following morning.

Jason's new creation was a clear winner. Once he caught up with production of the buns, along with items they'd need for their lunch rush, he planned to tackle another bakery tradition: the éclair. At this rate, Gwen thought, even if they never found another event to cater, it would take Jason at least a year to work his way through the standards.

But she wasn't giving up that easily. She'd caught Jason's enthusiasm for the catering arm of her bakery so she'd tossed and turned all night and arrived early with ideas for marketing pieces to place in the local paper. The holidays were coming up fast and, if they wanted to get some of that business, it was time to advertise. Grande Valley loved a party and Gwen knew there would be many opportunities to cater holiday events.

Ping!

Gwen glanced at her phone to see who was texting her, then realized it was Del.

Got a moment?

She picked up the phone and typed in her response.

Sure, want to call me?

Can't, sitting in a boring Board meeting listening to financials, but I'm in the back corner and can sneak in a text.

Gwen was curious what was so urgent Del was texting in a corner during a meeting.

What's up?

Carl is across the room. He's speaking next but he pulled me aside right before the meeting and

Gwen waited for Del to finish her sentence. The seconds passed and she started worrying just what Carl had pulled her aside for when at last Del returned.

Sorry-somebody stood behind me but he moved. Don't want anyone to read this!!

Now Gwen really was wondering what Carl wanted.

Got it. So, why did he pull you aside?

There was a moment's pause, three small dots filled the lower left corner of the screen as Del tapped out her answer.

OH!!! He just got back and he told me he's got a reservation for us for dinner Friday night at Chateau Noir!!!

Gwen knew the restaurant. It was very romantic and had a reputation for being the first stop on many steamy nights in Blue River. It was also a popular place to propose marriage. The staff went out of their way to accommodate whatever romantic plans might be laid. Gwen understood Del's concern, but she couldn't blame Carl. The guy had been put off long enough and clearly this was a play to move their relationship forward.

What did you tell him?

The bakery's chimes jangled and before she could look up Gwen heard Claire approaching.

"You won't believe what I've got in mind." Clearly excited, Claire plopped into the seat beside Gwen, ready to share.

"Hold that thought, we've got a Del emergency."

"Carl or Jimmy?"

"Carl. He's taking her to Chateau Noir Friday night."

"Whoa."

"I know."

"Is she excited?"

"More of a cornered deer-in-the-headlights reaction."

"That girl needs to make up her mind."

"Listen to you all of the sudden lecturing on making up your mind."

"I know." Claire leaned back in her chair, stretching her arms wide. "What can I say? It's been a life-changing few days. I've got to talk to you about something, though."

Ping!

"Okay, but let's get Del through this first." She leaned over to share the phone and Del's text with Claire.

Didn't have time to say yes or no—he whispered in my ear then somebody called him to the front so the meeting could get started. I have to tell him something as soon as it's over and it's almost over!!! HELP!!!!

"Give me that!" Claire reached for the phone.

Claire here. Listen kiddo, if Jimmy is in then give Carl the boot/ if Jimmy is out then give Carl a shot. U are a single independent woman & u are allowed to have some fun. Does Carl sound fun? It's not like you r marrying the guy. Expect fun & nothing more. It's ok to have fun.

Claire hit send and handed the phone back to Gwen who shrugged her shoulders and nodded agreement. Dots formed to signal Del was writing her response but long seconds passed until at last it arrived.

Ok

"That's it?" Gwen asked. "I thought for sure we'd get a long explanation of why she shouldn't go."

"I think she needed someone to say it was okay to go even if it wasn't serious. Del's an old fashioned kind of girl, after all. Playing around is a new concept. Hard to think of sex as just for fun and not something more."

"I guess I'm a little old fashioned, too. I'm not the playing around type; I want the emotional connection, commitment, that sort of thing."

"Sure. Most people do, but, until that comes along, you don't have to buy the amusement park to take a ride on the Ferris wheel." Claire grinned.

"You are lucky you found Bob." Gwen shook her head, laughing.

"I am lucky Bob found me. It's been a long time since I was looking for more than that ride on the Ferris wheel. I'd almost forgotten how nice it is to have more."

"You think Carl wants more?"

"Probably not. Carl doesn't seem like the marrying kind from what we've heard."

"I think you're right. If he hasn't married yet why would he now?"

"Oh, wait, almost forgot!" Claire took the phone back.

And be sure u have protection!

"Think she knows what you mean?" Gwen asked.
"She is an adult."
"I know, but—"

Ping!

Ok

Claire tapped again.

And have some friggin' fun!
Yes, sir!! THX!!! :)

"If she doesn't call on Saturday I will." Gwen put aside her phone. "I hope we haven't steered her down the road to depravity."

"More like the road of living it up a little. I think we can safely count on our Del to steer clear of depravity."

"I may not sleep Friday night."

"Let's hope Carl keeps her up all night," Claire said with a wicked grin on her lips.

"So what was your big news?"

"Oh, yes. Lattes all around!" Claire swept her arms to encompass all her fellow bakery patrons. "I may have actually figured out what the hell to do with myself. Or at least be on the way to it."

"Should I be afraid to ask?"

Claire folded her arms and shook her head. "While I understand your skepticism, you have nothing to fear. It's a genuine plan, not just an advanced yoga class or adding a more vigorous strain of zucchini to the garden."

"God forbid."

"Yes, we've had more than enough zucchini. It could be years before I can look another zucchini in the face...or bud or whatever."

"I certainly won't be making zucchini bread again anytime soon. So what's the genuine plan?"

"To begin with, we're holding Columbine Vineyards festival dinner at the Larson Sister's house. Or as I plan to rename it, The Larson Estate."

"I love it. And I love your plan. It's a wonderful use for the house and it solves a problem for the vineyard. But is there more beyond the dinner?"

"Oh, yes, much more, but I've only just begun to formulate my plans. I want the house to be a gathering place, an event center."

"That's a wonderful idea. I'll help spread the word. I'm working on putting together some marketing pieces to drum up catering business. I bet a lot of folks would love to have their holiday events in that lovely old home. Especially once you're done remodeling it."

"We could do some marketing together, Gwen, although you probably have room in here to host evening events if you wanted to." Claire looked around Gwen's bakery with new eyes, envisioning the possibilities and noticing for the first time the water color paintings that Carolyn had recently hung on the back wall. "Where did those come from?"

"Carolyn. She proposed making this back wall a little gallery for herself and other artists. See," she pointed to the corner of the nearest painting, "she's included a small tag on each piece with the price, the piece's name and her own, of course. It's a great marketing tool for her and it dresses up the bakery. She's even thinking of encouraging the town council to look into hosting a *plein air* festival in Grande Valley. Do you know what that is?"

"Yes, I was in Crested Butte one year for a convention when I noticed these artists with their easels set up all over town. They were painting the mountains, the town, horses beside streams. It was fascinating to watch them. I was sorry I didn't have more time. You know...the Larson Estate could host a *plein air* festival."

"What a wonderful idea. Carolyn could help you, too. She's sure to have contacts."

"I love the idea. And we might have an artist-in-residence series through-out the year. There are a few bedrooms upstairs that the artists could use. And I noticed that old Victorian on Oak Street is for sale. It's a fixer-upper but it would be a wonderful extension for the estate. Someplace in town where we could have exhibit space, perhaps the artists could teach classes—classes! Remember when I was talking with Jason about teaching cooking classes someday? He could do a series out at the house. If you didn't mind."

"Not at all, one more thing to keep him in town."

"I'm going to talk with him right now." Claire stood and started to the kitchen. "I'll be right back."

"Hey."

"What?" Claire stopped and looked back at her.

"Feels good to have a purpose again, huh?"

"Feels good to be back." She winked, then strode through the doors to the kitchen.

Gwen couldn't agree more. She'd missed the old Claire, although she thought Claire 2.0 had a much better shot at a happier life.

Twenty-Seven

DEL LOOKED AT HER REFLECTION in the mirror, nervously turning side-to-side, judging her appearance. She readjusted the thin scarf she'd wrapped lightly around her neck, trying to cover up a little of the décolleté revealed by the slender straps and draping neckline of her coral and cream silk dress. It fell to cocktail length above strappy high-heeled sandals that revealed her toes, their nails painted coral to match her dress.

She'd had her hair and nails done and spent more time than usual on her make-up, even dabbing on a very expensive perfume she saved for special occasions.

If she was finally going to be a woman of the world, she was going to do it with style! At least that was what she'd kept telling herself throughout the day. She need-ed to commit to giving Carl a chance or she'd never really know if he was worth it.

Del glanced at the clock: quarter to seven. Carl would be here soon. Her stomach growled and she remembered she'd skipped lunch, though she was too nervous to eat even if she'd had the time.

She'd driven Cara to a sleep-over at a friend's house.

Nate was on a nature retreat with his class-mates and wouldn't be home until Sunday afternoon. Finding Cara a sleep-over hadn't been hard. She was at the age where little girls were more than motivated to spend the night popping corn and watching a marathon of their favorite Disney pre-teen series.

Sandy, her straw-colored miniature poodle followed her to the kitchen, nails tapping on the wood floors along with the tap of Del's heels.

"We need to take you in for a grooming, little miss," she said, "only one of us should be this noisy as we walk." She stooped to scratch behind her ears, took the lid off a cookie jar decorated with silhouettes of dogs and pulled two biscuits that she held in the air above Sandy's head. The dog stood on her back legs, dancing and panting in anticipation of her treat. Satisfied at last, Sandy went off to find her water dish.

"Your tummy is happy, now how about mine." Del opened her refrigerator and stood, looking through its contents, then down at her dress. "Everything in here looks messy." She shut the door and opened a cupboard where she found a bag of small vanilla cookies. She popped a couple in her mouth, standing over the sink as she chewed and washing them down with a glass of water. She frowned, then opened another cupboard and retrieved a bottle of antacid tablets, popped two into her mouth, then drank a little more water.

The doorbell rang and Del's hands instantly pressed against her stomach, as if to keep the butterflies that filled it from exploding into the room. Sandy barked and raced from her to the door and back, happily anticipating whomever was on the other side.

"You're not much protection, are you?" Del slowly approached the door, anxious to get the evening started, but also for what it might hold. "You'd fold for the first cookie that came your way, wouldn't you? And then I'd be left alone to my own defenses." Sandy yipped merrily at the door. "What would happen then?" Del reached to open the door. "Well, I guess we'll see."

CLAIRE LOOKED AT THE NOTE in her hand, double checking the address of Cora and Evie's new villa at the Village.

"Claire!"

She turned to see Cora pushing a cart piled with towels, pots, sheets and pans that jostled and swayed their way along the sidewalk.

"What are you doing? I thought you had movers bringing things from the house."

"Indeed we do, but we'd already bought some things for our little temporary home and Mr. Trsander is so busy hanging pictures and rearranging furniture to Evie's specifications, I thought I'd help out with these few little things."

"Let me." Claire took over the handle of the cart.

"Thank you, dear."

"You've received some things from the restoration company? They got the smoke out of all your furniture, clothes?"

"Oh, yes, they've put some of it into storage until we decide what to keep at our new home...and if you want any at the house."

"I hadn't thought about that..."

"No rush dear, the storage company is most accommodating."

"For a price, I imagine."

"Well, isn't that so often the way. But Roger will take care of it all and, once we are settled in, we will hardly be any trouble at all to him, or to you, for that matter."

"You are definitely not any trouble to me. You're a pleasure, really." She stopped the cart for a moment and Cora looked up at her. "It's like...well, like—"

"Family," Cora finished her thought, smiling as she did.

Suddenly Claire felt herself choke up and could only smile back.

Cora gave Claire's arm a squeeze. "Evie and I feel the same way, dear. It's funny how the good Lord has a way of helping the right people find each other sometimes. Despite our friends, Evie and I were really on our own."

"I know how that feels."

"I know you do. But you're not alone anymore, not by any measure. You've built yourself a wonderful family here in the valley, I think, in addition to those you already had. And of course, now you have our home— *your* home."

"That's what I need to talk to you and Evie about. I have a plan now and I want to tell you about it. I guess I...want your approval."

"You will always have our approval, Claire. Now, our opinions may vary from time to time. We are women of prodigious opinions, I believe."

"I'd say I have that in common with you."

"Indeed. Maybe that's why Evie and I have come

to care so greatly for you. We see our younger selves in you."

"If I can age as gracefully as you and Evie have, I'll be a happy woman."

Cora held the door open as Claire pushed the cart through. From inside they could hear Evie's raised voice.

"Oh dear, Mr. Trsander, What have you done? I thought I'd asked you to move that pie safe closer to the kitchen but here I've found it in the guest room. What on God's green earth were you thinking?"

Cora winked at Claire. "Some days we're more graceful than others."

T HE WAITER FILLED DEL'S COFFEE cup and then Carl's. A second waiter stepped up to place a single crème Brule between them along with two spoons.

The evening had started out with a stimulating conversation over appetizers and aperitifs. They'd covered the daily details of each other's lives. Del told an attentive Carl about her progress on the holiday fundraising dinner, from table settings and dinner menus to donor invitations and silent auction contributions.

"It sounds like a rousing success, Delly." Carl had paused to smell the cork the waiter offered and nodding his approval of the wine he'd chosen. "You're a natural at this sort of thing; a regular Jackie Kennedy."

"Well, I don't think I'd compare my talents to hers, or a hospital fundraiser to hosting galas for world leaders."

"Same thing." He swirled his newly filled wine glass

and placed his nose as deep within the crystal vessel as possible, inhaling the vapors he'd released.

Del had always found the behavior of the dedicated wine connoisseur a little pretentious, but then, she supposed if she truly understood the nuisances Carl appeared to be detecting she might appreciate them more. She wondered if Bob might ever have the time to give her a little lesson about wine and then realized Carl would probably be happy to. He seemed to know his vintages, but Del felt uncomfortable admitting to him that she did not.

Carl finally took a sip, swirled it over his palette for a moment and then, swallowing, graced the sommelier with a satisfied smile and nod. Del's glass was then filled and Carl nodded toward her glass. "It's a very nice pinot noir. I think you'll like it."

She picked up the glass and paused to sniff its contents thoughtfully. Del smiled and nodded back, thinking to herself that, yes, it did smell like wine. She followed the sniff with a sip and had to admit that it not only tasted like wine, it tasted like cherries and wood smoke and other things so complex she couldn't put them into words.

Del had never had a wine like this. It flowed like a warm, earthy river across her tongue, satisfying all her taste buds along the way, leaving behind a residual desire that could only be quenched by another sip. It was a perfect complement to the chateaubriand Carl had ordered for them both.

Now, that bottle, and a second one safely put to rest, she wondered if the warm glow she felt was from the combination of wine, food and stimulating company or just more alcohol than she normally drank in a week. Despite all her misgivings about the evening, she had to admit she was having a wonderful time.

The waiter delivered crème Brule for two and Del eyed it with hesitation. Oh, my, I don't know that I have any more room for dessert, Carl. Everything is delicious, but filling." She took a sip of her coffee. "Their coffee is wonderful."

"They bring it in from Costa Rica. Dinner was perfect, as always. I have to hand it to the chef, he never disappoints. Nice change from all the chicken I've had lately." He dipped his spoon in a corner of the Brule. "You eat what you can, Delly, and I'll handle the rest. Might mean a few more sit-ups at the gym." He gave his abs a hard slap. "But it'll be worth it after tonight."

"You've really spoiled me. I don't eat like this often. And the atmosphere...and company." Del smiled over the rim of her coffee cup. "Well, it's been a delightful evening, Carl."

"I'm happy to hear you say so." He reached over to hold her free hand in his and running his thumb back and forth across her palm. "But it's not over yet." He smiled.

Del's breath caught, like deer in the headlights, the sensory overflow of wine, words and Carl's thumb gently stroking her palm told her mind to run while every nerve in her body wanted to fall into his arms.

"WHAT A MARVELOUS IDEA!" EVIE passed a plate of Lemon Sandies from Claire to Cora to Mr. Trsander as they stood in their new kitchen. The counters were cluttered with boxes and there was barely room for anything more than a cookie or two for a mid-moving snack.

Claire had explained her plans for the house and both sisters seemed enthusiastic.

"If there are painting classes I'm sure Evie would want to attend. She's always been the artistic one between us."

"Oh Cora, what about the Christmas wreath you made last year out of grape vines? That was so festive on our front door."

"LOOK ABOVE THE REFRIGERATOR." DEL pointed Carl toward the kitchen. "I'm not sure what's up there but maybe you can find something you'll like."

"Let's find something to warm you up." Carl took her hand in his then ran his free hand up the side of her bare arm where it was tucked beneath his suit jacket that he'd draped around her shoulders as they left the restaurant.

"Your jacket did the trick." Del started to take it off.

"No, honey, leave it on. You've still got goose bumps."

Indeed, she did still feel the chill up her arm but wondered if this time it was from Carl's touch rather than the stiff autumn wind that had blown in after sunset.

"I-I don't know why I didn't think to bring more than this thin wrap." Del held out a shear, creamy vanilla-colored sheath of silk. "I just didn't think it would be so c-cold."

"There, you see? Still shivering." Carl swept his arm beneath the coat, and wrapping it around her waist he pulled her closer. "Let me warm you up." His voice was low, his warm breath soothing the chill from her shoulders as he ran his lips along her neck and up to her ear.

"Oh, my. That is warm…oh, yes.…" Del closed her eyes, enjoying the nearness of another body to hers then, noticing the tap, tap of little dog toenails at the sliding glass door, remembered she'd let her little dog outside as soon as soon as they'd arrived. "Oh, Carl, I'm sorry." She pulled away. "I have to let Sandy back in. Why don't you check that cabinet? I'll get her and then I'll freshen up a little. I'll meet you in the living room, okay?"

"Don't be long. I'll see what I can find."

Sandy accompanied Del to her master bedroom and beyond to her bathroom. The little dog sat, looking up at her as she checked her reflection in the mirror and added a light bead of lipstick and a few dabs of blush. Not that she needed it, in spite of the cold, she was feeling flushed all over.

Dinner had been a great success and Carl's company pleasant in every way. True, he'd been a little condescending to the waiter when he was slow refilling their water glasses, and had insisted on a table closer to the window overlooking the garden after they'd been seated near the fireplace. Del longed for that fireplace as the evening wore on, but Carl insisted the garden view, with its man-made stream trickling along a cobblestone path that glowed as the evening went on, was the best seat in the house. It was nice, and the gentle trickle of the stream was pleasant until the wind picked up and the windows had to be closed.

That same wind had inspired Carl to drape his suit jacket around her on the walk to the car. He always looked so nice, Del thought, so put-together. His gray suit fit perfectly and beneath, he'd worn a charcoal button-down topped with a pale lavender tie. The affect was stunning, and made his tanned face beneath impeccably cut dark golden hair stand out. Carl's eyes, she noticed, weren't really blue, as she'd thought, but a pale gray. She'd never quite seen the color before in someone's eyes and wondered if they looked different in different light. She'd have to pay closer attention, she decided.

Well, wasn't that what she was doing this evening, she thought to herself, paying closer attention to Carl ?

Del looked down at Sandy and smiled, stooping to scratch her behind the miniature poodle's ears. Sandy had jumped up to greet Carl when he first came and he'd patted her head, but Del noticed he'd side-stepped to keep the dog away from his leg. She supposed that with his suit, which obviously looked hand-tailored. He wouldn't want dog hairs-or paws-mussing it. Still, she was a little disappointed that he didn't seem all that taken with little Sandy, not like Jimmy, when he'd come to the house. Sandy practically abandoned her when Jimmy was around, clearly knowing the extra treats and spoiling attention he always gave the little poodle.

Del shook her head, clearing away the memory. Carl wasn't Jimmy, she thought. Even Jimmy hadn't been who she thought he was in the end. He'd been distant after their break, but recently their interactions had felt cold, like he'd turned his back and his heart on her. Wasn't it time she moved on with a man who clearly found her fascinating and wanted to spend time with her? A man who wanted her. The chill returned, as did the flush.

"Hey, Delly, what's keeping you?" Carl called from the living room. "I've got just the thing to warm you up."

She pulled his jacket closer around her and smiled nervously at anticipation of the evening still ahead.

"THE ONLY THING IS..." CLAIRE hesitated as she watched Mr. Trsander return to the task of hanging several original oil paintings of the Book Cliffs on the living room wall.

"What is the only thing, dear?" Evie asked as both sisters stood looking at her.

Their expressions were suddenly filled with concern and Claire wondered how these two delightful people had become so close to her that they understood her moods perhaps better than she did.

"You know, I'm moving in with Bob, to take care of him while his leg heals."

"Of course." Cora nodded. "That only makes sense."

"It's just for now, but, if it goes okay, if we get along and don't drive each other nuts, well, then maybe I'll..."

"Make it permanent?" Evie asked. The smiles had returned to both of the sisters' faces.

"Yes. Maybe. But then, of course, I wouldn't be living at your house, my house I mean, well, *our* house." She smiled back at the sisters and decided right then that that was how she wanted to refer to the house from then on: our house. It made sense.

"But you would still be doing things with our house, wouldn't you? The events, perhaps artists in residence and such?" Cora asked.

"Of course."

"Then we're happy with the future of *our* former home, Claire. It will be a busy place and—"

"—a happy place." Evie finished her sister's thought. "That's what we wanted all along. We wanted you to feel at home and we wanted our home to always be a place full of happiness."

"A place that continued to matter, even when we were no longer there."

"It will." Claire said. "It absolutely will. In fact, I can see it being the center of a great deal of events and activities that matter very much to the whole valley."

"Just as we wished; just as our dear Papa would have wished. It's his legacy, after all."

"I'm going to call it the Larson House, so it will be a tribute to all of you, not just your father."

"Well, we did pay tribute to Papa when we named Elbe, didn't we?" Evie giggled at her sister.

"I hope Papa took his sense of humor with him to heaven, Evie. Though, speaking of Elbe, I suppose it's about time we brought him back home, isn't it dear?"

"Oh, my, yes."

"Of course," Claire said. "I don't know why I didn't think of that already."

In truth, Claire knew full well just why she would have forgotten. For all her insistence over the years that she live an independent life, Elbe had shown her just how wonderful it was to have someone there to greet you when you came home, to nuzzle you awake in the morning and snuggle up against you when you wrestled with life's challenges. She had to admit she would miss Elbe, but smiled when she thought of Bob. Maybe that sweet cat had helped melt her resistance just enough to allow her to see how wonderful it would be to have Bob in her life full-time, an idea that seemed more appealing every day.

"He's grown on you, hasn't he?" Evie asked.

"What?" Was Evie reading her thoughts about Bob?

"Our Elbe, you'll miss his company, I'm sure."

"I have to admit that I will."

Cora took her sister's arm in her own. "You must come and visit him anytime you like. And perhaps visit us as well?"

"You can count on that."

"JOIN ME." CARL PATTED THE spot beside him on Del's couch.

She sat down, leaving a few inches between them. Sandy ran to her little fleece bed beside the fireplace and turned two circles before curling up. "Oh, you turned on the fireplace. That's nice." Gold and orange flames blazed in the gray fieldstone hearth.

"I thought it would warm you up, so will this." Carl took two small brandy snifters from the coffee table and handed one to Del as he closed the gap between them. "You had a nice bottle of B&B."

Del sniffed the glass then took a small sip. The amber liquid felt hot going down and warm once it hit. "That does warm me up."

"That's just for starters, Delly." Carl took a large sip

from his snifter then set it down. He slid his arm across the back of the couch and wrapped it around her shoulder, pulling her closer. He played with a strand of her hair, swept his other hand onto her shoulder, his thumb playing across the line of the spaghetti strap that was already slipping from her other shoulder. "I don't need fine brandy to get me hot when I'm around you baby. You do it all by yourself."

Del took another sip for courage, then set the glass down beside Carl's. This was it, she told herself, time to move on, time to be 'all in' with Carl. She placed her hand on his chest and felt the hard, well-defined physique of a man who took very good care of his body. He'd loosened his tie and open the top button so Del pulled the tie through his collar, then undid three more buttons so she could see his chest. She ran her hand under the fabric and felt his warm skin beneath. Hadn't she seen pictures of him with his shirt off? Wasn't his chest hairy? But it was smooth to her touch.

"You're so smooth, did you shave?" she asked absentmindedly, letting her thoughts leak out. Del was instantly embarrassed by the question.

"Don't be ridiculous, beautiful."

"I know, it was silly of me to—"

"I'm getting it waxed these days."

"Really?" Del had never heard of a man waxing his chest and couldn't even imagine why he would remove all that wonderful chest hair.

"I got the idea when I was at a conference in the south of France," Carl explained while nibbling on Del's ear. "I noticed all the young guys doing it and the ladies seemed to appreciate it. Plus, it looks a lot better in photo ops. I figure it appeals to the younger demographic."

"Oh." Del wasn't quite sure what the younger demographic was or why Carl would want to appeal to it. "Doesn't it hurt? I mean, when they do it?"

"Like hell. I'm thinking of laser treatments next." Carl paused to look into her eyes. "But the upside, baby, is there's nothing between my body and yours." His thumb flicked the strap free from her shoulder and his fingertips grazed lightly over the top of her nearly freed breast.

"Carl..." Del quivered under his touch. She closed her eyes and moved her hand higher, wrapping around his neck and pulling him into a seductive kiss.

Carl's hand slid lower, then slipped under the fabric. Del leaned closer, tipping her head back onto the couch as his lips left hers and kissed their way down to replace his hand.

"Delly, you're so soft," he murmured before going in for more, his free hand now moving down along her thigh, then back up under her dress.

Del hardly knew what to say, the brandy and the evening had put her in a delightful state. She moaned at each increasing touch, feeling as if she floated on air with Carl beside her, kindling sensations too long unattended.

"Oh, Carl," she managed to whisper, "shouldn't we move to the bedroom?"

"No, baby, I want you now," he whispered back, his voice hoarse and deep, his hand pressing closer to the warm ache between her legs, sparking a heat that brought a desire to touch him as well.

Del reached for his belt, tugging blindly to undo it. "You're driving me crazy, I need you baby." He leaned in closer and together they toppled down until they lay together across the couch. "I can't wait any longer, I know we're gonna be a perfect fit."

"Yes, Carl, you feel so good already." Del felt the pressure of him against her, anxious for more intimacy. She felt his hands push her skirt higher, their bodies arching together in anticipation.

Carl paused, his face close to hers, their eyes meeting as if words were unnecessary. And then he said, "I don't mean just now, Delly, I mean together we're unbeatable. We're gonna go far."

"Um...far?" Del paused her anticipatory grinding and tried to focus through the alcohol and hormone rush that was swamping her. Was he proposing , she wondered?

"Yes, I was going to tell you later, after we made love, but I want you to know now, I want you to appreciate, along with me, what this moment means."

"Okay..."

"Right here and now, this is the start of something big. We're going to be one, together, and we're going to be unbeatable."

"Unbeatable?"

"Sure, I'm announcing it tomorrow. I want you beside me. It'll look great. Everybody loves you. You're so wholesome—hell, you raise money for a children's hospital, how much more wholesome can you get? And we look great together, imagine the photo spreads, the in-depth interviews. No more talk about me being a playboy. We'll talk about our growing attraction as we sat across the table creating fundraising events for a children's hospital wing, no less. It's gonna be great, I'm settling down and you're the one who's taming me.

The press will eat it up."

"P-press?" Del propped herself up on her elbows, the haze clearing just enough to realize this wasn't your standard pre-consummation pillow talk.

"Baby, I've got exciting news. I'm throwing my hat in the ring tomorrow; I'm running for governor. My handlers say I'm a sure thing so you can pretty much count on being Mrs. Governor. From there, who knows, maybe down the road, a run at the White House. We're going all the way, Delly, and the press will just eat you up, we'll look great together."

He moved in to kiss her and she didn't resist as it gave her a little time to think. Finally, Del pulled away, scooting into a sitting position and arranged her dress back into something at least resembling full coverage.

"Carl, is that what this is all about? Finding a running mate for your—your campaign?" Del tried not to yell but her voice did reach a higher octave than normal, squeaking as it did.

He looked at her, a bewildered expression on his face. Carl ran a hand through his hair as he sat up a little straighter. "That's not all it's about. You're a very sexy woman, after all. Once you let your hair down a little. I can't think of a better woman to settle down with than you. You're everything my critics say I lack. Having you by my side will make me a better man, and you know I'll treat you very well. You'd never lack for anything, I'd see to that."

Del stared at him, trying to sort out what she'd just heard. This wasn't a declaration of love or even passion. It was more like a job offer—with benefits!

"Maybe I didn't put that quite right."

"Oh, I think you put it right." Del stood as she

returned her dress straps into their upright positions and pulled her dress firmly back down. Wisps of hair seemed to dangle everywhere and Del pushed them out of the way as best she could as she got a clear-eyed view, perhaps for the first time, she realized, of the real Carl. No wonder she'd always felt a little hesitant about the man. She'd never really known him. There was a part of him, a plan he'd apparently had all along, that she hadn't been clued in on.

"Don't worry, baby. You don't have to do anything on your own. All the events will be with me. I'll do most of the talking, maybe there'll be a question or two for you but most of the focus will be on me. It'll be great P.R. for your fundraising too. But mostly you can sit back and enjoy the perks and, when we aren't campaigning, well..." He patted the couch beside him. "We can have some fun, a lifetime of fun, I promise."

When Del didn't budge but only continued to stare at him he added, "Oh, I get it, you want to make it official. That's understandable, a woman like you, I'd expect nothing less. We'll go ring shopping tomorrow. You pick out anything you want; whatever your heart desires."

"Whatever my heart desires." Del said it more to herself than to him. Just then Sandy perked up and ran over to Carl, jumping against his leg and panting for attention.

"Easy there." Carl pushed Sandy down. "Watch the paws, little fella, don't want to get grass stains on the pants, eh?"

Sandy sat, her head cocked, considering Carl's statement, then made her own statement, on his shoe, before running to Del, who swept the little dog into her arms. "Sandy isn't a fella, she's a little girl, Carl."

"Well, look what that little girl did to my shoe. These are Italian leather, they can't get wet." He grabbed Del's favorite cashmere wrap that was lying across the back of the couch and wiped his shoe dry. "I'll pay for the dry cleaning, baby," he added, tossing the wrap on the coffee table. "So, where were we?" He looked up at her.

"You know what, Carl? While I appreciate that I wouldn't have to *do anything on my own*, I like doing things on my own. I can talk for myself, I can have fun by myself, and I can definitely figure out what my heart desires, all by myself. And it doesn't desire you. I think you need to leave." She stepped away from the couch and pointed to the front door.

"What? baby, I think you misunderstood me."

"I understood you just fine—and don't call me baby!"

Twenty-Eight

"**H**E SAID WHAT?" GWEN YELLED into the phone as she entered the three-way call Claire had set up between the two of them and Del. Del had texted them both a brief description of her evening with Carl and, despite the late hour, the friends were on the phone within minutes.

Del had been restless and needed to talk to someone, so she'd started with a text to Claire, who she knew would be awake. Claire called and woke up Gwen because, clearly, this was not a normal *Del Development*. It required a late night pow-wow with her friends.

"He's running for governor and wanted me beside him, to make him look good." Del sat in her bed, Sandy snuggled up beside her. She ran her fingers through the pup's silky apricot fur, grateful she wasn't running her fingers through Carl's most-likely-dyed blonde locks instead.

"And he told you this in the middle of sex?" Claire asked for clarification.

"Yes! Well, almost, we were getting there...it was pretty hot, I have to admit, but then he told me, and believe you me, it was like ice water on my libido."

"I'll bet, sweetie." Gwen's voice was soothing but still tinged with signs of feminist ire.

"Why the hell couldn't he have at least saved it for after you got laid? I mean really, what a waste of a perfectly good seduction."

"Claire, that's terrible," Gwen said. "How would Del have felt afterward if she'd known he was just using her?"

"Satisfied? Satiated? Swept away? Shit, I don't know, but she was so close to getting it on with someone besides Jimmy."

"Claire!" Gwen chastised her.

"That's okay, Gwen. I know what Claire means. I have to admit, as mad as I was, I was also kind of sorry. I mean, it was so nice...until it wasn't."

"Until he opened his mouth and showed his true colors, you mean," Gwen said.

"Well, yeah, I guess so. I guess it's for the best. I mean, it wasn't the same as Jimmy, was it? With him, I never had a moment's doubt, but with Carl I've doubted all along. Turns out I was right."

"I suppose." Claire was forced to agree with her friends. "I guess your gut was trying to tell you something but your natural Pollyanna nature just wouldn't listen."

Del laughed. "I guess I am kind of a Pollyanna, when it comes down to it. I do think the best of everyone and I am always looking on the happy side. Maybe I need to stop that, huh? I mean, it makes it awful easy for guys like Carl to take advantage of me."

"You don't need to stop being who you are, kiddo. Who you are is great. But maybe pay a little more attention to that gut of yours."

"And your friends can be your backup," Gwen added. "That's what friends are for, right?"

"Where would I be without friends like you guys?"

"Definitely not taking a conference call at two fricken' a.m.!"

They all laughed at that and Del felt some of her frustration drain away. She couldn't help yawning once her body relaxed.

"I heard that," Gwen said. "Sounds like it's time for us all to get some sleep. I'll call you both tomorrow. I have an idea how we can all take a little break from reality and bolster Del's spirits at the same time."

"Count me in," said Claire.

"Me too! Oh, you guys are just the best. I am so lucky, I don't know how I could have ever been so low with friends like you two. It's—"

"Okay, already, Pollyanna, take that optimism and think happy thoughts while you catch some z's. I gotta check on Bob, I'll catch you guys tomorrow."

CLAIRE TIPPY-TOED BACK INTO BOB'S bedroom and slipped quietly under the covers beside him. She smiled to herself when she thought about how right it felt to be near him, whether awake or asleep. She heard his breathing change and he rolled over to face her.

"What was that all about?" he asked groggily.

"Del gave Carl his walking papers."

"What'd the guy do?"

"Showed his true colors and they stunk."

"Oh...Del okay?"

"Sure. And if she isn't she will be. She's strong."

"I think hanging out with you has made her stronger."

"Maybe..."

"And what has hanging out with her done for you?" He dug his elbow into his pillow and propped his head up on his hand?

"What do you mean?"

"Well, you were pretty entrenched when I met you. Remember that first time, at Gwen's bakery in Blue River? Andy and I were having coffee at a table nearby when you blew in to talk with Gwen, didn't even see me at first."

"I saw you." She propped her own head up then reached out and traced a finger across his forehead, pushing hair out of the way as she slowly trailed down along his cheek and ended at his mouth.

"Did not." Bob nibbled at the tip of her finger and smiled.

"Maybe not at first, but when I did," she leaned closer, her face inches from his, "you were hard to ignore." She traded her finger for her lips and kissed him lightly.

"You tried, though," Bob said as their lips parted.

"I did...and you're right, I know Del—and Gwen—made a difference. Otherwise, I probably would have run away from you as fast as I could."

"Tell me why."

"You know why."

"But I'd like to hear you say it." It was his turn to reach out, playing with her hair and tugging her face back for a brief kiss before their eyes met. Bob knew one of the secrets to unlocking Claire's thoughts was seeing into her eyes, letting her know he truly saw her, the real her inside.

"Because I knew you meant business."

"Business?"

"No one-night stands or brief flings for you. You were the all-or-nothing kind of guy. The one who likes to put a ring on it."

"Indeed I do." He grinned and pushed up so that he could reach out and pull open the drawer on the bedside table and pulled out a small box."

"What the—" Claire started to sit up but he reached out to keep her where she was.

"Don't move, this is the perfect moment for this." He settled back in beside her.

"Listen, Bob, I agree this is great, but, you know, it's all so new to me. I mean, just moving into your house—even for a little while—it's like, a big step already. I'm not sure I'm ready for—"

"Shut up a minute, Ace." He reached out a finger to still her mouth. "It's not quite what you think it is."

"It's not?" While relieved, she felt slightly let-down, which surprised her even more.

"Just open it." He handed her the small, black velvet box and she laid her head down on the pillow and held it aloft, cracking it open and tipping it to see its contents: a thin silver band encrusted with diamonds.

"Bob, this looks like..."

"But it's not. When you get an engagement ring from me you'll know it. You'll need sunglasses just to open the box." She smiled up at him. "It's a *promise ring*. I'm promising you that, if this new arrangement works out and you're happy, then there will be more down the road, when you *are* ready. Promise."

"Really?" She pulled the ring from its resting place and slipped it on her left ring finger then paused. "Maybe I should wear it on the other hand."

"Whatever you want, Ace, but I like seeing it there." He smiled and she left it where it was. It was ridiculous how good that ring felt on her finger. Its very presence conjured up a sense of contentment she'd never felt before.

A sudden glimpse of a long forgotten memory flashed in her mind. She saw her mother and father sitting together on the couch in their home, their heads tipped together in conversation, the occasional laugh, and her father pulling her mother in to give her a soft kiss before parting. He looked up and winked at Claire, who'd giggled at what she'd considered mushy adults. But the expression on her mother's face mirrored her own and for the first time she knew exactly how that moment had felt for them.

It made her smile to remember a happy moment between her parents before the accident. Her dreams of them always involved the plane. They'd overwhelmed her other memories, but now this simple, traditional band on her finger had pulled the veil away from memories she'd left untouched for too long. She thought of the Larson sisters. Their connection, though different from her parents', felt the same as this memory and never failed, as well, to make her smile.

"This is such a romantic, old-fashioned idea. Where'd this idea come from?"

"Evie...and Cora."

"I thought it had Larson sisters written all over it. Is that the secret you two had in the hospital?"

"Yes. The sisters, being somewhat old-fashioned,

felt a woman ought to have some sort of expectation when she moves in with a man. They made me promise but, really, they didn't have to twist my arm."

She felt his eyes on her as she held her hand aloft. She smiled as the moonlight filtering in through the window caught the diamonds and made them twinkle in the darkness.

"What's a little ring when you already have my heart?" he asked softly.

She pulled her gaze away from her hand and looked up at him, moonlight glinting on the tears that pooled in her eyes. "I love you, you know."

He wrapped his arm around her and pulled her closer and, before his lips took hers, whispered, "Old news, Ace, old news."

CLAIRE SWEPT THE CORNERS OF the kitchen in her little farmhouse. The last of her possessions had been moved to Bob's. She'd decided that if she was really going to give their relationship a serious shot she had to be all-in. That meant combining the few items of hers that she'd brought along to her *little home in the valley* with all of his in his elegantly rustic stone and wood home. In time, assuming this worked, they could talk about truly merging their homes—hers in Blue River and his here in Grand Valley.

Claire had already decided that Grand Valley was her new home. Moving back to Blue River would feel like a step into the past and these days she was all about the future. She smiled and shook her head as she thought about the new person she'd become; the new person she was still becoming. Glass-half-empty Claire was back in Blue River. Grand Valley Claire, with Bob, the Larson sisters, Gwen and Del, and all the excitement of her new career developing the Larson House and who knew what else, well, that was absolutely glass-half-full Claire. And that's how she liked her glass these days.

Elbie scooted into the house through the open kitchen door and ran over to sniff his empty food dish.

"Hey, buddy." Claire scooped him into her arms, the two nuzzling their faces together. "Looks like you are the last order of business for today. Time to go home to your new home, Elbie my friend. Your owners miss you very much." Elbie tapped her face lightly with his paw, then applied sandpaper kisses to her chin. "You're just sucking up to me for tuna, aren't you?" The cat began to purr and Claire's eye filled with tears. "I'll miss you too," she whispered.

🍷

"HELLO. ANYBODY HOME?" CLAIRE EASED open the door when the sisters didn't answered her knock. They'd given her a key and made it clear she should always feel free to come right in, as if it were her home away from home. And Claire was surprised to find that, more and more, it felt that way.

She'd called the night before to let them know she would be bringing Elbie home so she was surprised they weren't waiting anxiously by the door for her.

"Cora? Evie?" She thought she heard voices in one of the back rooms and started that direction when Cora came down the hall to greet her.

"We're here. We were distracted and didn't hear you

at first."

Claire could hear Evie giggling like a school girl somewhere out of sight.

"Oh, Elbie," Cora purred, taking the cat from Claire and wrapping him in her loving embrace. The cat purred back and the two commenced a mutual appreciation of nuzzles and kisses. "How we have missed this boy."

"Looks like he's missed you, too." Though sad that the day had finally come to return him, Claire was happy to see the reunited pair. "I've brought his things, they're right outside, let me bring them in. Where's Evie?"

"She'll be right out. Let's go find her, shall we, Elbie? Claire, could you put all of Elbie's things in the kitchen? We'll sort them out from there."

"Sure." Claire watched as Cora and Elbie disappeared back down the hall and wondered at the odd behavior of the sisters. She'd expected an excited greeting, both of them cooing and cuddling at their dear feline's long anticipated return. What she'd gotten felt almost like a brush-off.

She definitely got the impression Cora didn't want her in the back room and she couldn't help wondering why, but she busied herself bringing in the litter box and extra litter, and the few toys the cat arrived with in addition to a few more Claire had bought. As she set the last bag, filled with food and treats on the counter, Claire finally heard the sisters coming out.

"Claire," Evie said, "we're so delighted to have our dear boy back with us. Now it truly feels like home!"

Evie, now carrying Elbie, was followed by Cora and Mr. Trsander, who held a large box, topped with an equally large bow.

"We've gotten you a little something to thank you for caring for our Elbie. Can you set the box down here, Mr. Trsander?" Cora patted the top of their dining table.

"You betcha, Miss Cora." He gently set the box down, then, winking at Claire, he added, "This'll brighten your day, Missy."

"Oh Cora, a *little something*, how sweet." Evie giggled.

"You didn't have to do that."

"We felt compelled, and Bob agreed."

"Bob?" Claire wondered what compulsion required a conversation with Bob. She started to pick up the box and instantly felt its contents shift. "What the—I mean, what on earth..."

Claire set it back down, lifted the beribboned lid and out peeked a black and white kitten, its eyes sparkling as they met her own.

"How adorable," Claire said and realized that it was her turn to coo. She lifted it out and brought it up to meet eye-to-eye. "Well, who are you?"

Mew, the kitten responded and patted a paw against Claire's chin.

"Or maybe the better question is *whose* are you?"

"She's yours!" Evie practically bounced with excitement. "We know how close you've grown to our Elbie and thought you could use a little one of your own. We checked with Bob, to be sure he wasn't allergic to cats—"

"—and to be certain he wouldn't mind adding a cat to his household, of course," Cora added.

"He thought it was a marvelous idea, didn't he

pumpkins?" Evie reached her free hand out to scratch behind the kittens ears.

"He did, huh? What makes you two so sure I'd *want* a cat? I'm a busy woman after all; are you sure I have time to take care of...it?"

"She, dear, she's a little girl. And we knew a competent woman such as yourself was up to any challenge."

That, Claire thought, was what she'd call the *Cora Card*. And Cora had thrown it with finesse, giving Claire a gentle challenge that would be hard to refuse.

"And we knew how very much you've come to love our Elbie."

"I have?" Claire gave Evie a questioning look, but her smile betrayed her. "Okay, so maybe he's grown on me a little."

"You adore him, and you know it. Who wouldn't?" Evie placed a tidy kiss atop Elbie's head before setting him down. Elbie was clearly more interested in the kitten.

"She'll be a good companion to you, Claire. Even someone as wonderful as Bob can't be there all the time. Furry and unconditional love is good for one's soul." Now Cora reached out and scratched behind the kitten's ears, causing a soft purr to erupt.

"Well..." Claire rubbed her cheek against the furry little head. "I guess it would be nice to have one of my own."

"Of course it will. We will happily guide and assist you in her raising."

"And pets are such good training ground for couples to practice on before they have a family of their own." Evie smiled, her expression almost dreamy.

"Hey, let's not get carried away here, one step at

a time." Claire ran her hand down the soft back that curled in her other palm.

"Oh, my!" Evie took Claire's hand in hers, ran her thumb lightly over the crystal clear line of diamonds encircling the promise ring.

"Bob has very nice taste, I'd say." Cora nudged her sister's shoulder with her own. The two smiled conspiratorially.

"He told me everything. I'm not sure I should turn my back on you two the way you plot against me." Claire enjoyed teasing them but, in truth, she loved that these two put so much thought into her happiness.

"No Claire, we plot *for* you," Cora corrected her.

"For your best interest, we've got...what is it they say these days, Cora?"

"We've got Claire's back, Evie. And we do." Cora winked at Claire.

Claire couldn't help smiling. How could she be anything other than grateful at these two women who cared so much for her in every way? Between Bob and the sisters, not to mention Del and Gwen, she had to admit to herself that it was nice to have someone *have her back*. It had been a very long time since she'd felt so completely supported and cared for. She felt her initial hesitation at the kitten give way to delightful anticipation of its company—and sharing the surprise with Bob. In fact, even though Bob might have known about the plan, Claire found she was anxious to introduce him too... "What's her name?"

"We didn't name her, that's the owner's prerogative."

"But we've been calling her Adeline, after Momma," Evie said. "Since we already had Elbie after Papa."

"Nice...though maybe a little formal for me. How about Addie?" Claire looked at the sisters for approval and their broad smiles were answer enough. "Addie it is then."

She rubbed a small, fluffy paw between her fingers, feeling the soft pads and tiny claws. Soft and sharp, she thought to herself, she and Addie already had a lot in common.

Twenty-Nine

THE TENT'S WHITE SPIRES POKED into the sky beside the Larson House. Claire had anxiously watched as the crew erected it the day before, and then worked long into the night draping it in endless yards of artfully draped white silk and artificial grapevines intertwined with twinkle lights.

While the upper floors of the house still had work yet to be finished, she'd managed to nudge and prod her contractors into wrapping up the first floor only days before. That left her with barely enough time to decorate the space with a mix of the furniture the sisters had decided to leave along with a few items she'd purchased.

The rental company showed up early that morning with tables and chairs for Columbine Estates's Festival Dinner and the final rush was on to set the tables and prepare the space where Gwen and Jason would set up the buffet.

Del had arrived to help and ended up working deep into the night beside Claire then returning just after daybreak. Gwen had sent Becky over in the morning with sustaining coffees and pastries.

"Thank God for caffeine." Claire grabbed a second triple shot latte, pausing briefly from her duties placing centerpieces on each table. Terra had chosen tall white pillars surrounded by a mix of white roses and Colorado's state flower—and the flower that adorned the winery's logo—the blue and white columbine.

"I may never sleep again after all the coffee I've had in the last twenty-four hours." Del carried a check list as she went about the room determining what still needed attending to.

"That's why we'll switch to wine at dinner, sweetie."

"I'm usually a one glass kinda gal but I may need a whole bottle after this."

It had been a lot of work but Del was in her element. After all her worries and heartache it was nice to turn her attention to a good cause. The harder she worked the more she smiled. How long had it been since she'd spent a whole day with a smile on her face? Too long, she decided.

Del's years of volunteer work, both in planning and implementing Blue River's Women's League holiday fundraiser, made her the ideal person to understand everything from traffic flow around the buffet table to access to electrical outlets; from lighting bright enough to see where you were going but soft enough to give the large tent an intimate feel. She even gave the string quartet Claire had hired for the evening instructions regarding when to amp up the volume and when to tone it down.

Terra had decided a silent auction would jazz up the proceedings. Del agreed. She knew the casual mingling along the tables of available items served to break the ice among attendees. She'd spread the auction tables along the outside of the tent so that everyone's dinner table was near a table full of items available to bid on.

The winery had contributed several bottles of their reserve wines along with framed posters of their labels and baskets filled with more bottles of wine and glasses from the tasting room emblazoned with the Columbine Estate's logo. Gwen contributed gift certificates to the bakery and Claire and Terra had coerced several other businesses in town to contribute items for auction.

But a silent auction needed a cause and Claire had just the one. With the sister's permission she created the Larson Trust. Its proceeds would be used to sponsor the arts among youth in the valley. Claire was already imagining a youth centered art festival to be held on the grounds of the Larson House and, perhaps someday, they would sponsor scholarships to aspiring artists and musicians. She understood that good wine and the arts was a combination that lent itself nicely to a very successful fundraiser.

The wine festival fell during a particularly beautiful time on the Colorado calendar, when the aspens were turning in the high country and, if you were lucky, the warm days with their brilliant blues skies and cool nights that hinted at what was to come would linger deep into October. Or it might snow.

The unknown was what kept Claire watching the weather reports and the sky itself. So far, neither had let her down and now, as the sun started its slow dip beyond the horizon and the late afternoon clouds turned first gold, then orange in anticipation of the richer crimson and plums that preceded the night, she was starting to breathe a sigh of relief.

"I think you're going to pull it off." Del stood beside her outside the tent, her arm wrapped through Claire's. They'd just managed to change out of their work clothes and slip into something more party appropriate before the guests arrived. Del wore a sleeveless dress in a deep shade of tangerine with a cream colored sweater draped casually over her shoulders. Claire had decided on black silk pants with a short white top she'd had custom embroidered with a spray of columbines done in tiny black beads.

"Thank God. Can you imagine the mud bath we'd have had if it had rained?" They'd managed to clean up the yard fairly well, what with the constant construction traffic, but there were still several places where lengths of artificial turf had been strewn in paths to protect the fashionable footwear of the attendees.

"I was thinking about the nightmare of moving the whole thing inside if the temperature dropped and it started to snow."

"Oh, we've got all those space heaters. They'd get us through dinner...after that we'd probably have shivering attendees heading for the house and hot toddies."

"Well, I think that worry is past; looks like we have a beautiful evening in store. You pulled it off, Claire."

"We all pulled it off. This was definitely a team effort." She nodded toward the buffet tables where Gwen and Jason were arranging trays of appetizers. Andy had come early too, helping with the myriad of little last minute things that Del had warned always came up. And she'd been right.

Claire was thankful for Del's expertise in this area. She'd learned a great deal from her in the last few days about party prep and assembly, not to mention the inner workings of the mind of a fundraiser attendee. These were all useful lessons that Claire was only just beginning to imagine a variety of ways she could put to use. Fundraising for worthwhile causes was a new facet of her ever evolving future.

"Bob looks happy." Del nodded toward the entrance of the tent. Andy had joined Bob, who stood, with the help of a cane, greeting the first guests as they arrived.

"He's in his element."

"Is it your element too?"

"You know what? I think it is."

In all the years of selling homes Claire couldn't remember anything approaching the sense of satisfaction she felt tonight. And contentment, that was a new sensation and she thought she could get used to it.

"Hey, if you guys don't have anything else to do I'll find you something." Gwen joined them. Over an azure blue dress with long sleeves and a graciously scooped neckline she'd tied a burgundy apron with neat little embroidery at the top left corner. It read, in a simple script, Gwen's Bakery and Catering.

"Sweet apron." Claire smiled.

"Jason actually had them made up. He thought we would look more professional. He's wearing a chef's coat, since he's serving, but his assistants wear these. Guess I'm an assistant rather than the boss tonight, which is fine by me."

"Don't you have helpers?" Claire asked.

"Becky's here, but Carolyn is actually attending the event."

"It's business for her," Claire said. "I've hung her paintings all over the house. It was nice of her to loan them, and she even contributed a small framed water color for the auction. It's good advertising for her, and for the Larson House Plein Air Art Festival we're having in the summer."

"It's official then? I'll have to plan a trip over here for that. I think it would be a lot of fun to watch artists painting all over town. Watch their process. I've always envied people who have that kind of talent."

"We'll have classes, Del. You can take one while you're here. Who knows, maybe you have a hidden talent."

"I doubt it..." But Del pondered the possibility.

"Before you start planning that trip, don't forget our trip to New York City."

"Oh! I'm so excited. I've never even been to the Big Apple, and here we're going to go right during the holidays. Think of the Christmas lights, the holiday window displays, that huge tree in Rockefeller Center."

"The shopping," Claire added. "I haven't had any time to even think about that and it will be Christmas before we know it. What am I going to get for Bob? I'm new to this stuff. I need help, you two."

"I think you've already given Bob all he could ever dream of for Christmas." Gwen smiled at Claire as they watched Bob chatting amiably with his guests.

He turned for a moment, caught Claire's eye, winked, then turned back.

"He's the happiest I've even seen him," Gwen said.

"So." Del reached down for Claire's hand, running her fingers over the promise ring and smiling up at Claire. "Do you think you'll find a bigger version under the tree this year?"

Claire pulled her hand back, admiring the ring for herself. "Let's not get too carried away quite yet. I like this one just fine. It's a lot like me these days, and Bob and I too. Full of promise."

"Hey, Chef!" Jason called across the tent, "I need your help over here for a minute."

"Gotta go." Gwen took a step then turned back toward her friends. "Forgot to tell you, Jason got us a reservation at a very nice restaurant during our trip. The owner is a friend and he says dinner will *blow us away*. And it's Jason's treat."

"That's so sweet." Del said.

"He said it was his way of saying thank you for all we've done for him here."

"What have we done?" Claire looked over at Jason. He was clearly in his element behind the buffet, greeting guests, serving up platings with the élan of a professional chef. At the end of the table stood Terra, sipping a glass of wine and smiling as she watched him work.

"I asked him that too. He said we'd helped him find his place."

"Sounds like he'll be staying." Claire said, nodded toward the young chef. "And not just for the work. They've been over to the house a few times to see Bob. Jason made dinner one night. Those two are a good fit; it's obvious when you see them together."

"It sounds to me like you don't have to worry about losing him anymore, Gwen."

"I'd better go see what he needs. I'll catch you guys later." Gwen started away once more then stopped again and came back. "Hey, I just want to say thank you, to both of you."

"What for, kiddo?"

"I'm not sure, maybe everything. It seems like you've both been a part of everything that's brought me to this point. You know, it's hard for me to remember a time when we weren't all friends."

"I know what you mean," Claire said. "I wouldn't have gotten to this place without you guys, either."

"Me too. Oh, we've got to do a group hug thingie now—you're making me cry." Del started to pull the friends into a hug.

"Chef!"

"Saved by the cook," Claire whispered to Gwen.

"Really gotta go!" Gwen hurried away at last, leaving her friends where she'd found them.

"Hey, look." Del pointed to the darkening sky. "The stars are coming out, isn't that wonderful? How magical, don't you think?"

Claire looked at the canopy of stars peeking out above them, then back inside the tent. She saw Gwen and her team serving the first of what she knew would be many events at the Larson Home and beyond.

She saw Bob as he greeted the sisters, who had just arrived. Evie's arm was linked in Cora's, just as Del's was in hers. Both sisters smiled and laughed as they looked up at the twinkling lights of the tent, then, spotting Claire, they waved excitedly.

"Magic? You know what kiddo," Claire said, as they went to meet them, "I think there's a lot of that going around these days."

If you enjoyed this book...

...please consider leaving a short review on Amazon or Goodreads. Reviews are the grease that keep our little writing world moving...and they're pretty darned nice, too. Want to pick up where this story left off? Watch for the third and final installment—Del's story—coming soon. If you missed the first installment, of **The Keeper Series,** *The Shell Keeper*, or want to discover the first installment of my **Kay Conroy mystery series,** *Framed*, plus be among the first to get all the latest news on new releases, etc., follow me on my website at *https://robinnolet.blogspot.com/*

Acknowledgements

Particular thanks to Lana Williams—friend, fellow author and awesome critique buddy. Her good eye, wise council and patience with my rambling emails are always appreciated.

To Julie Becket, of JujuBeckCreative, who patiently takes my rambling emails full of thoughts about design (etc!) and always comes up with the most lovely cover art for all of my books.

To Jennifer Jakes, with The Killion Group, Inc., for her patience in taking my rambling emails and coming up with incredibly formatted interiors for my books.

And of course, to my family, for their patience (do you notice a theme?) and encouragement for this rambling day dreamer and story weaver. They make it possible.

Special acknowledgement to the wisdom found within the pages of Anne Morrow Lindbergh's *Gift From The Sea*. Every woman should have this book in her arsenal of life's lessons learned.

Blog, Facebook and Goodreads—Oh, my!

Visit my website, *https://robinnolet.blogspot.com/* to find me on Twitter, Facebook or Goodreads and learn more about new releases and to share your thoughts.